MUSICK
FOR THE KING

A Historical Novel

BARRIE DOYLE

MUSICK FOR THE KING
Copyright © 2020 by Barrie Doyle

Print ISBN: 978-1-4866-1979-5
eBook ISBN: 978-1-4866-1980-1

Word Alive Press
119 De Baets Street, Winnipeg, MB R2J 3R9
www.wordalivepress.ca

WORD ALIVE
—PRESS—

Cataloguing in Publication may be obtained through Library and Archives Canada

For those creative people—musicians, writers and artists—who help us transcend our ordinary lives and touch the immortal.
SDG: Soli Deo Gloria

PROLOGUE

The darkened room was still. Only the ticking of the ornate gilt French bracket clock in the hallway broke the silence. On the red velvet four-poster bed, a figure stirred as the door opened quietly and a greying man in his fifties wearing soft-soled shoes slipped in, shuffling along on the polished wooden floor.

The blanket shifted as the balding, grey-faced figure under it turned his head slowly and peered through unseeing eyes, following as he heard his servant walk quietly around the foot of the bed to the windows to draw the curtains aside. Rays of sunshine chased the darkness out of the plainly furnished room, leaving only shadows in the corners. The bedridden man couldn't see the light but felt the warmth of the sun on his face and smiled.

The bed exploded into color, its voluptuous scarlet-draped bedspread and velvet curtains hanging down the side of the huge four-poster.

"What day is it, John?" the old man asked as he struggled to raise his body.

The servant bustled around the room. "Saturday, sir. April 14. It is late afternoon. You slept well."

John looked gently over at his master, once vibrant and full of life, churning out masterpiece after masterpiece, but now blind and frail.

"And tomorrow is Easter?" the old man asked.

"Yes, sir."

"It would have been a good thing to die on Good Friday, the same day my Savior died. But just as good to join him now and rejoice in the resurrection with him tomorrow. Don't you think?" Without waiting for a response, he took a deep, labored breath. "What kind of day is it?"

"Bright and sunny, sir. If you like, I could open the window, so you can feel the freshness of the air and the warmth of the sun."

The old man shook his head. "Thank you, but no. I fear the noise of the street will disturb my meditation and prayers."

"Would you like me to sit with you a while? There are many letters and notes from friends and well-wishers who wish to be remembered to you. I can read them."

"Later, perhaps." The man paused a moment. "The King. How fares the King?"

"His Majesty is well, I trust, sir. He sent a message just yesterday expressing his high regard for you and his hope that you will recover."

The figure on the bed smiled. "His Majesty has been a good patron. He has favored me with much over the years. I am extremely grateful to him."

He closed his sightless eyes once again and began quietly humming. John strained to hear the tune, and then grinned as he recognized the strains of "Worthy Is the Lamb." Before John could comment, however, the humming stopped abruptly and the old man's eyes popped open. A large smile creased his face, a sigh escaping him as he slumped over onto the glistening white pillow, his right arm dropping onto the vivid red bedspread.

John cried out and rushed over, but it was too late. Gently he closed his master's eyelids, then reached over and rang the handbell kept on the tiny round table beside the bed, tears flowing down his face.

A maid appeared at the bedroom door.

Hearing her enter, John looked up. "Send the footman to St. James' Palace with a message for His Majesty. Tell them that this day, the great musical genius George Frederik Handel has passed into the arms of the King of Kings."

PART THE FIRST

IN WHICH THE GREAT COMPOSER GEORGE FREDERIK HANDEL SUFFERS PHYSICAL INFIRMITY, FINANCIAL LOSS, AND CREATIVE RIDICULE AND HUMILIATION

CHAPTER ONE

IN WHICH MR. HANDEL CONFESSES CONCERNS

A glistening black carriage, drawn by two matching blacks, jerked and bumped over the cobblestones, clattering to a halt in front of a modest red brick townhouse that was so typical of the newly built district of Mayfair. On the carriage door, the coat of arms proudly announced its aristocratic ownership. Inside, a tall and elegantly dressed thin man adjusted his fashionable brown curled wig. He waited patiently as the liveried footman, clad in brilliant white-trimmed red coat and breeches, jumped down from the rear of the carriage, crossed the narrow paving stones, and strode up the stone steps. He knocked imperiously.

Ignoring the steady cold drizzle that seeped down the neck of his coat, the footman bowed slightly to the young serving girl who answered.

"Milord His Grace the Duke of Devonshire, to call upon Mr. Handel," the footman said. He handed her a calling card.

As the door opened wider, William Cavendish, third Duke of Devonshire, jumped out of the carriage and rushed into the house, sweeping off his cloak and tricorn hat. He handed both, along with his gold-tipped walking stick, to the hovering maid.

Bowing profusely, the butler ushered him to the formal drawing room. The duke smoothed his deep blue coat and matching britches that emphasized his white silk stockings and gold-buckled black leather shoes.

A few candles flickered, fighting against the dreary gloom of the rainy spring afternoon. The duke cast his eyes critically, noting that for every candle lit even more remained unused or sat partially burned in their holders. The oil lamps were unlit, a distinct change for a room that had normally blazed with light. Dark maroon curtains had been pulled as wide as possible in the front windows, held open by ornate yellow woolen ties that contrasted starkly with the light grey walls.

Minutes later, a heavyset man, sweating profusely and limping in pain, entered. His drab brown outfit was topped by a fashionably coiffed white wig sitting tall and slightly askew on his head.

Devonshire suppressed a slight smile. Handel had never been overly fastidious about his appearance. If he was dressed and wore a wig, that was good enough. No matter if the clothes were mismatched or the wig ill-fitting; his brilliant mind was too busy composing arias and concertos to worry about sartorial details.

"Your Grace, my apologies for keeping you waiting, but you surprise me," said George Frederik Handel. "I did not expect the pleasure of entertaining you in my modest premises. I remember your kind visit last spring. It is a delight to see you again. I trust Her Grace the duchess is well?"

Handel bowed formally and gestured the duke toward a well-appointed deep green settee.

Although he smiled at his guest, Handel's deep-set brown eyes were heavy with worry. Where they had once sparkled with gusto and enjoyment, they were now lined and drawn, outlined by dark circles. Sleepless nights had robbed him of the pleasure his life and music had so often brought him.

As the duke sat, Handel hobbled slowly over to a facing chair.

Devonshire waved his hand airily to dismiss Handel's apology. "I'm given to understand you closed your latest opera after only three performances. Why? *Deidamia* was an excellent work and your music was, as always, sublime."

"You are too kind, Your Grace—"

Devonshire flipped his hand up quickly. "William, if you please. We are surely past the formalities in our long friendship, at least in private."

Handel smiled in agreement. "Very well then, William. But not everyone agrees with your generous assessment of my operas these days." Glumly, he added, "In fact, very few at all. Most of those who do attend my presentations spend their time cat-calling and hooting throughout the performance."

"I was there when you opened. Yes, the audience was thin and very rowdy, but it was a foul night. I expected the crowds to build over the next several weeks. You advertised well, did you not?"

"I did. I did indeed," Handel said bitterly. "Posters and bills handed out and placed across the city, but as fast as they were put up, paid gangs tore them down. Just last week, a mob burst into my printer's establishment, stealing hundreds of bills right off the press and burning them in the alley behind. Of course, they were gone before the watchmen showed up. Not that those lazy drunken excuses for the law could have done anything. Beyond that, my rivals mock me, say atrocious things, and sabotage my presentations. There are many who wish to see me destroyed and forced to leave England." Handel sighed heavily and slumped in his seat. "To leave it to the English."

He scowled angrily, then turned as he heard the door open. Clacking footsteps on the wooden floor preceded the appearance of his butler, brandishing a canter of wine, two glasses, and a plate of sweet cakes. Handel remained silent while the butler poured wine and offered cakes to the duke.

As Devonshire accepted, he noticed that Handel took nothing for himself.

"Not like you, George, to pass up a nice glass of wine and cakes." Devonshire sipped. "And a good wine it is, too. German, no doubt?"

"Italian, sir, Italian." A brief smile crossed Handel's face. Then a wince of pain. "My gout." He grunted and pointed to his right foot, which rested delicately on a footstool. "Have to stay away from rich food and drink. Damn pain keeps me up at night." He gestured with his left hand. "Not to mention the palsy I suffered a few years back. It still nags at my right arm from time to time, like an old fishwife. I am a wreck, Your Grace. A physical and creative wreck."

Handel looked up at his butler.

"Thank you, John," he said, waving his man away and waiting for the door to close before shifting forward on the chair as delicately as he could. He gave an audible wince.

Devonshire knew what a sacrifice it was for Handel to restrain his enthusiastic and notorious desire for the finest food and drink. The gout must indeed be bothering him.

Stories had flourished about Handel's prodigious appetite. Ever since the days of good Queen Anne, Handel's cheerful willingness to enjoy the hospitality of noble families and provide entertainment had been matched by his equal willingness to partake of the hearty feasts.

Devonshire thought back to one particularly lavish and boisterous evening at the Duke of Waverly's house. Handel had been challenged to compose a short piece on the spot in return for a flagon of the finest Italian wine, a brace of pheasants for his own table, and a platter full of sweet delectable pastries. Grinning, Handel had promptly sat at the duke's pianoforte and produced a sparkling number that delighted his adoring audience.

No, Devonshire thought. Turning down excellent food and drink was definitely outside the norm for Handel.

"Is the gout an aftereffect of your recent palsy, I wonder?"

"They say not. My physics believe it is a result of stress and rich foods." Handel flipped his hand. "The fools don't seem to understand that life is to be lived to the full... or at least it did."

The man's voice trailed off into a whisper, then silence. After a moment, he moved his foot off the stool and leaned forward, his head bowed in defeat and cradled in his hands, elbows driving into his fleshy knees.

"I am a failure," Handel said, his quiet voice oozing despair. "I am finished, Your Grace... I mean, William. Three performances! That's all I could afford without strong audience support. Especially since I had to close *Imeneo* after only two performances in December." He raised his eyes to meet the Duke's. "I cannot underwrite these performances any longer. With no money coming in, I cannot pay the performers, the musicians, or the backstage people, let alone rent the theater."

"But many, including the King, love your music. He is your patron."

Handel nodded. "His Majesty has been generous in the past and has certainly favored me. His generous stipend of two hundred guineas a year is all that has kept me from debtor's prison these last few months. That which I borrowed to finance the productions, I am slowly paying back." He paused. "And I will pay you yours as well, Your Grace. You have my word."

Devonshire nodded his acknowledgement of the promise, but his bushy eyebrows rose in astonishment at the intimate revelation. George Handel, darling of the London theater crowd and favored composer of the current monarch, as well as King George I and Queen Anne before him, was confessing to near poverty.

He couldn't help a quick glance at a side table covered with what he now realized were bills, obviously unpaid.

Handel, head down and rubbing his ailing leg, did not notice the duke's startled reaction. "My audiences don't like my music anymore. I don't understand it. Each time I produce even more magnificent operas and concertos. But where they once loved, now they hate. My jealous enemies undermine my very existence in this city and, except for a very few like yourself, even my friends keep their distance."

Devonshire opened his mouth to argue the point, but his host was now well into pouring out the fears and dashed hopes he'd been bottling up for months. Handel's German accent, normally softened, grew broader and louder as his pent-up anger and frustration emptied out.

Handel was notorious for his short temper and rages. Once, during a rehearsal, he'd been so furious with a featured soprano that he'd literally picked her up and held her out the upper rehearsal hall window of the Covent Garden Theater. Only when the diva had agreed to sing the piece the way Handel wanted did he relent and bring her back inside.

The candles flickered, and the fast approaching dusk darkened the room to match Handel's mood. He was building up to another of his legendary furies.

He looked up at Devonshire suddenly, punching his fists together. "I'm nothing more than a pawn in the battle between His Majesty and the Prince of Wales. I am even told by the prince's lapdogs that I am the embodiment of the old German heritage and European culture—all that the King represents—while the prince and his entourage are the personification of a new and glorious England."

Handle spat the prince's name, his dark eyes flashing with anger, and glared at Devonshire in defiance. He raised his hand, jabbing at the air with his forefinger.

"I speak no treason, sirrah, but you must surely realize that the prince and his followers have poisoned many people against the King. He has built his own opposition court, whipping up anger and disloyalty under the guise of culture. His newspaper friends rail against my operas, calling them old-fashioned and unworthy of modern England, while they promote their own English operas and composers. They want to show that I am out of touch. I am a mere stand-in for the King in that battle!"

"You never did like *The Beggar's Opera*, did you, George?" Devonshire said, trying to lighten Handel's mood.

From its first performance, *Beggar's Opera* had turned London's musical scene on its ear. Where once the nobility and emerging merchant class had reveled in the stylish Italian operas, especially those churned out by the proliferate Handel, John Gay's composition, the first fully English language opera, had been a satirical parody of modern English society. It had been a wild success instantly, embraced by many as the new form of music.

"Out with the old, in with the new." Handel's face reddened in fury and Devonshire hastily moved to diffuse it.

"I grant you, this hostility between His Majesty and the prince becomes more and more bitter by the day. But there are political forces at work here. It is not just about music and culture. Not even your sublime music, my dear George."

Handel struggled to his feet and hobbled over to the window, staring balefully out at the drizzle-covered street. Street vendors walked slowly along, calling out their wares but finding few takers along a mostly empty Brook Street. A street urchin strayed too close to the duke's carriage, skillfully dodging the slice of the driver's long whip before scampering away. As other carriages and wagons rattled by, the duke's horses snorted and breathed steam into the cooling late evening air.

Two chairmen struggled across the cobbles, trying to keep their sedan chair and its overweight occupant level and bump-free as they hurried along.

Handel sighed, speaking morosely to the window as if he'd forgotten the duke was present. "Perhaps if I were like Johann Bach in Leipzig, things would not be so bleak. As Kapellmeister, all he has to do is sit back and write wonderful church music for the church and his master. As long as they are happy, he is happy. But I…!" he suddenly roared, slamming his hand atop the sideboard, rattling its china plates and ornaments. "I create music for all to enjoy—nobility, merchants, bankers, churchmen, tradesmen—whoever can afford the small cost of attending the theater. I seek to entertain people!" He sighed, staring sightlessly out the window. "It also means I am subject to the whims of a fickle audience. These days they are lured away by the prince's associates and their lies. And when that doesn't work, they disrupt and destroy."

He turned and tried to pace the room as he normally did when thinking through a problem, except it was more of a wincing, painful, stuttering motion this day. He shook his finger at the duke.

"The prince surrounds himself with bootlickers who encourage his split with his father and make me the object of his anger. Then they have the audacity to send their hooligans to disrupt my performances…"

Handel's fuming voice tailed off and Devonshire remained quiet, saddened to hear the depth of Handel's anger and despair.

"Perhaps, George, if you had engaged Mrs. Cibber for the role of Deidamia instead of Elisabeth Duparc?"

Handel vigorously shook his head. "Susannah is as much outcast in this town now as I am, and you know it. That court case exposed her private life for all to see. She wants nothing to do with London. She told me so herself." He waved his hand vaguely. "And I don't blame her!"

Devonshire finished his wine, nodded, and rubbed his fingers slowly along the arm of the settee. Ever since Theo Cibber had brought that adultery lawsuit against his wife Susannah and her lover William Sloper, she'd been the talk of the town. The scandal had fed the ever-greedy public appetite for gossip—indeed, at a greater level than any before or since—and opinion swayed between pity for the wildly popular Susannah and fascination with the lurid details of the story's unprecedented violence and sexual abuse. Stories of Theo Cibber's twisted appetites had disgusted the court, and many others normally impervious to such bizarre and deplorable behavior. Susannah's own reputation had taken a massive blow as the public became aware of the depths of her less-than-moral character.

The sophisticates of London had nodded in understanding of her predicament, even as many of them also cavorted in adultery. They publicly disapproved of her, but her biggest sin, to them, was allowing the affair to become public knowledge. Discretion, above all, was their motto.

However, for some in the church there was no middle ground of consideration. In Westminster Abbey one Sunday, Devonshire himself had endured a particularly venomous sermon by the Bishop of London, Edmund Gibson, that railed against Mrs. Cibber's adultery as an example of the dissoluteness of English society.

While he understood her desire to escape London's penetrating public gaze, Devonshire also mourned her loss to music and the stage.

"She is a sublime singer and would have done the role well," Devonshire replied.

"Pah!" Handel sat forcefully on his chair and grimaced as shards of pain lanced up his leg. He aggressively rubbed the leg again, trying to ease the agony, his face reddening with both pain and anger. "She would have indeed, William. She has the talent and voice to make any role come alive in front of an audience. It is her divine gift. But the crowds attending those paltry performances would have destroyed her, so venomous were they."

The pain in his leg grew fiercer.

"Laudanum! John, bring me my laudanum," Handel shouted at the door, hoping his butler would hear. "I have an inclination to remove myself from this godforsaken city and its intrigues. Perhaps there are others who would appreciate my most excellent music."

Handel struggled to his feet once again and shuffled over to a small desk against the wall behind Devonshire. He rummaged through some papers and picked one up, handing it to the duke.

"You've seen this?" Handel asked.

With one glance, Devonshire nodded. In his hand was a reproduction of a caricature of Handel that had been making its way around the hearths of London's nobility. Titled "The Charming Brute," it showed a bloated Handel, complete with a pig's face and snout, seated on a wine barrel at a pipe organ overflowing with fruits, hams, roast fowl, and bottles of wine.

"My erstwhile friend Joseph Goupy did this," Handel said listlessly. "If my friends mock me thus, you can guess what my opponents do." He shook his head suddenly, then stared at Devonshire as if seeing his guest for the first time. "My manners, Your Gr… William. I beg your forgiveness for the bleating of an old man."

Devonshire tut-tutted the apology just as the door opened and the butler hustled in with a small bottle and glass. Handel downed the potent painkiller and tried to persuade his caller to dine with him.

"My thanks, George, but no," Devonshire said. "I have a previous engagement at the Duke of Reddingham's in Piccadilly this evening, which is why I stopped here on the way. Before you decide to leave London, do me the honor of waiting. I have an idea that might suffice. In the meantime, I would like to commission a concerto for a garden party at my Chatsworth estate. I would pay the usual fee, of course."

"You leave for Ireland, then?" Handel knew that as Lord Lieutenant of Ireland—in effect, the King's Viceroy—the duke needed to visit Ireland on a regular basis, to oversee the Irish Parliament and perform the varied tasks required of the King's representative.

Devonshire nodded and rose. "If you would allow me the indulgence of giving some advice, my friend." He paused at the door, waiting while the butler hurried to get the duke's cloak and hat. "Make no hasty decisions to return to Germany or Italy. I'm sure these momentary issues will resolve themselves and the music of the great George Frederik Handel will once again enthrall the people of this city and this land."

Despite Handel's initial reluctance to accept the assignment and his arguments that he didn't want the duke tainted by his perceived fall from grace, Devonshire was adamant. He assured Handel that his music was well worth his suggested meagre sum.

After promising that his man would appear in the morning with a partial payment, Devonshire climbed into his carriage and left.

Handel stood by the window unmoving, Goupy's caricature still in hand, reacting only as his butler started to light more lamps.

"Leave them, John. Put them all out. I am retiring upstairs to my bedroom. No more visitors tonight."

He shuffled out of the room, ripped off his wig, and handed it to his man. Then, slowly and painfully, he climbed the stairs.

CHAPTER TWO

IN WHICH MRS. CIBBER SUFFERS FROM SHAME
AND PONDERS CHANGE

Susannah Cibber stood at the corner, peeking out from the window's green curtains. The bustling street was full and noisy as usual, with traders hawking their wares at the top of their voices, jockeying with the shouts of irritated waggoneers as they forced their way through the crowds. Most people strode purposefully past the house, intent on their business.

As Susannah took in the scene, she knew they would be there—somewhere on the street.

Sure enough, she spotted them through the throng across the street and two doors down, two men and one woman standing stock still amidst the flowing crowd, staring at her house. The woman held a fan to her face as if in shock as one of the men pointed first at the house and then at the window where Susannah stood.

She stepped away quickly and summoned her maid to close the curtains.

"Enough. I have had enough!" she shouted as she stormed out of the room, crying into her lace handkerchief. Her long brown curls bounced as she ran.

William Sloper met her in the hall just outside his study and held her as she sobbed into his shoulder. "My dear!"

"They're outside again, William."

"Who, my dear?" he asked, knowing full well the response.

"Ignorant, curious, damnable fools, that's who. They're always out there, pointing and looking at the house. Waiting to see if the whore of Drury Lane is at home and if they can catch a glimpse of her."

Sloper put his arms around her and led her into the drawing room, begging her to sit. He called the maid to attend to her mistress.

"Susannah, you were so strong at court. You didn't let them beat you then. Don't let them beat you now."

She snuffled a bit more and patted the lace handkerchief against her eyes to dry the remaining tears. "I know, William. I know. It's just that sometimes I feel so devastated and violated."

They continued to talk quietly as Susannah calmed down. It was the same nearly every day; curious snoops whose salacious interest in the Cibber scandal drew together like moths to a flame. They poked around the Drury Lane Theater, eager to see Theo Cibber the actor, theater manager, and depraved husband come and go. They dawdled and crisscrossed the street in front of Sloper's rented townhouse, trying to glimpse Theo's estranged wife and possibly even William Sloper, the third party of the sordid love triangle that still captivated them.

William looked over at his lover and sighed to himself. He did love her, despite the ignoble and painful outcome of their affair. He hadn't meant for it to happen; it had violated the morals that had been instilled in him but which he'd allowed to lapse.

Moving to London had opened many doors in terms of his career and living life to the fullest. With more than sufficient income from his wealthy merchant father to underwrite his extravagant lifestyle, he'd thrown himself into the city's enchantments with gusto. It was his appetite for the theater that had brought him into contact first with Theo Cibber and then with Susannah.

He'd admired the famed actor and manager at first. Soon the two were drinking and partying, but it quickly became obvious that Theo's drinking and extravagance far outpaced his ability to pay. In desperation, Theo had prevailed upon his new, wealthy friend to rent part of the house he shared with Susannah, thus supplementing the family income.

The opportunity to live with a great actor and his equally talented actress-singer wife was almost too good to be true. Indeed, he later ruefully acknowledged, it had been too good to be true. Sloper was soon witness to the violent and abusive side of Theo Cibber, the side prudently hidden far away from fawning audiences.

One evening, he'd returned to his quarters to find Susannah disheveled, her clothing ripped and red bloody stripes along her arm and back where her husband had beat her. He'd tried to comfort her but run afoul of Theo's violent temper himself. Driven off on the occasion, he became more and more aware of the turmoil and misery Susannah suffered. He marveled nevertheless at the astonishing change that came over her once she stepped onto the stage. From a beaten terrified woman, she became an animated, powerful soloist and actress who drew in her audience and melted them.

As the days passed, Susannah had begun to confide in him. While she earned a goodly sum as the lead actress at the theater, Theo seized her salary and parceled out only a few meager shillings to her, putting the rest into the theater or the production, at least ostensibly. In reality, he used the money to wine and dine his layabout friends and grovelers.

One day, on Sloper's birthday, he had invited Theo and Susannah to dine with him at a new tavern in Piccadilly. He'd asked Susannah to wear a particularly stunning dress to mark the special occasion. Instead she had worn a pretty but unremarkable gown. Only after much wheedling had he discovered that Theo had sold her other dress and many of her newer clothes in order to pay off some of his debts.

Sloper had commiserated with her and comforted her, which had soon, inevitably, led to their affair. At first Theo had ignored it, preferring instead to increase Sloper's rent and collect more of the merchant's money. Only when Theo's own friends and acquaintances noticed and began joking that his wife's attentions were falling elsewhere did Theo finally take action, launching a lawsuit designed to force a divorce that would pay him at least five thousand pounds in damages.

Testimony of Susannah's constant beatings when Cibber was drunk or displeased had shocked even a London society bred to believe that women were merely a husband's chattel. Cibber had forced Susannah into constant work, giving her little opportunity for rest. As a husband he had provoked, ridiculed, and exploited her, beating her on the slightest excuse, ensuring that only her stunning good looks were left undamaged.

Susannah's near slavery and Cibber's corruption had been splashed across the daily broadsheets while London ate up the sickening details. Disgust for Theo Cibber had risen and raucous demonstrations in court became the order of the day when Cibber testified. He was hooted at and jeered by the crowds as he left the courtroom.

Ultimately, the court had no choice but to find in Cibber's favor, although the judge's ruling left no doubt about his loathing of Theo Cibber; he awarded the man a grand total of just five pounds in damages.

She and Sloper had fled to the small townhouse Sloper had rented on the edge of fashionable Piccadilly. But even here, the curious crowds persisted and made her days unpleasant.

Susanna's mercurial temperament had rocked between abject misery and depression, punctuated by times of utter determination. There were days when she'd announced she wanted to be back on the stage. There were days when she wept uncontrollably, convinced her acting and singing days were over. Often the latter occurred when she saw people outside her house staring and pointing. There were even a few brave souls who knocked on the yellow-painted door, daring to ask for autographs—only to have the door slammed in their faces by the maid.

"Perhaps Mr. Handel could employ you in another of his operas?" Sloper remarked casually, watching her expression. "After all, it has been a while since the case was heard. Most of the public have shifted to other people and other interests."

"And have the crowds stopped jeering? No. Has the church forgiven? No. Are the lords and ladies of London society ready to embrace me back into their fold? No." Susannah's temper began to boil once again. "Besides, Mr. Handel is in no better position these days than I am. His operas are failing. The crowds mock him. His own friends are deserting him. There are even rumors that he will soon flee England and return to Germany."

"Surely not, my dear. His musical genius is loved by all. Even His Majesty adores his music."

Susannah fanned herself with her delicate lace fan. "The Prince of Wales hates the King and anyone His Majesty likes, so the prince and his entourage stand against anything the King supports. Mr. Handel is the substitute for their hatred."

"I think you're putting altogether too much upon the prince. He may be flighty and a bit scatterbrained, but I doubt he has that much power over what the masses think and like." Sloper walked across the room and rang a tiny handbell. "No, I think Mr. Handel's decline in popularity may say more about the fact that people want their music, their operas, in English. Not Italian."

Susannah huffed as the maid entered the room.

"Prepare the lunch for one half-hour, Polly." Sloper then dismissed the maid and turned again to Susannah, now fully recovered from her mini tantrum. "A spot of tea and a hearty lunch will do you good, m'dear. Take your mind off all this worry."

"Perhaps so, William. Perhaps so. But I don't want to stay in London any longer. I want to get away. Can we go somewhere else, my love? Anywhere, as long as it's away from here."

"What about your brother? He's been very supportive. Could he not use you in one of his productions?"

"Thomas is a dear, and he has been a great bulwark for me. But he too has to tread lightly. He has built a great following with his music and his productions at Covent Garden. Already 'Rule Britannia' has become popular among the masses and the nobility. The name Thomas Arne is now connected tightly with the best in music. Alas, I fear were he to put me in one of his productions it might severely damage his reputation just as he is beginning to soar like the genius he is." She paused and unconsciously dabbed some tears from her eyes. "Thomas, in fact, is the one who is urging me to leave London and establish myself elsewhere."

By the time the meal was over, Sloper was partially convinced that Susannah was right. Getting away from London might be the best thing that could happen. As she'd pointed out, offers of acting or singing parts had dried up. Even her brother was obviously reluctant to use her. Nobody wanted to be the first to take back the notorious Susannah Cibber and put her on stage again.

Also, despite the revulsion many had for Theo, he was still a force to be reckoned with in the theater world. Offering Susannah a part would put that brave impresario, whoever he was, in a vicious fight with Theo, not to mention the mobs.

"Do you still want to be on stage?" William asked her quietly.

There was a long pause before she answered.

"Yes. Yes, I do. I love to sing and act. I strongly feel the person I am portraying. I take them into my being and give them life. It is a wonderful feeling. And to see the audience react and understand what I am trying to portray about my character's life or conflict is a powerful thing." She looked up at him. "So yes, I want to be on stage again. But I know that it has been taken from me. My life on stage has been shattered."

She suddenly realized how her words must sound to the man who'd made love to her, taken her away from her lawful husband, and been a party to that travesty of a divorce trial. She smiled up to him and raised her hands to his face, planting a lingering kiss on his lips.

"I willingly accept it, of course. William, I love you. You rescued me from that beast, and for that alone I would give up all my fame and acclamation." She lowered her eyes. "But I confess, I yearn to perform."

William nodded. He understood how difficult it was for her. The affair, torrid though it had been, had also meant a diversion in his own plans. He'd come from Bristol as the chief representative for his father's company, but the bigger attraction had been his love for the theater. As he'd spent time in the capital and socialized with the various nobles he did business with, however, he had realized that politics and a seat in Parliament had become his driving ambition.

The affair with Susannah would have been forgiven by the lords and nobles who controlled the affairs of government—if it had been left simply at that. Instead he'd chosen to run away with Susannah and live with her. That, he now found, was a difficult obstacle to overcome.

He had quite obviously blotted his copy book as far as his government mentors were concerned, which put him in a difficult position. He cared for Susannah and wanted to be with her. But if he stayed with her, he jeopardized his political ambitions. Further, his father was furious with him from both a moral and business perspective. The notoriety Sloper now brought to the family business had become a detriment to commercial growth. And that, his father reminded him in letter after letter, would not be allowed to continue.

He had no doubts his father would remove him from his London position in the blink of an eye, except that William's latest purchase of Virginia tobacco had turned a more than decent profit for the company. His father had grudgingly sent his thanks. But William knew he was standing on a very thin eggshell. One more crack and he'd be banished to the colonies, no doubt.

If he took Susannah away, where would they go? It had to be a place where she could regain her confidence and he too could continue his career. A return to Bristol and his father would be a confession of failure, and in any case he'd be rejected by his father, who could not abide the thought of Susannah and he cohabiting.

They could of course move to the country. But unless he could secure a parliamentary seat and strong support from the local nobility, he could not afford it. And there was no telling how people would react to having Susannah in their midst.

It was a dilemma. But they couldn't stay in London much longer. That much was obvious.

"You said Thomas advised you to start somewhere else. Did he have any ideas?"

Susannah stared wistfully at her lover. "The continent, of course, and he said he would provide me with letters of recommendation." She stopped. "But his first suggestion was Dublin."

"Dublin?"

William wracked his brain. All he'd heard about it was the port and the city's rough and ready nature. He vaguely recalled that his father had an outpost in the Irish city, but in his youthful brashness he'd ignored everything about the business except for the operations in London he'd desperately wanted to lead. Older now, and somewhat wiser, he wished he'd paid more attention when his father had outlined the other warehouses and offices in his merchant empire.

Susannah carefully sized up his reaction, expecting to see him look down his nose. His seriousness surprised her.

"Yes," she hastily continued. "It really is the second largest arts center in the kingdom. The Lord Lieutenant, the Duke of Devonshire, is a great patron of the arts." Now that she had his attention, her enthusiasm gained steam. "And he's a great admirer of Mr. Handel as well. I understand that Dubliners enjoy lots of concerts of all kinds during the season there. Thomas was quite positive about the place. In fact, he's even spoken about going there to perform himself."

"Hmm. Dublin, eh?" He stared past her to the nondescript painting on the wall, lost in thought.

CHAPTER THREE

IN WHICH MR. HANDEL'S ENEMIES PLOT HIS END

The previous day's cold rains turned overnight into dry, sunny weather. Josiah Clegg welcomed the change as he walked briskly along Piccadilly, dodging the crowded commotion of the busy street. He couldn't wipe the smile from his face as his short, pudgy legs pushed through the many flower-sellers, barrow-pushers, and pie salesmen. Stepping around numerous piles of horse manure, he crossed the street and made his way down the Haymarket. At Suffolk Street, he passed by the magnificent structure of the King's Theater. His smile grew broader as he thought about his coming evening and which tavern he would bless with his presence and which of the many willing women in London he would enjoy.

Business first, though. He stepped into a building and climbed the rickety wooden stairs to the third level before pushing open a door and entering a tiny office lined with shelves piled high with papers and leather-bound books. A few beams of light snuck through the narrow window, revealing the bend head of a blading man hunched over his desk. All Clegg could see was his hand, clad in a half-glove, ink-stained fingers exposed, flying quickly over a paper.

Clegg shifted a pile of papers onto the floor and plunked himself down onto a hard, cheaply made wooden seat, waiting patiently. The man's hand moved so swiftly that the lone candle lighting the desk flickered every time he forcefully moved the quill. There were no sounds in the office other than the muted noise of the street and the *scratch-scratch* of the pen.

Finally, the man laid down his pen and blew softly on the paper before methodically sanding it. He gazed at Clegg, unspeaking, then reached down and opened a drawer. From it he pulled a small leather pouch, weighed it in his hand, and tossed it towards Clegg. A clink of coins broke the silence.

Greedily Clegg pulled the pouch open and tipped the coins into his hands. He counted them quickly, then looked up. "This is short. I was promised ten shillings for the job."

The balding man shrugged. "You were paid to ensure that Mr. Handel was shut down. We anticipated it would take much longer than three performances. It did not. You have been rewarded adequately for the small amount of time and effort it cost you." He raised his hand in caution, noting the anger building in Clegg's face. "Before you make idle threats, remember who you are working for. If I need you again, you will be contacted."

With that, the man turned his back on Clegg and picked up the quill, waving his hand in dismissal.

Clegg sat unmoving. "Sir, I must remind you that my expenses in this endeavor were quite substantial, considering the number of men and women I hired to disrupt the performances, not to mention the men I used to enter the printer's establishment and destroy the posters."

After a long pause, and without a word, the man opened the drawer again and pulled out another, larger pouch. He poured out some of the coins, selected two, and, turning slightly, tossed them in Clegg's general direction. Adroitly, Clegg caught both and added them to his small hoard.

"Never let it be said that your master is not both generous and considerate." The man turned back to his work.

Clegg, realizing he would get no more, clutched the coins and left the room as silently as he'd entered.

When he was gone, the man, named Grinton, stopped writing and laid the quill on the desktop. He picked up the note that had been delivered just before Clegg arrived and read it again. Despite Clegg's interruption, he still had twenty minutes. He reached up for a hat he'd dropped onto a shelf and placed it on his head, selected a long green woolen scarf and grey cloak, and clattered down the stairs.

As he opened the front door of the building, the man stopped and searched the street, making sure that Clegg had gone.

Satisfied, Grinton pulled the cloak and scarf around him and headed off. A brisk walk took him up Hedge Lane and across Leicester Fields. His cloak covered the threadbare patches on his breeches but couldn't keep the muck and manure kicked up by passing wagons from staining them. He stopped three times to brush the dirt and manure off as best he could, stepping around the cow turds. He had to look reasonably groomed, he told himself as he continued to brush as he walked, considering the man he was about to meet.

He turned at a red brick townhouse and knocked loudly on its garish green door. He glanced over at Leicester House along the north side of the unkempt meadow. Sheep grazed in the middle of the field while a cowherd shouted and directed a small herd of cows towards a small city dairy for milking. Rumor was that the Prince of Wales had his eyes on buying the House with the intent of creating an alternate court to his father down at St. James' Palace. That would certainly lift the tone of the entire area, he thought as he waited for the door to open.

A footman opened the door and sniffed haughtily, but on orders from his master he led Grinton to a small, well-stocked library where Lord Dawlish sat behind an immaculate and ornate desk. The sort, somewhat portly red-faced man was poring over a single leather-bound accounts book that lay open in front of him. To Dawlish's right, a small handbell completed the desk's furnishings.

Dawlish pursed his tight pale lips and peered through hooded eyes over his aquiline nose at his visitor. He remained seated, not offering Mr. Grinton a seat, leaving the little man to stand awkwardly, gripping his grubby hands. The man's smell, of the city streets and cesspools, offended him and he regretted having arranged this meeting at his own home. But, he philosophized, needs must. He propped his elbows on the desk, folding his hands into a prayer-like posture, fingertips barely touching his lips.

"You did well, Mr. Grinton," Dawlish began. "I hear Meinheer Handel has closed his opera and is near destitution. My partners will be pleased."

"Yes, my lord, I was able to hire some—"

"I do not want to know the methods you employed or who you hired. It is enough for us that the deed was done." A cold smile creased across Dawlish's face, although it disappeared immediately.

Grinton nodded his head and said no more. Life had looked up ever since Lord Dawlish had sought him out the previous year and hired him for what his lordship had called "sundry duties." It mattered not a whit to Grinton what those duties were, even if they crossed into the grey or even black shadows of the law. For too long he'd scrambled and scratched out a meagre living from the dregs of London, offering up the fruits of his legal knowledge. Did it really matter to his normal clients that his legal training was the result of a mere six months of work as a barely capable clerk to a near-blind aging lawyer in Dartford? He didn't care. When the old codger had finally died, Grinton stole the man's legal books and disappeared into the depths of the city's infamous crime-infested slum known as the Rookery. Two months later, the one-time clerk and petty thief named Gilbert Snowley had emerged as the lawyer Edward Grinton, having also stolen his former employer's name.

Even so, between slapdash and suspect legal advice for even the more suspect individuals, he'd only barely survived.

Then, in October, Lord Dawlish had sought him out one night and hired him. His rising ego hadn't questioned why one of the new-money noblemen of the realm would dip into the dregs of London for his help. All that mattered was that the guinea he'd received each month for his services provided welcome relief. It meant he could eat reasonably well and pay the rent on his ramshackle rooms.

Dawlish had judged his creature well. Greed and a lack of moral compass, plus connections among the London underworld, had made Grinton the perfect choice for some of the more sordid activities the prince required. Grinton was also someone he could deny knowledge of, or even dispose of easily.

"We now require more of your expertise, Mr. Grinton," Dawlish said. "We want you to find us much information as you can about Mr. Handel's debts, his lifestyle, his close friends, and whatever else you can about him. And when you secure such information, provide it to Mr. Zephaniah Randford."

Grinton's head snapped up. "The owner of *The Weekly Gazette?*" Without waiting for an answer, his greedy mind began to calculate how much more he could squeeze out of the aristocrat. "It would, of course, require a considerable investment to obtain such information."

"You are already adequately paid, Mr. Grinton," Dawlish snapped coldly. "Do not press your luck. There are others we can deal with."

Dawlish rang his handbell. A footman who'd been hovering just outside the door entered and unceremoniously escorted Grinton out.

Moments later, Dawlish penned a brief note to his mentor, explaining that the next phase of the campaign against Handel had begun. He instructed his footman to ensure its delivery as quickly as possible.

In Mayfair, a mile or so west of Dawlish's house, George Frederik Handel gingerly eased himself through his front door and down the stone steps into a waiting sedan chair. The days when he could afford his own carriage had fled and he could no longer walk the distance to St. George's on Hanover Square. At least the warm spring sun had swept away the cold rains and drizzle that had assaulted the city for more than a week.

Handel stepped into the chair, instructing the chairmen to take him to the church.

It was a short trip, just along Brook Street to Hanover Square and down Great George Street. As he labored up the steps through the lofty Grecian columns that fronted the church, he felt his spirit uplift. He quietly entered the sanctuary and stopped at the top of the center aisle, as he always did, to drink in the beauty of the stained-glass windows.

The curate saw him and immediately came over. "Mr. Handel, it is good to see you in God's house yet again. Do you wish to play?" He gestured toward the great pipe organ above them.

"Thank you, Henry. I will in a moment. First, I pray."

Handel made his way to a pew and sat a moment, drinking in the warmth of the rich dark wooden pews and decorations throughout the church, complemented by the equally rich wooden balcony that swept around all three sides facing the high altar. His snow-white wig flowed around his shoulders as he knelt and bowed his head.

His prayer was more resigned than it had been on previous mornings when he'd railed against his enemies and misfortune, calling upon God to smite them and restore him to the favor of the people. Today, it was a simple prayer. He reached into one of his voluminous coat pockets and gripped his personal Book of Prayer. For ten minutes he knelt, head bowed, beseeching God to accept him, a penitent.

"I have railed against my enemies, O God," he murmured. "Take away mine anger. I thank thee for the music you have given me, for the talent you have blessed me with. I thank thee but ask forgiveness for taking it so lightly. My enemies have shown me how fleeting it all is; how fickle people are. Thou hast blest me, O God, and I bend in supplication before thee. If thou doth desire my removal from London, then blessed be thy name. I seek, Lord, for thy divine guidance. Money, health, and fame are thine to proffer to thy servants. I have lost them all, but I now accept their loss, O mighty God. May I be found worthy in thy sight. The Lord giveth and the Lord taketh away. Blessed be the name of the Lord."

He sat back on the sturdy pew, eyes closed in contemplation, and enjoyed the solitude broken only by the shuffling of feet and the occasional creaking of pews. His journey from Lutheranism to Anglican had been easy, he reflected, and symbolic of his decision years ago to become a nationalized Englishman. But the deepening journey of his faith had turned out to be a lot bumpier and trickier as he fought his own carnal self—his ego, his love of the fine life of foods and wine, his anger, and his impatience—on the way to a profound sense of God.

After lingering in contemplation a few more minutes, he rose and made his way slowly up the stairs and along the back of the church, finally sitting down at the great keyboard in front of the massive pipe organ.

In moments, the church was flooded with the sound of the marvelous instrument in the hands of a master. Old hymns and new creations poured from his hands and mind as he soared heavenward with the notes. Below him, unseen, people walked quietly into the sanctuary and sat in the pews, transfixed by the artistry of the music. Some, the regulars at St. George's, nodded profoundly; Mr. Handel was back at the organ. All was well in their world.

Handel played for more than an hour. Whether florid, heavy, light, soft, complex, or simple, each offering resonated throughout the building. His fingers flew over the keys as he played like a man possessed. His own compositions alternated and flowed into Bach, Haydn, and even Telemann, only to morph into works by newer composers such as Charles Wesley and Isaac Watts. It was as if he were taking out his frustrations at his situation and contrasting them to his deep underlying faith. That he had faith, even his critics agreed. What they could not agree on was whether the bulk of his faith was in God or in himself.

Finally, the last ringing notes echoed through the beautifully acoustic church. He got up and, for the first time, looked down in astonishment to witness a crowd of men and women sitting in the pews below. As he watched, they began to applaud, quietly at first then gaining in enthusiasm and volume. He hesitated, then bowed slightly and moved away from the mighty organ.

At the back of one of the pews, a well-dressed man sat with his hands on his knees, refusing to participate in the applause. He stiffened as the crowd reacted, instead watching carefully as Handel stepped down off the staircase and entered the main sanctuary. His eyes narrowed as the composer acknowledged the crowd again before hurrying out of the church.

The man, Lord Ilchester, followed far behind Handel, pushing through the crowd who fell back as they perceived his aristocratic demeanor. Ilchester's footmen rushed up beside him to protect him from the masses. He idly flicked dust from his coffee-colored coat, leaning heavily on his walking stick. He noted Handel calling over a sedan chair, then heading back up Great George towards his house.

As Ilchester stood on the church steps watching Handel's departure and waiting for his own carriage to draw up, he heard a thin wheezy voice beside him.

"Well, Lord Ilchester, you leave the same premises as our esteemed Mr. Handel. Are we to draw any conclusions?"

Ilchester spun around, sneering at the small, weasel-like man standing beside him, wigless but with his greying brown hair tied back with a black ribbon. A long woolen scarf was wrapped around his neck with two ends hanging in unruly fashion.

"Crysdale!" Ilchester exclaimed. "Is your broadsheet newspaper so eager to scrape under the dung heap that they must send you out to annoy your betters?"

John Crysdale, editor of *The Tarrier*, gave a cold smile in return, flashing his yellowed, crooked teeth.

"My lord, forgive me for bothering you. I merely noted your presence in St. George's as Mr. Handle performed. I wondered to myself if you were moving away from your previous criticisms of him. Certainly, from what I heard in there, his music enjoyed a profound response. Lots of applause. And very loud and prolonged too!"

Ilchester glared at the little man with undisguised disdain. "Then you will also have noted that I did not join in the ovation, Mr. Crysdale. That alone should tell you something."

Without waiting for a response, Ilchester strode quickly towards the carriage, its door already held open by his footman.

Smiling, Crysdale watched as the carriage disappeared down St. George Street. For all the animosity he felt towards the nobleman and his ilk, he was intrigued to find that the Prince of Wales' supporters such oozed dislike for Handel. Crysdale did not know why, nor did he probe too deeply to find out. He was merely pleased that it existed, thereby providing him with lots of fodder for his paper.

He shrugged and began walking, pulling his coat and scarf tighter against him as a cool wind picked up and blew along the street in defiance of the warming sun. Now that the furor over the Cibber marriage was over, scandal and intrigue in the city seemed to have dissipated. All that remained was the increasing acrimony between the King and his son, a war played out by the small battles that embroiled each's favorites. Music, art, or theater didn't matter much, only insofar as they defined which side members of the aristocracy came down on.

Commonplace scandals, or crimes such as murder or the latest actions of the vicious highwaymen roaming the open countryside, were not for Crysdale and *The Tarrier*. No. For him, it was the intrigue and posturing of the nobility. Their failings and foibles were the meat on which his readers preferred to dine. Clearly this was a meal would be ongoing.

He smiled to himself again and walked on.

CHAPTER FOUR

IN WHICH MR. HANDEL'S FRIENDS TRY TO HELP

Charles Jennens stepped out of his deep burgundy carriage and walked quickly into the large townhouse he owned on Great Ormond Street. Two footmen followed, struggling with a large cloth-covered painting, the latest in Mr. Jennens' considerable and admired collection.

The large red-bricked house fit in nicely with its gentrified surroundings. The area attracted the newly wealthy merchant class. They flitted around the edges of the nobility's preferred neighborhoods, such as Piccadilly, although, truth be told, the merchant's houses were often grander, more modern, and more luxurious than many of those owned by the nobility.

In his toasty warm library, sitting by the roaring fire, Jennens cared little about such frivolities as houses and material goods. He had bought the house not because of his neighbors but for its proximity to Covent Garden and Haymarket, to Lincoln Fields and Drury Lane, his beloved theater district where he could enjoy and patronize the finest in operas and stage productions.

His great wealth was a mere steppingstone to the three things he cared about above all else: the protection of the Christian faith, his love of music and the arts, and finally the restoration of the rightful monarch. His stance, as well as that of many of his friends, was that he objected to the ousting of King James II in what had been called The Glorious Revolution. God had ordained the Stuarts to rule, and man could not gainsay God's legitimate rulers. William of Orange and his wife Mary, however related, had not been direct heirs. Therefore, they and their descendants were not legitimate rulers. It was not right, in his mind, especially the tenuous links that had made George, Elector of Hanover, King of England.

Despite those firm beliefs, Jennens was no rebellious Jacobite, ready to take up arms against the monarchy. He just stood on his principles, that the Stuart line, not Hanover, should rule. It had led to Jennens and his friends being labelled non-jurors, for their refusal to swear allegiance to what they considered the Hanoverian usurper, King George I and his son, now King George II. It meant Jennens was now excluded from any hope of service to the nation. Like all non-jurors, he couldn't enter Parliament nor join the army or navy, because he wouldn't swear allegiance to King George. Neither could he become a clergyman, join one of the great trading companies, or join the Bank of England as a director. He and his fellow non-jurors were banned from public service of any kind.

While some friends chafed under these restrictions, Jennens himself didn't care. Being a non-juror merely freed him to pursue his many interests and gave him unique opportunities to promulgate the faith in his own way. Temporal matters such as governments and power were not on his horizons. He paid little attention even to the source of his father's great wealth, forged in the ironmaking industry. The thousands of tons of iron being cast in the Midlands even now needed wood to become charcoal. His father had assiduously bought thousands of acres of woodland across England, Wales, and Ireland, as well as across Europe, to feed the money-making fires.

After his father's death, Jennens had merely hired a capable and honest man to oversee the vast estates and ensure continued revenue while he concentrated on his own pursuits.

As he sat before the fire, he picked up one of his favorite pamphlets, Jonathan Swift's *Argument Against Abolishing Christianity*, and lovingly caressed its arguments in his mind. The book had planted a thought several months ago, and Jennens had pursued the idea patiently, as was his wont, letting it swirl around in his mind, oblivious to how long it might take. What mattered was that the idea he pursued had time to germinate and come to fruition in its own time.

And time he had in abundance.

Jennens was perfectly aware of the dichotomy in his own being. He loved living in London with its hustle and bustle and lively cultural pursuits, but all the time he enjoyed the city he yearned for the tranquility and beauty of the family estate at Gopsall Hall in Leicestershire. Yet when he was in Gopsall, riding across the verdant fields and through the woods, his heart remained in his equally beloved London.

Such was the pull in his mind between his enthusiasms. He enjoyed rich, lively debate with friends about theology, philosophy, and governance, but his mind would already be appreciating the beauty of the latest painting he'd acquired or replaying the stirring performance he'd just attended. As he read, viewed art, or listened in rapt attention to a musical masterpiece, his focus was always split between it and the next debate or project he had in mind.

Even now, as he scoured Swift, his mind raced. He worried about the latest gossip he'd heard about his friend Handel.

A soft knock on the library door broke his thoughts. At his command, the door opened. His butler, Henry, approached with a small silver plate.

"Some letters from Gopsall, sir, and an invitation from the Duke of Devonshire."

Jennens picked the card and letters up off the plate. He quickly perused the letter, noting his mother's request to return to Gopsall as soon as he deemed possible. A second letter, from his estate manager, mildly concerned him. Although his mother hadn't said so directly in her letter, it seemed she was ailing again. The manager suggested that an early visit might be advisable. The third item was an invitation to attend a dinner party at the Duke of Devonshire's London home on Piccadilly for Tuesday next.

"Henry, send my thanks to His Grace and inform him I will attend."

Jennens then dismissed the butler and put the letters aside. His mother was often prone to illness and demanding his presence. More often than not, he found her in perfect health when he arrived. Yet it was an excuse to return to Gopsall and enjoy its bucolic attractions, especially now that Mr. Handel had cancelled his latest production.

He would have to think more about this.

The thought of the cancelled opera reminded him again of the disturbing talk he'd heard, that Handel was leaving England—for good, his informant had declared.

Jennens was troubled by the news. Two days ago, he had sent a note around to Handel's Brook Street home expressing his concern, but negotiations for his latest painting acquisitions had precluded a personal visit. Besides, he'd been told that Handel was seeing very few people these days, friends or otherwise.

He picked up the duke's invitation again and studied it. Devonshire was a long-time friend, Jennens' non-juror status notwithstanding. They saw eye to eye on most things. In conversation with the duke, Jennens had been forced to admit he even liked King George, especially his patronage of the arts, but he could never accept or swear allegiance to the man.

"I just cannot see it, my dear Charles," the duke had once said. "On the one hand, you are an ardent Protestant, yet you reject the Protestant king and embrace the Roman Catholicism of the Jacobites!"

Jennens' response, affirming the divine succession of kings as opposed to mankind's selection of kings, had not swayed the duke.

Nevertheless, putting aside the philosophical argument of kingly succession, Jennens and Devonshire genuinely liked each other and shared many of the same passions.

His mind suddenly made up, Jennens called Henry and asked him to have the carriage brought around as quickly as possible.

Less than an hour later, Jennens pulled up in front of the duke's London residence, Devonshire House, which graced the north side of Piccadilly. Once inside, he was directed to the duke's drawing room where he got right to the point.

"William, I'm gravely concerned. I've heard from several different sources that our dear friend Handel is considering leaving us and returning either to Germany or Italy. If true, this is devastating! His genius, his mastery of so many different kinds of music, his talent on the keys, and his virtuosity in composition, is unparalleled in our nation. The loss to our culture could never be replaced!"

Devonshire held up his hand to stem the flow of words. "My dear Charles, I totally agree. Losing Handel cannot be allowed to happen."

"What can we do then, William? What can I do?"

While he shepherded Jennens to a seat, Devonshire gestured to the butler for some wine. "Here, Charles. Enjoy this fine Italian red I just received. Then we can talk."

While they sipped, Devonshire reported on his own visit to Handel the previous evening.

"He is not doing well at all, Charles. His health issues, gout, and particularly the paralysis that affected him the past while have taken him down physically. And he does certainly have severe financial concerns. He lost a lot of money on those two damned operas. And he's a pawn in the battle between the King and prince, aided and abetted by jealous musicians, theater owners, and lower-class broadsheet press. But it's more than that, I think. His confidence is gone, or at least on its last legs."

"Confidence has never been a problem for George," Jennens challenged. "He may have lacked money at times, and he may lack friends and health. But confidence? Never. He is the most confident man I know. He is great, and he know it. In fact, he revels in it."

Devonshire nodded. "True, George has never been shy about himself. Do you remember when someone accused him of borrowing material from Bononcini? George told everyone that the material was actually too good for the Italian maestro." The duke chuckled at the memory. "Handel said Bononcini didn't know what to do with his own music at all. Fortunately, I did."

They both laughed.

"Yes, and do you remember the time Handel and I went for a meal at The Golden Goose after one of his operas?" Jennens added. "We waited and waited for our meal until finally Handel demanded an explanation for the delay. I thought he would explode when the landlord said they were still waiting for more company to arrive. 'Deliver the meal *prestissimo!*' Handel shouted. '*I am* the company!'" Jennens mimicked the composer perfectly, right down to the man's German accent and pronunciation.

Still chortling, Devonshire agreed. "That's the point, Charles. Ego and confidence have never been Handel's problem. But now?" He gestured futilely. "He seems defeated. He seems to have given up." He slapped Jennens' knee as he got up to refill his glass. "And that, my dear friend, is why we have to re-cultivate his self-confidence."

Together they talked well into afternoon. Devonshire told Jennens that he'd personally commissioned a small concerto for a summer fete. He added that he'd also met with the King on other matters.

"I discreetly suggested to His Majesty that he commission a new, special piece by Handel to celebrate twenty-five years of the Hanoverian dynasty," Devonshire said. "Even if a year late, it would be good for the nation. Alas, His Majesty did not respond."

Back and forth they threw out ideas and just as quickly dismissed them.

"He needs a triumph, Charles," the duke insisted. "One that will transcend the petty bickering between the King and the prince. One that will immobilize the sycophants in the prince's retinue and lift our friend out of the slimy mire of their schemes."

"Unless His Majesty is willing to pay for a huge extravaganza, I don't think it will happen," Jennens replied. Needing a triumph and producing it were two different things. "His late father, George I, took that brilliant barge trip down the Thames. Handel's 'Water Music' was perfect for the occasion and caused his reputation to soar to new levels. He'll need something like that, and soon, before it's too late."

Devonshire agreed but worried his own ability to help would necessarily be minimal. His posting to Dublin as Lord Lieutenant of Ireland required his time and presence on that island. London and its intrigues would be far away.

"But you could help with another libretto," Devonshire said. "You did the one for *Saul*, and it was a great success."

Jennens flushed with pleasure at the duke's words.

Devonshire poked his friend and added slyly, "Mind you, anyone with half a brain could see you intended it as a lament for the execution of King Charles." He grinned. "You're lucky we live in modern times and that King George didn't see your libretto as treason, my friend."

Jennens looked up, startled.

"Actually, my friends at court said the King quite enjoyed *Saul*," Devonshire added hastily.

Jennens said nothing but looked worriedly at the duke. "I have never hidden my loyalties, but you and everyone knows I have accepted the Hanovers, even if I do not swear allegiance."

The duke dismissed the comment with a wave of his hand. "You miss my point, my dear Charles. Do you have a libretto you could give to Handel? One that would feed the fires of his creativity and challenge his musical genius?"

Jennens was silent for a moment, then dropped his head. "No. I don't."

But even as he said the words, the idea that had been whispering to him sporadically suddenly began to frame itself. Nevertheless, he said nothing, preferring to let the idea shape itself further before uttering a word.

There was silence between them as they contemplated their friend's dilemma.

"That is sad then," Devonshire said. "Both of us desire to help our friend and keep his genius in Britain, but neither of us has yet found the key. It seems unlikely either of us will be able to help him."

Dusk was falling as they waited for Jennens' carriage to be brought around. The duke apologized for not entertaining his guest further, but he explained that he'd planned a rare supper at home with his wife and family. Besides, there was much planning to do for the upcoming move to Ireland, and he wanted to spend time at Chatsworth before crossing the Irish Sea.

After a hearty invitation to join him at Chatsworth before summer, they parted.

By morning, Jennens had made a decision.

With Handel's opera closed down and few new productions in the offing, he would return to Gopsall House. He expected his mother to be hale and hearty when he arrived, but the trip would give him the excuse to take his newest acquisitions home. He was particularly proud of the Van Dyke he'd bought three weeks ago, as well two of the Dutch painter Pieter Rijsbrack's English landscapes. Indeed, he was so impressed with the Dutchman's work he was considering commissioning him to do a landscape of Gopsall. Plus, he told himself, Gopsall was handy to Chatsworth. He'd be able to spend some more time with Devonshire and perhaps come up with a plan for Handel.

A frenzy of activity followed for the next week as he began to close the Bloomsbury house. Wagons came early on the third day and the wagoneer's men, as well as two of Jennens' footmen, loaded everything carefully. Jennens fussed around them as they worked, making sure the artwork was well covered and protected for the long trip north. He examined the wagons carefully and inspected the massive Clydesdales that would haul his trove of paintings, statues, and other newly bought possessions.

As much as he fussed over the paintings, he obsessed over the latest books he'd purchased. All books were like treasure to him, but they were also old, well-loved friends. His library at Gopsall now exceeded eight thousand volumes, and to him they were like a well worn, comfortable cloak. The library gave him great pleasure, embraced him, warmed him, and comforted him. His latest volumes, some already devoured, would go north too. As he contemplated the road ahead, he reminded himself to put aside a number of his books to take with him personally in the carriage to sustain him on the arduous journey.

"Now, mind you sleep with the wagons at each inn," Jennens reminded the two footmen who would accompany the wagons. "You must guard the load with your lives."

The footmen, long used to Jennens' habit of repeating instructions and fretting over every detail from previous trips to and from Gopsall, merely acknowledged his orders and went back to finishing the loading.

He pulled one aside. "I will leave next Thursday and, God- and weather-permitting, should arrive at Gopsall no later than the following Tuesday. Tell Simmonds I have said he is not to hang the paintings at all, nor position the statues in any way. That is something I want to do myself."

He had no intention of letting his chief butler at Gopsall hustle to put everything away or hang paintings so that everything was perfect for his arrival. The pleasure of placing everything in its perfect place was one he relished and intended for himself and himself alone.

After giving final instructions to the master of the wagons, he watched from his stone front steps as the wagons lumbered along the street, pushing their way through the crowds, until he could see them no more.

Inside, while the remaining staff bustled around preparing a meal, he adjourned to the library and picked up Swift again. In his typical satirical way, Swift demolished a variety of assaults, some sincere and others fatuous, against the faith. Although Swift had penned the satire more than thirty years ago, Jennens still perceived the same anti-religious feelings in society today. Only yesterday he'd warned a small group of friends, "The ongoing dissolution in society is caused by their rejection, or at the very least ignorance, of God and the church."

The lively debate that'd ensued had begun to solidify a thought.

"What Britain needs," he'd declared to his raucous friends, "is a strong declaration as to the efficacy of the word of God. He has shown his love to man, but man must accept him at his word. And that word is Scripture!"

As they had enjoyed another glass of port, they'd discussed Jennens' arguments.

"People today attend church because they have to, not because they want to or are drawn," shouted one. "They don't even listen to the Archbishop of Canterbury, let alone the local vicar."

Others had pointed out that, especially in crowded London, Sunday was much like any other day. There were no compelling reasons to attend church, so most did not. Still another argued that as the population grew, hundreds, perhaps thousands, of children were being raised without ever entering a church other than for baptism or burial.

They had glumly agreed that deism and belief in a vague Supreme Being was supplanting the solidity of the Christian faith and impregnating even the arts and intellectual sphere with its undefined beliefs. The concepts of divine intervention or biblical revelation were sneeringly dismissed. Instead, a sense of "natural" religion, where God was seen in nature, had begun to develop. But this natural religion outright rejected the supernatural, miracles, and prophecy that was so integral to the Christian faith and so strongly espoused in Scripture.

He thought all night about their discussion, and as he did his last conversation with the Duke of Devonshire reverberated in his mind. For Jennens, a strong, abiding faith was imperative. It drove him. It sustained him. Had he not declared himself a non-juror, he might well have pursued a theological career or become a clergyman. But his status had demanded he find another way of sharing his faith. The Bible was the rock on which his faith rested. It was solid, unmovable, unimpacted by the changing vagaries of people's likes and dislikes. It overrode culture, career, status, wealth, and yes, even monarchs. Especially those who disposed of the divine right of kings.

One comment by his friend Richard Fitzsimmons particularly niggled away in his mind: "If people read their Bibles and absorbed it the way our dear friend

Charles absorbs his operas and concerts, many would likely rebuild their faith and return to the church."

At his breakfast the next morning, Jennens glanced at Swift again, then put it aside. Instead he reached over to a side table and grasped a smooth leather-bound Bible. Reverently, he picked it up and began to read. The Bible was his foundation. He found comfort in its simple liturgical cadences and language.

But as he read, the ideas that floated and danced around his mind formed into the whisper of an idea. His thoughts returned to the librettos he'd provided Handel in the past. Even *Saul*, Jennens conceded, had revolved around the dramatic story of a biblical character that the compose had used to promote an earthly concept—sorrow over a doomed king.

As he reviewed his previous librettos for operas and oratorios and the ideas behind them, he realized that many were shallow compared with the concept now forming in his mind. They'd lacked purpose and real cohesion.

He thumbed through the Bible, reading his favorite passages. What if he wrote a libretto so that it rose above simple biblical stories like Saul and Esther, and instead laid out a sound theological teaching? What if he could create a unified and authoritative thread that told the story of man's redemption through careful use of selected portions of Scripture? Would such a libretto challenge Handel enough to shake him out of his despair?

His mind began to churn even as he turned to other pressing matters. He determined to use his days in the carriage to think about and begin collecting various passages he could use. And above all, he would use the time to pray—for himself, Handel, and most importantly the truths he yearned to share with the masses.

CHAPTER FIVE

IN WHICH MR. HANDEL'S ENEMIES
PLOT TO DESTROY HIM

The footman knocked quietly on the door, waiting for permission to proceed. "Enter!"

With that word, his white-gloved hands pushed open the door. He stood aside, rigid in his royal blue, gold-trimmed frockcoat and breeches, meticulous white wig, and white waistcoat.

"Your Royal Highness, the Right Honorable the Lord Ilchester, Earl of Bromsgrove, and Lord Dawlish."

Ilchester and Dawlish had dusted themselves off as much as they could after their before-dawn carriage ride from London to the prince's palace. As the men bowed and approached, before extending their white-stockinged left legs and bowing deeply again, a gesture known as "showing the leg," the footman carefully and silently backed out, gently closing the door behind him.

"Gentlemen, be seated," said Frederick, the Prince of Wales. "Welcome once again to Cliveden."

The prince gestured lazily to a settee and himself took a seat in an ornate, throne-like, scarlet armchair laden with gold filigree and ornamentation. He'd commissioned it deliberately to reinforce his belief that he headed a second and alternative court to his father, George II. The chair dominated the room, sitting upon a small red-carpeted dais that matched the rest of the room's flooring. The rich wooden walls had been ornately decorated with portraits and landscapes by some of the finest artists that Europe, and especially England, had produced. They were part of the prince's own personal collection.

Frederick's somewhat smaller stature was diminished in the great chair even though his girth filled the seat quite well. Ilchester was aware that his own six-foot height left him looking down upon the prince, especially when they stood next to each other. He also noted the prince's slightly disheveled appearance this early in the morning. It spoke either to a raucous drunken party the night before, or a quick morning assignation with his latest mistress, interrupted by their arrival.

When the Prince reached over to a side table and lifted a half-filled jug of claret, poured some into his glass, and took a long deep drink, Ilchester knew it was the former. This was confirmed moments later as the prince wiped his mouth with his lace sleeve.

"Had a wonderful celebration last night." Frederick burped and waved a half-hearted apology. "Seems His Majesty is upset that I am challenging him in Parliament for a greater allowance." He slurred his words slightly. "I spoke to some of the lords and supporters and we are going to press my case in Parliament."

Ilchester knew that money was a blazing fire at the heart of the father and son's hatred for each other. The King refused to offer even a modest increase to the prince's already stringent allowance. The prince, meanwhile, was profligate, reck-lessly spending thousands of pounds he did not have, counting on friends such as Ilchester and especially his wealthy confidante George Dodington to lend him the funds needed to stave off those he owed.

"Your Royal Highness, is that wise? Parliament only raised your allowance a slight amount back in '37 after a great furor…"

Before he could say more, the prince jumped to his feet and flung his glass against the nearest cabinet, scattering glass shards across the room.

"Damn you, man, don't you dare contradict me," the prince raged. He swore and paced the room, shaking his fists and subjecting the two men to a tirade about the King for his parsimonious and unwarranted treatment of his heir.

As soon as Frederick rose, both Ilchester and Dawlish also stood, blanching under the profanity-laced tirade.

When the prince swayed and stumbled back into his seat, Ilchester tried again. "Sir, I meant no disrespect. I merely wanted to suggest that you not be so visible in the request this time. I beg you, sir, let your friends and supporters build the case for you and approach the prime minister ourselves on your behalf."

Mollified somewhat, Frederick weakly waved a hand at them. "You would do this?"

"Yes, sir. Allow us to speak to Mr. Walpole, and especially those members of Parliament who strongly support you and wish to see you treated and com-pensated as a prince of the Kingdom." Seeing the prince's eye fixed on him, he pushed a little harder. "You have most certainly been treated unfairly by His Maj-esty. All Britain can see that. Let us persuade Parliament that you are a jewel to be treasured, and rewarded as such. You are the heir to the throne and deserve to be treated accordingly, sir. Far better that such arguments come from others than from Your Royal Highness."

Suddenly, Frederick smiled at the tall, thin man standing before him. "Mayhap you are right, Ilchester. You will speak to Walpole?"

"I will, sir. And the Lord Chancellor and Lord Privy Seal, to start with. We will prevail, sir."

Frederick drummed his fingers on the arms of his chair. His quick glance at the shards of glass showed his regret that his sudden temper had deprived him of his claret. He glanced around, saw the nearby jug, and smiled. He then picked it up and drank lustily, an action even Ilchester found uncouth, although it was typical of the weak spendthrift before him.

The prince drank deeply and wiped his mouth with sleeve yet again. Drunk, he most certainly was. Add to that the fact that the prince was uncouth and immoral, a womanizing gambler more connected to lies than truth. For Ilchester's purposes, the prince was the ideal tool to rid the nation of the German Hanovers. Not to bring back the ill-fated Stuarts, no, but to restore the greatness of English-born rulers, descendants of the old families, to begin a new dynasty. Ilchester was still mulling over which to support. For now, the goal was to shake the foundations of the Hanoverians. Then he would be ready to take the next steps.

Before he could comment further on the prince's ever-present financial woes, Frederick scrutinized the men intently. "And do you bring me good news regarding Handel?"

Ilchester glanced over at Dawlish and nodded at him slightly, giving him permission to speak.

Grinning, Dawlish began. "Your Royal Highness, we have closed the play *Deidamia* after only three performances—"

Frederick swore and waved his hand in dismissal. "I know that, you fool. We are not isolated here at Cliveden, sir. I would thank you not to waste my time with trivia I already know. The issue is, have you forced Handel into debtors' prison or out of the country? That, sir, is what I want to know!"

The smile dropped off Dawlish's face. "Your Royal Highness, we are much closer to that result than we were last week—"

Again, a furious Prince interrupted. "I don't want close, Lord Dawlish, I want gone. Finished. Destroyed." He raged against Handel, comparing him to a foreign pustule sucking money out of the country while importing other foreign singers, musicians, and actors. "He crushes opportunities for good English people to take these roles. Don't we have talented musicians? Don't we have excellent composers, like Thomas Arne?" he bleated. "As long as Handel is around, he stifles all others. We must destroy him."

Dawlish attempted once more. "Sir, he was within days of the debtors' prison when he received a commission from the Duke of Devonshire to help pay off his immediate debts." He braced himself for another tirade and added, "His Majesty also gave him a small grant to produce some music for a dinner he's holding at St. James' Palace. But the rumors are that he will be leaving London soon."

"I don't want rumors, Dawlish. I want certainty! I want proof that he has left our shores, and the sooner you get it done, the better."

Frederick then bellowed at the footman, who, waiting patiently behind the door, flung the door open, bowed, and stepped inside.

"Handel bores me. His music bores me. He's a relic of the past and must be gotten rid of." Frederick shot a quick grin at the two men. "Besides, even if he didn't bore me, I couldn't like him. My father likes him, and I cannot like anything or anyone my father likes. I am held to a piddly amount of funds by an ungenerous government guided to do so by my parsimonious father, yet I hear that the next Italian opera will be staged at the Haymarket this autumn and the cost will exceed some six thousand pounds. Gad, 'pon my honor, gentlemen, is this country not in a sad state when we can fling away such sums for a parcel of squeaking, capering, and fiddling Italians and foreign buffoons?"

Ilchester leaned forward and quietly and discreetly tried to correct the prince. "But Mr. Handel has nothing to do with these performances, Your Highness."

"Not personally, perhaps," the prince bellowed, "but he is the leader of that pack. He is the one who inflicted Italian music upon us, to the exclusion of fine English music like Purcell or Arne or any hundreds of others. Gad, sir, yes, I blame Handel and his poltroons, for they are an insult to our nation. And the King supports them!"

Frederick had spun himself into full-fledged rage, fueled by the alcohol. Considering discretion the better part of valor, Ilchester merely nodded, learned back, and let the storm blow.

Finally, exhausted by his rant, the prince sank into his chair. He turned to the footman. "See these gentlemen out." He paused and glared at both guests. "And pass the word that they are not welcome back at Cliveden until they have positive tidings for me."

He got up and lurched towards the door leading to his inner rooms as Ilchester and Dawlish backed up, bowing and showing a leg as they did so until they were out the door.

The footman said nothing as he closed the door, turned, and led the two men back to the main entrance where their carriage waited.

Neither spoke until the carriage passed through the gates of Cliveden House and turned onto the rough, muddy roads towards London.

"You told me that Handel was leaving," Ilchester hissed as he stared straight ahead. His quiet anger had festered throughout the audience between the Prince and Dawlish. "I would not have countenanced a meeting with His Royal Highness otherwise. There have been rumors of Handel's departure for months."

"My lord, my employees in this enterprise assure me it is only a matter of time before the man does indeed leave London. That, sir, is a certainty. He will leave. Only the day and destination are in question. I assure you, Handel is finished."

Ilchester said nothing as the carriage bounced along the rutted roads. The uncomfortable silence and gloom inside emphasized the darkening clouds and rain that lashed down at them as they made their way to London.

The carriage finally arrived in Leicester Fields and drew up at Dawlish's house.

As the man began to get out, Ilchester reached over and gripped his companion's arm. "No more ifs and maybes, Dawlish. Do not bother me until you have good news. And do not fail me." He pointed at the old Leicester House, now undergoing construction. "The prince will soon be my neighbor. I pray that I might be a good one to him and serve him well. That means you must give me the results both he and I desire."

Dawlish opened the carriage door latch and stepped out onto the ground. Flushed, he looked at Ilchester, bowed, and watched as the carriage rolled away. He turned and mounted the stone steps into his own townhouse, raging with fury and impatient to take it out on his unsuspecting staff.

A relatively short walk from Leicester Fields, but a thousand miles away in atmosphere, the man bearing the unwieldy title George the Second, by the Grace of God, King of Great Britain, France and Ireland, Defender of the Faith, Duke of Brunswick-Luneburg, Arch Treasurer and Prince Elector of the Holy Roman Empire paced the floor, just as he had for the past ten minutes.

He didn't particularly like St. James' Palace, even if it was the principle royal residence. He preferred Kensington Palace but avoided it ever since his wife Queen Caroline had died there three years ago. Kensington had been her favorite. He couldn't bear to visit its memory-laden rooms. Kew Palace, he'd given to his son, a wastrel womanizer. He would not enter that place again, either, even though it had also been a favorite at one time. So the drafty old Tudor palace, St. James', was his only London refuge.

A sharp knock on the ornate carved door stopped his pacing. He waited as the door slowly opened and a liveried footman stepped in, bowed, and proclaimed, "Your Majesty. The Right Honourable Sir Robert Walpole."

The footman stepped back as Prime Minister Walpole walked through, stopped, bowed, and stepped confidently forward. He bowed again and waited, as protocol dictated, for the King to speak first.

"Sir Robert, thank you for your quick response to my summons."

"Your Majesty. I am yours to command at all times."

The King looked at him carefully. "I hear the Prince of Wales is agitating Parliament for another increase in his allowance." It was said quietly and very neutrally.

Walpole held the King's gaze. "He has made a request, yes. But Parliament has not acted."

"Then get Parliament to act and say no. Immediately. Waste no more of the government's time on this."

"Your Majesty, this is a very delicate situation," Walpole said, despite the King's glower. "His Royal Highness has created a fair amount of support amongst the people. A simple dismissal of his request, as you command, would only fire up the rabble and undermine Your Majesty's position."

"Who governs this country, Walpole? The rabble? You? The King?" George growled, then sat at his massive baroque desk, aware that protocol demanded that Walpole stand as long as he did. He waved at Walpole to be seated.

"Your Majesty, I only mean that we must proceed carefully and examine all the options and rationales to giving or refusing the increase for His Royal Highness before making a final decision. We can take our time doing that in order to probe and understand how strong his support really is. In the meantime, there is no increase for him."

"He deserves nothing, Walpole. Do you hear me? Nothing. He is a wastrel who will take any additional monies and spend it on women, drinking, partying, and gambling. Is that how the rabble wants the country to use its taxes?"

The volume increased as George got further into the argument. "He's a liar, Walpole. You know that he spread lies about my death twice in the past five years. He planted rumors that I'd died crossing the Channel in that horrible storm, and then, when it was obvious I had not drowned, he later claimed I died of cholic and fever. That was just three and a half years ago, Walpole! The leopard cannot change his spots."

The King glared at Walpole, defying him to argue. Instead Walpole merely nodded agreement.

"I will do what I can, sir. You know you can count on that."

"See that you do, Walpole. See that you do." George drummed his fingers on the arms of his chair. "You want to know how strong his support is? I'll tell you. He undermines all I have done for this nation. He ridicules and dismisses the culture, the music, the good I have done. He has turned the people against the very things that make this country strong and vibrant. My own sources in his court tell me he has spread lies and instigated rumors against the great Mr. Handel, a man whose incredible music has made this nation proud and renowned throughout Europe." He pointed at Walpole. "His hatred for me is such that he tries to destroy anything I touch, like, or support. My sources in his court even tell me he has paid for gangs to disrupt Mr. Handel's productions! That's where the money will go if he gets his increase, Walpole." The King pounded his fist on the arm. "He's the heir to the throne. He should be preparing for that instead of rutting and drinking around town. It's no wonder his mother refused to see him, even when she was dying. She wanted nothing to do with him. Nor do I. That's why I banished him from my court."

The King drummed his fingers harder, still fuming.

Walpole waited for him to finish. "Your Majesty, we will be very vigilant and careful before making decisions on this delicate matter, you may be sure. And Your Majesty's views will certainly be a key part of our deliberation."

The King grunted. "Keep me informed." He relaxed slightly. "Now tell me the latest news from Europe. How badly did Prussia defeat the Austrians at Mollwitz?"

"It was very close, sir. King Frederic of Prussia is obviously inexperienced in warfare and is fortunate his infantry is well trained and well led by Field Marshall Von Shwerin. Our reports indicate, however, that his cavalry and other forces did not comport themselves as excellently. Had it not been for the infantry, Austria might well have won the battle."

George pulled a map onto his desk and beckoned the prime minister to show him how the Austrian Hapsburg forces and Prussians had dueled in the spring snows of central Europe. After an hour discussing how Britain might use the European war to increase its influence, and on the side protect George's Hanover interests, the King nodded at Walpole's suggestions on the diplomatic front, particularly with the disturbing news that Prussia and France were negotiating a peace treaty that would inevitably force the Austrians into a two-front war.

"This is what my idiot son should be worrying about. Not his women and wine. And certainly not Mr. Handel and his music!"

CHAPTER SIX

IN WHICH MRS. CIBBER MAKES A DECISION
AND MR. JENNENS BRINGS MR. HANDEL
A NEW OPPORTUNITY

The previous night's row had been fearsome. More fearsome than any that had preceded it.

Sloper had received an offer, almost an order, from his father to leave London and what he called "its insidious temptations" to manage his father's wide-ranging enterprises in the Caribbean and British colonies in the Americas. It was, Sloper decided, an excellent opportunity to rebuild his career, ingratiate himself with his father once again, and remove Susannah from the ridicule and gossip of London. There they would raise a family and live an idyllic life on a plantation.

Except Susannah had refused. She wanted to get away from London, yes, but not that far. Recently, Theo had been making threats and he was, as she reminded Sloper often, a man not averse to duels, criminal activity, and revenge. The courts may have rejected his demand that Susannah live with him, but he was not above kidnapping. Both she and Sloper knew full well the depths of Theo's hatred and desire to avenge what he had considered an outrageous court decision. Especially since he was now himself the butt of scorn and ridicule, and therefore receiving fewer opportunities on the stage and in productions. He was hurting for money and wanted to lash out.

The more she thought about it, the more Susannah did want to escape London. But she also wanted to find a way back onto the stage, and those opportunities wouldn't exist in the new world. Her brother's suggestion of Dublin was becoming a more inviting prospect, and given the vibrant cultural scene in Britain's second city the chances of some productions were great.

The couple's disagreement between the Caribbean and Dublin grew more fractious as the two argued the various merits of their desires. It was dragging them apart psychologically, and now, it seemed inevitable, physically as well.

After the previous night's quarrel, Sloper had offered a compromise at breakfast. They would part for a while, he to the Caribbean and she to Dublin, for two years. It was now June 1741. They would maintain their relationship by letters and agree to return to London no later than June 1743. There, depending on what had happened with both their careers, they would reconsider their positions.

It wasn't what she wanted. Or was it? Certainly, it meant separation from William, who'd rescued her from an intolerable situation and respected her as a person, not a slave. But it also meant she would be hidden away, afraid to leave the house for the scorn and ridicule she knew she would face. And she was barred from her love of the theater.

Susannah had finally admitted her burning desire to return to the stage in the middle of last night's argument. Her vehemence on the topic had shocked William and even surprised her.

"I need it, William," she'd said. "I need the validation that I am worthwhile, that I still have value to people and that I am not just an object of contempt. I want people to see past my sins and that horrible court case, to see me as a talented, welcomed actress and singer again."

As in any argument, harsh words and criticisms had been hurled. William had apologized this morning for his hard words, and she too had confessed her overly dramatic and unkind statements.

It was then he had offered his suggestion: "The separation would meet both our immediate needs. I can make enough money to perhaps break away from dependence upon Father. You will perhaps find opportunities to act and sing."

William had then left, ostensibly on business, but she knew he planned to enjoy a long stay at the coffeehouse, conversing with friends, reading the latest news sheets, and thinking about his own plans.

She was musing the dilemma when the maid entered, carrying a letter. Susannah took it with some trepidation, fearing another anonymous attack but found instead a delightful and warm letter from her old friend and performing mentor, Peggy Turncastle.

After light and breezy comments about her current situation, Peggy got down to business. It was an invitation to visit her in Dublin for a while. Susannah quickly read Peggy's enthusiastic comments about the musical and theater scene in the Irish city. All Peggy wrote confirmed Susannah's brother's assertions. Dublin had an exciting theater scene, with new theatre managers and new players who would invigorate her professionally. No doubt news of her adultery had made it to

Dublin, but the London vitriol would be absent; she could perhaps engage them with her acting and singing and wipe away their assumptions.

By the time tea was served, she'd made up her mind. She would venture alone to Dublin and pray that William was kept safe in the new world and achieve the success he so badly wanted. For her, it represented the chance to leave her shame behind. It was the promise of a new life.

Jennens worked feverishly for two months. The idea that had been sparked in his mind during his discussion with the Duke of Devonshire now merged with a half-finished pamphlet he'd been working on that would tell the whole story of Jesus Christ, his foretelling through to his extension of eternal life to all mankind. Jennens planned it as his masterpiece, a persuasive and sound document that was theologically unassailable.

The more he thought about it, however, the more he realized that instead of a pamphlet he would turn it into a libretto and offer it to Handel to let him work his magic. It wouldn't be a dramatic libretto such as he'd produced for *Saul* and the other works he'd given Handel. No. In this work, he would let the Bible do the persuading for him. He would not argue, cajole, or explain. Scripture would speak for itself.

Since the gospel was a story of hope for mankind, he would emphasize that message through a judicious selection of verses. But to tell the story, he had to delve through both the Old and New Testaments, revealing the single thread running from Genesis through to Revelation, that God's plan for human redemption would be through the coming, life, death and resurrection of Jesus Christ.

This was the challenge. There were twenty-three thousand verses in the entire Bible, almost eight thousand in the New Testament alone.

Now that he was in Gopsall, he dropped into a solid routine. After breakfast he took an hour's ride over the parklands, then he had a quick word with his estate manager and a visit with Mother—as he'd expected, she was in relatively good health and just wanted his company. Afterwards he retired to his library and spent hours at his desk poring over the Bible, verse after verse, discarding and considering each in turn.

The first part of the libretto had to set the stage, showing the vast sweep of Scripture leading up to the proclamation that God would provide a Savior for the nations. The starting point was critical; it had to evoke the vastness of the need as well as the vastness of God's response. And it had to give hope. He struggled over which verses could encompass this enormous need.

As he read, reviewed, discarded, and contemplated his own knowledge of the Bible, he was drawn more and more to the prophecies of Isaiah. So many of the prophet's words concerned the coming Savior. Inexorably he was drawn to the strength and warmth of Isaiah's fortieth chapter, which projected hope into a people desperate for salvation.

He had found the opening thrust of his great story.

Rapidly, he dipped his quill into the ink and began to write:

Comfort ye, comfort ye my people, saith your God. Speak ye comfortably to Jerusalem, and cry unto her, that her warfare is accomplished, that her iniquity is pardoned: for she hath received of the Lord's hand double for all her sins. The voice of him that crieth in the wilderness. Prepare ye the way of the Lord, make straight in the desert a highway for our God.

The struggle to begin had passed and the work began to flow more smoothly. Handel would make those words come alive, Jennens was sure, and give them life and power.

In the meantime, he scoured the Bible, selecting the most meaningful verses to move the libretto forward. Other verses from Isaiah and the so-called minor prophets led into the rousing story of the birth of the Savior found in the gospels.

His routine soon changed. Gone was the ride through the estate. His dealings with the manager became limited to occasional notes, or, if required, a meeting right after breakfast. He explained to this mother that he was engaged in a "vast and meaningful work" and could not be disturbed.

Jennens persevered through a bout of the ague. He declined Devonshire's invitation to a farewell dinner at Chatsworth, pleading illness and indicating that he was preparing a libretto for their friend Handel. He wished the duke Godspeed on his time in Ireland.

Knowing how Jennens could not be diverted once he had the bit in his teeth, Devonshire sent a swift reply accepted his explanations and asked what name Jennens was putting on the new work. It was a question Jennens had been asking himself. Normally his librettos were easily named because they told the story of an individual life. He was proudest of *Saul*, but he'd produced many other librettos, most of them still stored in drawers in his library and intended for his own use and pleasure. Each had focused on the main character, or characters, and bore those names.

This particular work, though, he instinctively realized, was grander and more profound. It was an explanation of his own faith and deep desire to persuade people away from their self-centered, pleasure-seeking, and often sin-soaked lives. Jennens was convinced that Jesus Christ was the solution to all problems, personal and societal, and was excited to present that solution to the people in a fresh and entertaining way.

Handel, he was sure, would match the magnificence of the story with a score to entertain as well as inspire people and lift them up. As such, it deserved a grand title, one that encompassed its full range. Calling it "Jesus" would not work. Nor would something as ponderous as "The Redemption of Mankind" or "The Story of Redemption" capture the public imagination. He was stumped.

Tirelessly, he worked through the days and well into the evenings. He sought out verses to demonstrate the overwhelming agreement between the Old and New Testaments in their prophecies and fulfillment of the birth of Christ. Isaiah's words that a virgin would conceive and that the child would be called Immanuel rang in his head. In a flash of inspiration, he combined that verse with another from the gospel of St. Matthew, one which repeated the prophecy and the name, cleverly linking both sections of Scripture.

Pleased, he capped the inkwell, picked up a lamp, and retired. He pulled the covers around the four-poster bed and settled in for the night. Sleep eluded him, though, as his mind struggled with the vexatious problem of titling the work.

He liked to end his day's effort on a positive note and reflected again on the proclamations of Christ's birth. He studied the verses, in particular the name Immanuel, and pondered its meaning.

He was just drifting off to sleep when he suddenly sat bolt upright. Immanuel! It was the name used to proclaim Jesus as Messiah, the coming savior.

Messiah, that's who he is, he realized. *This is his story. The story is Messiah.*

He jumped out of bed, lit a small lamp, and, clad only in a white nightshirt and nightcap, rushed out of his room, almost leaping down the stairs, and dashed into the library. He placed the candlestick on the desk and unscrewed the inkwell. With a fresh sheet of paper, he delicately inscribed the name *Messiah*. Underneath, he wrote *A Sacred Oratorio.*

A weight lifted off his shoulders as he headed back to bed. Although he'd known the general thrust of the work, now that he had a title—a good and meaningful one—he knew the rest of the work would proceed faster.

With Part One completed, he swiftly moved into Part Two. His dilemma was his desire to convey the eternal story and repercussion of the passion of Christ without delving into the specific details. He knew that audiences, whether religious or not, were already aware of the whats and whos, but he was convinced they were not fully aware of the whys.

The opening phrases in one verse in the gospel of St. John jumped out at him: *Behold, the Lamb of God*. It was an ideal start to revealing the purpose of the passion and set the stage for Part Two of *Messiah*.

Steadily he worked away. Piles of paper crumpled and otherwise lay at his feet as portions were eliminated, then written back into the manuscript before being discarded once again. The more he read, the more he studied, and the harder he worked, the more it seemed to him that the hours and days flew by.

Part Three fell into place as he blended the poignant words of Job, *I know that my Redeemer liveth*, with the stirring words from St. Paul: *now Christ is risen*. Promises of the second coming and its announcement, that a trumpet would sound and the dead would be raised, helped him build the story to a climax. He found the culmination in the Book of Revelation, which proclaimed, *Worthy is the Lamb*.

On a hot afternoon in late May, Jennens finally laid down his quill, his grand work finished. He sat back, pleased and happily anticipating what Handel might do with it.

He was about to get up when a thought struck him. He'd missed something in his excitement. The last few words of the verse stood out, and he picked up the quill again. He dipped it in the ink and added one more word: *Amen!*

Two weeks later, Jennens found himself on Brook Street in London again. He stared up at the fashionable brick house, hesitant to approach the door. The entire trip from Leicestershire he'd been in an ebullient mood. Nothing dimmed his excitement, not the rains and muddy roads, nor even losing a carriage wheel outside Coventry. Yet now, yards away from Handel's house, his confidence dropped. Would the great musician like the work? Would he realize the massive scope of the libretto? Would Handel even want to write the score for it?

Doubts and niggling fears swirled through his mind as he knocked on the door and waited for the butler to admit him. Inside, he was shown into the front parlor.

"My dear Jennens, what a delightful surprise." Handel walked into the room, his voice booming a welcome. Jennens noticed a slight limp, though not of the magnitude of the one described to him by Devonshire.

As the two arranged themselves in chairs, Jennens nodded towards the man's leg. "You have a slight limp, my friend. Nothing serious, I trust?"

Handel waived his hand in dismissal. "Pah. My physics call it gout, but it's a lot better now. Hardly notice it at all." He grinned. "Back to eating as I want instead of the morsels of food and ounces of wine I was allowed."

As they spoke, Jennens noticed that while Handel projected a happy, confident mood, there was a hesitancy he hadn't noticed before. "You seem distracted, George. Did the cancellation of *Deidamia* impact you that much?"

Knowing the answer, even he was surprised at Handel's honest response.

"It did, Charles, it did. It almost put me in debtors' prison, no thanks to the Prince of Wales and his lackeys. Their attempts to destroy me almost succeeded, my friend. I have little money to launch a new production, even if I had one in mind. In any case, they would shut me down if I did." Handel reached over to a bottle and offered Jennens some wine. As they sipped, a sober expression crossed the composer's face. "If not for the generosity of His Majesty and some other friends, I would no doubt be suffering in prison right now. My only hope is that it was not just an act of charity and that they truly consider my music adequate. As it is, I am covering my daily expenses, for which God be thanked."

Jennens leaned forward, wondering how to broach the subject delicately. "I'm sure the works were well worth every penny they paid you, George. Don't underestimate yourself, sirrah." He paused. "There have been rumors around town the past few months that you might be leaving London and going back to Germany, or perhaps Italy."

There, he'd said it.

Handel tipped back his head and roared with laughter, shaking so much that his wig began slipping and sliding, creating an unusual sight. Still laughing, Handel nodded and had to adjust the wig.

"Yes, I've heard the rumors as well. Wishful thinking amongst the prince's tools, largely. They were hoping I'd either disappear into prison or Europe." He suddenly regained seriousness. "I confess, my dear Jennens, I did indeed consider it. To be back in Italy, writing grand operas and the like." He took another sip. "But I am now too British, you might say. I feel that I have not yet touched the British soul; I have not given the nation that has been so good to me the music it deserves and which I have yet inside me."

He stood up, adjusted his wig again and then in frustration removed it and tossed it on the sideboard. He crossed the room and opened the door, calling for John to provide some food for him and his guest.

"I am leaving London, though." Handel dropped the news without prelude. Jennens' jaw dropped to protest, but Handel cut him off. "It's all right, Charles. I'm only going as far as Dublin, thanks to the kind invitation of His Grace the Duke of Devonshire."

Handel seated himself again and waited while John served up some meats and cheese. The composer explained the duke's proposal to bring his concerts and presentations to the gentry and good people of Ireland.

"This is good news then?" asked Jennens.

"Oh, most definitely, my dear Charles. It seems I am very popular in Dublin still. The prince's tendrils have not yet destroyed me outside this city. I'm quite looking forward to it. I shall reprise *Saul*, of course, Charles, and many others as well. His Grace has invited me to do an entire season this winter, so I shall be gone from the autumn onwards. So you'll have to find other theatrical and operatic enterprises for your London season."

He popped some more cheese into his mouth and wiped it with a small laced towel.

Jennens leaned forward and pulled his leather satchel up to his knees. "Perhaps then you'd be interested in a new libretto I have prepared just for you, George. I can think of no one who can do this the justice and majesty it deserves."

"Thank you, my friend, but I have no plans to develop new works for the presentations. The duke assures me that all the people want is their old favorites. They've seen local productions of my work, but now they desire the real thing. They want to see me creating and conducting all my old works and Italian operas."

"I meant that you could work on this new libretto and debut it in London upon your return."

At Handel's insistence that he was not contemplating new productions, Jennens' face dropped. He protested, but Handel was adamant. He had neither the current enthusiasm or time to write an entirely new production.

"I must leave no later than October and then I will be busy hiring theatres, musicians, and performers... and then of course there are rehearsals. Not to mention the amount of time I will be required to spend with the lords and ladies of that land. No, I will not have time to write new works."

By then, Jennens had drawn the manuscript out of the satchel.

Handel glanced at him and sighed. "Let me see it then. Perhaps when I get back from Ireland next year, we could consider this."

He reached out his hand and read the title page. He looked askance at Jennens, then proceeded to leaf through the remaining sheaves of paper.

"Most unusual, Charles. I have never worked with material such as this. This might be something that Johann Bach in Leipzig might want, no?"

Jennens shook his head, Disappointment flooding through him. His expectations and enthusiasms were crushed. He had thought Handel would rejoice at receiving such a challenge, that he would seize the opportunity to raise his musical genius to the level the work demanded.

"I know. It is not a drama, but it is not like your other oratorios either. The subject matter is immense. It is the story of God's plan of redemption from the beginning and into the eternity his love has provided."

Handel nodded seriously, sensing he had somehow offended Jennens with his less than wholehearted response. "Let me look at it further. If Dublin is a success, perhaps we can produce this to launch my return to London after all." He summoned John once again. "Now, tell me how things are at Gopsall. I have enjoyed so many wonderful times there. How is your dear lady mother? Have you taken down that copse of wood and extended the parklands yet?"

An hour later, Jennens left the Handel house and summoned a sedan chair to take him home. He had been crushed at Handel's off-hand response.

Once at home, in his study, he began writing a letter to his friend Edward Holdsworth, a fellow non-juror with whom he'd shared an inkling of his hopes.

Handel says he will do nothing next Winter, but I hope I will persuade him with the Scripture Collection I have made for him. I hope he will lay his whole genius and skill upon it, that the composition may excel all his former compositions as the subject excels every other subject. The subject is Messiah.

He finished the letter and gave it to his man to deliver. Tired and emotionally spent, he picked up a lamp and retired to his room. After his man had helped him undress, he knelt before the bed as he did every night and prayed.

CHAPTER SEVEN

IN WHICH MR. HANDEL'S ENEMIES CONSPIRE AND
HE CONSIDERS MR. JENNENS' LIBRETTO

L
ord Ilchester waited nervously. After waiting days, he'd finally received the
command he'd requested, to present himself at Cliveden. Finally he impart-
ed his news to a stern-looking, and this time sober, prince seated grandly on
his mock throne.

Silence followed Ilchester's report. As the silence drew out, the more nervous
he became.

Finally, Frederick glared at him with a seething anger rather than his usual
volcanic eruptions. "I said I wanted him driven from Britain. Dublin is in Britain,
is it not, Ilchester? At least on my maps it still is. Unless my father and Parliament
have made some unknown changes. Is that what happened, sirrah?"

His cold, flat tone created even more anxiety in Ilchester.

Frederick stood, stepped down from the platform and began to pace. Ilchester said nothing but, knowing from his look that the prince had yet more to say,
stayed silent.

"This is not what I wanted to hear, sir. I want Handel and his foreign influences gone from these lands. For good. It will show my father that his old ways and
reliance on European culture is not the future of this land. Not in culture. Not in
heritage. Not in power. A new Britain, stronger and independent of all overseas
impacts, will—indeed must—be our way forward." The prince turned and stopped
suddenly in front of Ilchester. "Well, sir. What do you have to say?"

"Your Royal Highness, certainly Dublin is still in Britain, but at least Handel is removed from London as you wished. We set the standards for the entire
country here in London, so if his influence is removed from London it will allow
English composers, musicians, and artists to shine. And that, in turn, will impact
the nation. Once that happens, he will have no option but to return to Germany
or Italy."

The prince digested this information slowly, then grunted. "Maybe you're right, Ilchester, maybe you're right. But what the devil made him decide on Dublin rather than Florence or Rome or Brandenburg or somewhere like that?"

Relieved at the lessening of Frederick's anger and acceptance of his argument, Ilchester relaxed slightly. "My understanding, Your Highness, is that the Duke of Devonshire invited him for the winter season to conduct a series of subscription performances."

Frederic grunted again. "When I become king, my first act will be to remove Devonshire as Lord Lieutenant of Ireland. Mark it, sir. He will not last a day in that post once I ascend the throne." He resumed pacing while Ilchester remained rooted to his spot. "Send that crony of yours, Dawlish, over to Ireland to do his work there. Maybe a little disruption at the performances might yet persuade Herr Handel that his future lies in Europe, not in our fair nation."

Ilchester bowed in acknowledgement, wondering all the while how he could convince Dawlish to comply.

"Come then, enough of Handel," Frederick said. "He is, after all, a minor, if irritating, inconvenience. How is the proposal to increase my allowance coming? Have those blockheads in Parliament made any progress yet?"

The prince gestured for Ilchester to take a seat and called for one of the footmen to bring some coffee and sweetmeats. As they waited, he offered Ilchester some of his finest snuff.

When Ilchester finally left Cliveden, it was obvious that the prince was in a foul mood.

News that his push for money was stalled in the House of Commons with only lukewarm support from the prime minister had sent him into a furious diatribe. He'd lashed out at Walpole's indifference to the prince's pleas for more money.

"I am the future of Britain, Ilchester. Does the fool not realize this? I am leading this nation into a new and exciting future, where Britain is first and foremost in our minds and hearts. We will celebrate our Englishness and sever our reliance on the dated culture and philosophies of Germany, Italy, and France. We will look ahead, not behind. And these dolts of parliamentarians don't seem to realize it. If we have to, we'll get rid of them."

The rage, fueled by copious amounts of wine, had continued unabated for almost twenty minutes. Finally, the fatigued prince had dropped into his chair and curtly told Ilchester to get out and get Dawlish to work.

Back in his Mayfair home, Ilchester sat in his library, thinking. How could he get Dawlish to go to Dublin? Dawlish was, after all, merely seeking Ilchester's favors, willing to undertake disreputable tasks for the privilege of nesting under Ilchester's wings. He was not a servant.

That raised a troubling question for Ilchester. How far was he willing to go to placate the prince? His past few meetings with Frederick had shown the man to be increasingly volatile and at times an unreasonable personality linked to an unstable concept of just how powerful and respected he was. Certainly, he was the public personification of a new and strong British image. His patronage of English artists and composers, as well as his support for new concepts of culture as a harbinger of political and economic power, fit into Ilchester's own desires and thoughts.

But the prince increasingly showed his tendencies to revert to the age-old concept of the divine right of kings and the lessening of power of both Parliament and the people. Charles I had lost his head over such beliefs. But it seemed Frederick was ignoring the lessons of the ill-fated Stuarts. Too close an affiliation with these extreme demands by the prince might undermine Ilchester's own standing.

It bore thinking about.

Susannah stood on the Bristol pier, watching as the ship bearing William made its way into the main channel of the Avon River, headed to Avonmouth, the Bristol Channel, and beyond to the Americas.

She watched until it disappeared around a bend, then lifted her skirts and turned to the carriage William's father had arranged for her. He'd been coolly polite when they first met but, she had to admit, extremely generous. Perhaps it was relief that his son was separating from this fallen woman, she wryly noted, but he'd established them in a fine townhome while the arrangements were made. He even invited her to a small gathering of the family and persuaded her to sing. When she finished, she saw him nod appreciatively, applauding and smiling. She may not have won him over, but she had certainly thawed the relationship. In the days to follow, he'd given her a number of gifts as well, as an allowance to visit dressmakers and seamstresses.

He stood by the carriage and assisted her in.

"My ship, the *Arabella*, will set sail tomorrow on the high tide," he said. "The accommodations may not be luxurious, but she will get you to Dublin by the next day. Far better than taking a stagecoach to Holyhead and the packet over to Dublin. Save you more than two weeks, especially if the packet is delayed in sailing."

He closed the carriage door behind her as she entered.

She leaned out, her hand extended to shake his. "I thank you again, most pro-fusely, sir, for your thoughtfulness and generosity. You are most kind." As she spoke, he added a quiet smile, stepped back, and signaled to the coachman, who wheeled the carriage and matching pair of bays off the pier and back to the townhouse.

Inside, she bustled around, directing the servants as they packed her final items into large trunks, ready for the next day's voyage. She knew very little of what to expect in Dublin. Her friend Peggy assured her it was a civilized and vibrant city. But it was not London, so apprehension was a constant companion.

William had already arranged a small dwelling for her close to Peggy. He'd settled with his bank to provide a regular allowance for her and told her to feel comfortable about moving to a different place if she wasn't comfortable in the one he'd organized for her.

In truth, these last few weeks in Bristol had refreshed her, body and soul. She'd not been the figure of scorn and had been able to wander the streets, popping into shops at will without stern looks from customers and shopkeepers. She would miss William, she knew, but she eagerly anticipated the relaunch of her career. Peg-gy was already working to set up recitals for her, and yesterday another letter from her friend had brought both joy and hope.

My dear, let me impart to you the most exciting news! It has been gossip for some weeks now but confirmed on Saturday. The great and glorious Mr. Handel is coming to Dublin! Yes, he is. And he will be here for the entire winter season. Oh, I am already planning to attend every perfor-mance he gives. As soon as subscriptions are available, I will be first in line I promise you. You've worked with him, have you not? Perhaps he might be able to hire you again for his Dublin concerts. Wouldn't that be marvelous!

The letter had continued with other gossip and plans to introduce Susannah to Dublin, but Susannah was oblivious to the rest of the news. Handel would be in Dublin. Surely, he would indeed want to include her in some of his productions. But perhaps not. He was all too aware of her reputation. She would have to seize every opportunity and recital Peggy was able to arrange for her and hope that Handel would notice her and consider her again.

The thought that her new life would begin in just a few days was the one bright spark that burst through the gloom of the past few years. She was beginning to understand how much the pain had drilled deeply into her very soul. From the abuse she'd suffered at Theo's hands to the public humiliation of the trial and its aftermath, to the scandal of her relationship with William and being the object of public curiosity and scorn, all had drained her physically and emotionally. It had been enhanced the past few weeks with her realization that William, the rock of her life since those days under Theo's control, was also leaving her. Would their relationship withstand the prolonged separation? She did not know.

Peggy's letter had opened a door, however slightly. As she went to sleep that night, she determined that whatever she could do to pry that door open even further, she would do.

"You jest, sir!" Lord Dawlish stiffened and sat upright. "I support your lordship in all things, but I remind you, sir, that I am not your lackey. I have no reason or desire to go to that damnable place, and even less so to that backwater city."

Ilchester looked at him patiently. "I do not ask you to go to Dublin as a lackey, my dear fellow. I am making a straight business proposition that will make a lot of money for both of us."

He explained again that he needed an agent to oversee the arrival of some goods. The nature of the goods and their method of arrival meant delicate dealings with the ship's captain directly, since the items would be taken from the ship in a small bay near the coastal village of Wicklow and taken ashore. Dawlish would be responsible for ensuring the security of the goods once unloaded and forwarding them to Dublin, and eventually London.

"Smuggling. That's something for others, not me!" Dawlish cried out. "I am no wrecker or smuggler. Leave that for those in the wilds of Devon and Cornwall, or smuggling brandy from France. I will not soil myself with it, sir. Not at all!"

"It's not smuggling or anything like that. Not at all, Dawlish. Not at all," Ilchester snapped. "You will merely oversee the transport of the goods and confirm that they are cleared through the revenue officers in Dublin. Everything is, and must be, entirely legal. These are goods I want to keep secret from some competitors. It would be impossible to bring them straight to London. Even landing at the harbor in Dublin might prove difficult, thus the arrangements I've made for Wicklow." He stared directly at Dawlish. "Once the customs officers have quietly approved, it will be too late for the competition. The items would be landed and on their way to London weeks, nay months, ahead of any others. I merely need someone trustworthy to oversee the entire operation. An agent who will ensure that all is correct and legal."

Dawlish smoldered still, but a greedy glint began to spark in his eyes. "And you say my share would be one hundred pounds?"

"At the very least. If the goods sell for a better price, you will receive more since you are the agent in charge."

He offered Dawlish some of his finest snuff. They both imbibed.

They discussed the issue for several more minutes. Ilchester cannily noted that the conversation evolved from outrage and posturing into negotiations over payment. How easily the lure of money overpowered the man's worries and moral cares, he reflected.

Finally, all was settled. Dawlish agreed to travel to Dublin in the autumn, as soon as he could make arrangements for his other business and property interests.

Dawlish then grumbled about crossing the Irish Sea at a time it was known to be stormy and treacherous. The addition of further bonuses and the promise of first-class transportation on the swift postal vessels called packets that carried vital mail and passengers to Dublin sealed the agreement.

"Oh, and one thing more, my dear fellow," Ilchester added. "As you may know, our prince's nemesis Handel will be in Dublin over the winter season. While you are there, I will require you to arrange for the usual disruptions and see that none of his performances are successful. I will, of course, provide extra payment for you to ensure this."

"Aha!" Dawlish leaned forward, a sneer on his face. "Now we get to the heart of the matter. That's why you really want me in Dublin, isn't it, milord? Anyone else could handle the business of the shipping transfer, but you need someone you can trust to do whatever it takes to destroy Handel." He leaned back smugly. "And I'm your man, am I not?"

"Don't be so damned smug, Dawlish," Ilchester snapped angrily. "It ill suits you. There are many others I could call on to do these jobs. I am simply giving you the first opportunity, but if you refuse, so be it. There are others."

He leaned back in his chair, staring at Dawlish, defying him to respond. As he expected, Dawlish's anger wilted.

"Very well, Lord Ilchester. I will see what I can do."

"Remember, I want your best efforts to interrupt Handel's season. He must be forced to leave Dublin in disgrace. I am counting on it. So is the Prince of Wales." He leaned forward and put his hand on Dawlish's knee. "I've heard whispers that there might be a dukedom in it for you once His Royal Highness ascends the throne. And judging by the King's age and health, that may be sooner rather than later!"

A grin creased Dawlish's face from ear to ear. "Never fear, milord. I will turn Dublin against him."

Handel decided to walk back to his house from the church rather than take a chair, since his gout had improved so greatly. Maybe it was the warm sunny days, or maybe it was the mounting excitement of his forthcoming Dublin venture, but he felt much better these days; better physically and more like his old self in outlook.

As he walked, he contemplated what he could stage. Certainly, he would offer a variety from his operas—and, at Devonshire's special request, some of his "Water Music." He felt invigorated. An hour playing the massive 1,500-pipe organ at St. Georges always lifted him emotionally and spiritually, but today it seemed to focus his thoughts even more.

He crossed Hanover Square into Brook Street, almost oblivious to the early summer warmth and crowded street. Without thinking, he stepped around the piles of horse manure and the jostling passersby. He ignored the smells as well as the shouts of the streetsellers and their many offerings of apples, flowers, breads, pots, pans, and a myriad of other items. His mind was a world away, filled with music and random thoughts of programs.

Inside the house, he immediately asked his manservant for stew and bread to be brought up from the kitchens to the drawing room.

While he waited, he paced the room, still struggling with the problem of the Dublin performances. Naturally, he could present a variety of his concertos and some of his successful works, such as *Saul* or *Rinaldo*, but the operas required talented and capable actor-singers, not to mention elaborate stage settings. Devonshire's wife, in particular, had asked for *Ombra mai fu* from his short-lived opera *Serse*.

He had no idea what kind of talent existed in Dublin, nor the ability of the theatre people there to stage an opera successfully. He pored over a list of his many cantatas, arias, operas, concerto grossi, orchestral works, keyboard works, and sonatas.

The duke had assured him that the musicians were as fine as any in London, and then the duke connected him by correspondence with Matthew Dubourg, Master of the State Music at Dublin Castle. Devonshire considered him the finest violinist in Britain.

Through Dubourg, Handel learned much about the strengths and weaknesses of various Dublin musicians. Even so, he would have to engage London musicians to supplement them, along with principal soloists. Dubourg informed him, however, that there were excellent choirs at both Christ Church Cathedral and St. Patrick's Cathedral who would provide the core of any chorus he needed, or even soloists. The boy sopranos, he declared, were excellent.

Handel, always generous to a fault, had also received and accepted a request for a special charitable performance. The three chosen charities included the Mercer Hospital, an infirmary, and one for the relief of imprisoned debtors. Shuddering at the thought of how close he'd been, and still was, to an impoverished debtor himself, he readily agreed.

There was still the problem of halls and theatres. He had no idea what quality might be available. A recent letter from Dubourg indicated that a brand-new, up-to-the-minute hall—Neal's Musick Hall, near the River Liffey—had just been completed. Dubourg said it was excellent in terms of both accommodation and acoustics. It was, perhaps, a venue he could obtain for use at a cheaper rate. Always looking to keep his expenses down, the businessman in him reasoned that the hall managers would be delighted to host a series of concerts by Britain's most renowned composer. And they'd likely be willing to accept a lower rental rate for the privilege.

As he sat to eat, he sighed. Some of his concerns could not really be addressed until he actually arrived in the city. He must therefore patiently put these issues to the back of his mind until then, he warned himself.

Patience, however, was not an attribute he possessed in abundance, he wryly admitted as he dipped the bread in the stew.

Still, he wanted—no, needed—to create a presence in Dublin that would overwhelm the Irish with its magnificence, do the Duke of Devonshire proud, and re-establish his stature as Britain's composer and musical personality. The trouble was, it was already the end of the first week of August and decisions needed to be made immediately. He planned to be in Dublin by the beginning of November at the very latest.

He broke off another handful of bread to dip into the tasty broth. He ate heartily and soon requested a plate of roast beef and nice red wine, along with some pastries and other delicacies. Thinking, he found, greatly expanded his appetite, not to mention his stomach.

By the time he was ready for bed, he'd prepared a tentative list of pieces he thought would entertain and please the Dubliners. He would, he decided, feature one main piece at each concert. *Acis and Galatea,* one of his most popular works, would certainly be among them. This would be accompanied by various smaller works, such as concertos for various instruments. His uncanny sense of what the public wanted and enjoyed remained intact, even though he'd faltered over the past few years in London. Or had he, he wondered? Was it that he'd lost his touch, or was it simply that the Prince of Wales' determination to undermine his public popularity, and therefore the King's, had succeeded?

Unlike most nights, when he fell asleep almost immediately, this evening he tossed and turned, his mind whirling with both anticipation and concern about Dublin. He'd gleaned information about the city from numerous friends as well as from the duke's missives and was aware of the Dubliners' firm conviction that they were equal, if not superior, to the cultural and musical appreciations found in London. That pride indicated that an astute and discerning audience awaited him. Nothing but his best would do.

At two o'clock in the morning, he arose, lit a candle, and quietly made his way down one floor from his bedroom and entered his composing room. He placed the candlestick on his tall composing desk and began to rummage around the many sheaves of musical manuscripts. Thankfully, his faithful servant John had tried to keep some order to them. As it was, only the latest compositions were present. The rest were stored in a cupboard just off the servant's quarters in the attic. Going up there now would disturb John and he would insist on waking and helping his master.

Handel rummaged around some more. On the floor just behind the door he discovered a pile of manuscripts including librettos various people had offered him in hopes that the great composer would set their creations to music. He sifted through them, looking for one that might capture his imagination. Nothing did, and with a grunt he placed them back on the pile, making a mental note as he did so to have John send them back to their owners with a note that reflected Mr. Handel's great appreciation of their offer, and yet at this time he was not contemplating composing for it.

He entered his music room and headed for the small comfortable chair that sat beside the window and placed the candle on the sideboard next to it, intending to read some of the material he clutched in his hands. Even at this hour he could hear the rattle and clatter of carriages and wagons making their way along Brook Street, bringing produce from the countryside into the great market that was the city. He closed his eyes, not seeking sleep but merely relief from the spinning, tumbling thoughts in his head.

John found him the next morning, sound asleep still in the chair.

Handel chuckled when John woke him. "Damme me, I thought to stay awake and pray, but it seems my body decided otherwise." He stretched.

"Sir, this letter was delivered just moments ago." John handed it to his master and set bustling about with the breakfast preparations. "Lovely fresh fish this morning, sir, along with fresh breads and new-bought honey."

Handel read the letter carefully. "John, a number of weeks ago Mr. Jennens visited us. He left a libretto for me. Do you know where I put it?"

"Bless me, sir, I think you placed it in the cupboard in the front parlor. I have not seen it since."

With instructions for John to bring it with him when he brought the breakfast, Handel sat down again in the chair. The confusion of the night had gone; a clarity of mind now guided him. The letter was from Jennens, inquiring about the manuscript. It confirmed in Handel's mind that he must at least look seriously at it. After all, he'd been searching for something different to debut in Dublin and he at least owed his friend more than the scant perusal he'd initially given.

When John brought the manuscript, he also delivered a steaming cup of one of his master's extravagances, coffee. Since he'd first had coffee at one of the city's coffeehouses, Handel had enjoyed sipping the aromatic brew, particularly in the morning. He'd bought coffee beans and sent John for instruction on how to make the heady drink.

Handel took a long, contemplative sip, then picked up the manuscript. He read the opening pages, noting that they contained quotations from the Old Testament. Jennens had told him this was different from most oratorios and plays. There were no named characters. Rather, it was more of a reflective meditation that walked through the entire story of God's plan for the redemption of man.

As he read, he began to feel a stirring in his mind. Automatically, it seemed, his brain was casting about for moods and tones to fit the words.

"John," he shouted, pushing his dirty plates and glasses away in order to clear table space, "bring my Bible immediately."

It was not that he didn't trust Jennens' vast knowledge of Scripture or meticulous adherence to the accuracy of copying verses; it was merely that he himself wanted to read the words within the context of the passages around them.

Context, in music, in life, as well as in his faith, had been drummed into him by his father when he was still hoping young George would put aside the silliness of music and follow a career in law.

"Understand the whole, not just the part," his father had often admonished. "Only then can you get to the heart of the matter."

He began to read Jennens' libretto side by side with his own well-worn and hand-annotated Bible.

CHAPTER EIGHT

IN WHICH MR. HANDEL COMPOSES

For more than a week, Handel read and reread Jennens' libretto. The more he did, the more he appreciated the skill with which Jennens had brought the main themes together. Although not written as a drama, it had all the elements of one. It was breathtaking and massively inspiring with its varied scenes of tragedy, triumph, sorrow, and hope.

Jennens had divided *Messiah* into three distinct parts. The first covered the many prophecies of redemption for a mankind that had sinned, creating a vast division between God and man. The second explored the passion and sacrificial death of his chosen one, the Messiah. Finally, it was all brought together in the third part, where the triumph of the resurrection and eternal reign of the Messiah reconciled man and God.

It was unusual. Nothing like it had been presented before. It brought faith and religion into the forefront of everyday life. It broke through the barriers between church and everyday life, where faith was normally exercised on Sundays only, never to fully impact the lives of people from Mondays to Saturdays.

It was inspired, and Handel was convinced that Jennens was likely correct. He, George Frederik Handel, was the only one who could do this libretto the justice of great music, to bring it alive in front of audiences.

The challenge was before him. He accepted.

He attended St. George's for the regular Sunday services. As always, it was uplifting. But he needed time to prepare himself spiritually for the task before him. His lingering Lutheranism wanted to drive him to work immediately; his deep Anglicanism held him back, pushing him to contemplate before rushing in.

Now that the excitement and creative fervor had gripped him, he made his normal preparation. He recognized the symptoms. At times like this it was as if a fever seized him and would not let go until he had finished. Speed was essential.

Speed in getting the tunes and music out of his wildly spinning head and onto paper. He'd done it before, but never on such a monumental and, he instinctively realized, important work. It would require his best work, his best thinking, his best imagination. Above all, he needed inspiration.

He gave strict orders to John that he was not to be disturbed.

Handel closed the doors from the small hallway to his comfortable music room and starkly furnished composing room. Until the work was finished, these rooms would be his entire world. He even had John arrange a blanket and pillows for the great leather chair in the music room so that, if needed, he could sleep.

Handel carefully noted the date: August 22, 1741. He stood at his desk in the composing room, holding the quill, and paused. He'd never felt this way before when beginning a composition. The enormity of the subject matter overwhelmed him. He closed his eyes, still clutching the quill.

The normally confident Handel suddenly and unexpectedly felt small and lacking adequacy for the task. It wasn't the insecurity he'd struggled with after the *Deidamia* fiasco. This was different. He knew deep within his heart and mind that he was good—very good—but was he good enough? Indeed, was anyone, Bach included?

"Guide me," he blurted out, eyes still closed.

He paused a moment longer, opened his eyes, and began writing. He carefully wrote the date at the top of the first page, as he always did. It provided a measure of his progress, noting the dates at significant points in the preparation and writing of a major work. This time, he decided, he would note the date each time he began one of Jennens' three parts.

By the time he realized he needed to light the lamps, he'd written in a swirl of activity. His designed opening movement, a Sinfonia, existed to remind his listeners that this was a solemn, regal moment. It's slow, dirge-like opening bars, replete with winds, horns, and strings, evoked a calm, grave tone which hinted at the majestic nature of the story about to be unveiled. It then moved into a sprightly and joyous celebration. It told listeners, he thought, that this was a story of royalty, of sorrow and suffering. The final movement took a gentle triumphant tone. In all, it laid out the entire work in a single piece of music. It was a good start.

Handel swiftly reviewed the Sinfonia, conducting the imaginary orchestra that played in his head. As he conducted, he made adjustments and changes on the sheet to better suit the mood he wanted to create.

He then turned to the first of Jennens' texts, a prophecy from Isaiah. In contrast with the pomp and ceremony hinted at in the Sinfonia, he assigned a tenor voice for the first words—a simple promise of hope: "Comfort ye, comfort ye my people."

The notes flowed in his mind from a simplicity of statement to the comforting reminder that the promise came from one source: "Thus saith the Lord."

He wrapped the words in repetition and contrasting motifs, all designed to emphasize the hope inherent in the promise, before moving into the joyous exclamation: "*Every valley shall be exalted.*"

Finally, he finished the scene with a jubilant choral piece declaring that the glory of the Lord would indeed be revealed.

He barely touched the sparse meals before him. At times he dashed into the music room and worked out particularly challenging sections of the score on his harpsichord, then rushed back to the desk, correcting or changing the score.

And so it continued, day and night. Brief sleep, when it came, came easily, despite his mental and intellectual exhaustion. Yet when he woke it was a refreshed and energetic wakefulness.

The days and nights flew by. It was always thus when he was creating; the music resounded and composed itself in his head. His hand barely seemed to write the notes and annotations fast enough. It was, however, the time he enjoyed most, as he heard and watched his creation come to life.

This time, with *Messiah*, it seemed that while the frenzy and speed remained, the structure came to him more quickly than ever before. He was taking the words into his heart and mind along with the music. The choruses, recitatives, and airs were no longer just words; more than with any other of his operas or oratorios, this time the words drove the music itself. The emotions and content they contained were just as vital as the music itself.

The joyous celebration of the Messiah's birth found its power in two choruses: the first announcing the birth and proclaiming that his name was wonderful, counselor, mighty God, everlasting father and Prince of Peace. The second gave voice to the angelic proclamation of glory to God and peace on earth.

Back in his room, he finished the annotations on a chorus that ended Jennens' first part, with Jesus' own words from Matthew's gospels that his yoke was easy. This epitomized how the words dictated the music as he conveyed a light, easy feel. Handel noted that Jennens had changed the pronoun from the first person to the third, thus better enabling the story to be told in an observational way.

He stopped and contemplated. The second part would lead into the deepest, darkest portion of the story. He picked up the quill, dipped it in ink, and added a slow, ominous ending to contrast the initial promise of ease and freedom. The cost that the yoke would demand was heavy and filled with pain and grief. He needed to remind the audience that tragedy was forthcoming.

On a fresh sheet, he carefully wrote the words August 28.

To him, the mournful opening bars of the chorus "Behold the Lamb of God" previewed the painful time to come. It had to set the tone of this middle portion of the story.

This part of the oratorio's composition proved just as frenzied and productive as the first. It was the most profound, critical, and deeply moving portion of Jennens' libretto. As he wrote, he often wept, struggling to comprehend the deep intensity of the Scripture before him and fearing he might not do justice to it at all.

Many evenings Handel curled up on the chair in the music room and wrapped a blanket around him, trying to doze. He couldn't. He would stretch, open the window, and breathe in fresh air. When he entered the music room to pick out a piece on his harpsichord, he would vaguely note that there was always a plate of food and mug of drink on the table. Most often it was left barely touched.

John, troubled that his master wasn't eating or drinking as he should, often heard the sobbing from behind the door. He was used to the frenzied composing rigor Handel often employed, but this perplexed him. Never had he known his master to be so lackadaisical about food and drink. And never had he heard him moved to tears by the work he was producing.

Long before he actually began to write the music, Handel had struggled with the second section of the libretto. The dramatist and theatrical producer in him realized that many of the key elements of the story, the dramatic and earth-shattering events culminating in the crucifixion, were missing. Rather, Jennens had emphasized the impact and meaning rather than the specific events. The chosen verses from the book of Psalms as well as the prophecies of Isaiah reinforced the harsh reality that God demanded a penalty for sin and therefore rejected and rebuked the one he had called to bear the sins of the lost and redeem them.

As he read the verses in context and meditated upon them, Handel noticed another feature of the libretto. All along, he'd understood that there were to be no named characters, unlike other operas and even oratorios. The performers were not acting out personas but voicing Scripture. It was simple and effective.

Only as he worked through the second part of the libretto did Handel suddenly realize that the main character himself, Jesus Christ, was never actually named. Instinctively he caught the genius of Jennens' libretto. The subject matter went beyond names, thus avoiding the act of reducing the account to the base level of humanity and human understanding. Instead, using the title *Messiah* and not the name Jesus Christ, allowed the listener to concentrate solely on the indomitable story being revealed. It lifted it to a higher plane, where the listener contemplated the spiritual ramifications of the great sacrifice of the Messiah.

As he came to grips with the profound subtleties of the work, Handel found his own creativity being impacted. Tunes and melodies he'd composed and used before in his operas, concertos and incidental music, now wound up reworked, improved and rejuvenated. Combined with melodies from folk songs and other tunes he'd come across in Italy and Germany, they were transformed and given new life. They became new, fresh, and powerful.

It was in the early morning hours that he glimpsed what was happening.

I've been creating my music and basking in it, but it is as if I were operating from the back side of the loom, he thought. *The wool is there, in discernable patterns, but I could only see the rough, unpolished picture.* He picked up the sheets of music he'd just finished and reviewed them. *But now I am seeing them from the other side, from the proper side. I am seeing the whole picture as it should be, not as I thought it was.*

The revelation both surprised and pleased him. Instinctively he realized his current effort was producing music that, in his mind, went beyond anything he or any composer, even Bach, had ever attempted. He was entering a realm beyond anything he'd ever dreamed of.

The libretto pushed him, drove him, demanded of him a level of musical expertise that he sought to surpass with each separate piece. And he was content despite the tears he shed. The proud composer who had embraced public adulation receded. He was pleased with the music he was writing and knew instinctively it was excellent. But if the public disagreed, he would still be content. More importantly, he was convinced that God was pleased. It was enough.

He approached the end of the second part, the choruses, airs, and recitatives having already outlined how nations and kings fought against and rejected the Messiah. Deliberately, he assigned a contemplative promise from the Psalms to the tenor voice, predicting that God would "break them with a rod of iron and dash them into pieces like a potter's vessel." Rejection of the Messiah would lead to ultimate destruction.

In the late evening, he reviewed the verses chosen to end the second part. They were verses from the mysterious and sometimes hard to decipher Book of Revelation, yet they projected a note of triumph, announcing that the work of Messiah was finished, and promising the future rule of the Messiah King.

Intuitively he knew this was a crucial point in the overall work. The promise of redemption and eternal life was about to be revealed to the audience. Of all, surely this was the climactic piece. He knew it had to be superlative. It had to transcend what he had produced thus far. He'd written anthems for monarchs before, but this must rise well above those works.

He paused. All along, he'd prayed for illumination as he wrote. This was different. He laid down the quill and knelt on the floor beside the desk, praying fervently for guidance.

At first it went slowly, with lots of stops and starts. Pages were tossed aside, some with inkblots of frustration. Handel struggled with the exact feeling and emotion he wanted to convey. It wasn't just another anthem. *Zadok the Priest* was the epitome of his coronation anthems, written for King George II back in 1727. But this was not a coronation. It was more. It had to convey a sense not only of kingship itself but of rejoicing in the ultimate victory of the Messiah.

He labored on into the night. From time to time he'd rush to the harpsichord and play with melodies and counter melodies, changing the musical phrases and altering the assignments from bass to tenors and back again, from sopranos to altos and back again.

As he worked, he grew more sure of the path he was pursuing. The opening cries of "Hallelujah!" echoed at all levels, setting a tone of victory and elation, rising to crescendos of acclamation that the King of Kings and Lord of Lords now reigned.

A smile of peace and joy creased his face as he worked faster and faster, writing the notes furiously. He grabbed the sheaf of papers and ran to the harpsichord. He sat and began playing with his left hand while singing the various parts as he wrote notes with his right. He stopped only to dip his quill in the ink.

Finally, he finished. He leaned back from the instrument and read the music once again in its entirety. He lifted the harpsichord's music stand to its upright position and arranged the music. He closed his eyes and began playing and singing, eyes still closed. He finished and then repeated it.

A sense of ecstasy came over him. He played it four more times, singing all the parts, even the highest soprano notes in falsetto, then dropping into the tenor, alto, and bass parts. As he sang, tears flooded down his face.

He shouted hallelujah numerous times, both before, after, and during his repetitions of the new piece. Joy flooded out of him as he sang. He sang and shouted louder and louder.

Awakened by the noise and fearing the worst, John hurried down the narrow dark back stairs from his loft room. He burst into the composing room just as Handel, laughing with excitement, with tears still streaming down his face, appeared in the entrance to the music room. He stopped when he saw his butler's frightened expression.

"Nothing, my dear John. It is nothing." A huge grin spread across his face. "Yet it is everything."

He was laughing, crying, and talking at such a pace that his Germanic accent broke through.

"Mein Gott, John. I did think that I saw all heaven in all its glory before me. And the great God himself!" He collapsed to his knees, shaking with ecstasy, hands and arms spread wide. "It was magnificent. The music is magnificent. I am a mere tool. I did not compose such music in all my life, yet my hands were driven by the music in my head. Ach, mein Gott! It is glorious!"

John helped him to his feet and led him back to the large music room chair. "You must eat, sir. And drink. You have not taken care of your needs well these past few weeks."

Handel looked up and noted John's concern. "I have no need, no need at all. I am being sustained in ways I cannot describe."

"Let me get some food and coffee at least."

Handel nodded and John scurried out.

Pulling himself together, Handel picked up the newly completed chorus and moved back into the darkened composing room. He picked up a fresh sheet, dipped his quill.

At the top of the page he wrote: September 6, 1741.

Gratefully, he munched on a cold chicken drumstick and began the first piece of the final portion of Jennens' script. This was the shortest part of the entire libretto, but it had the potential to be the most powerful and glorious, reminding listeners that God was eternal and his promises everlasting. This was the triumph over death. This was the fulfilment of hope.

Feverishly now, and energized in a way he'd never felt before, he spent the following days and nights carefully marrying the stark verses in Jennens' script with the passions and emotions inherent in them. Music, he knew, could convey emotion in profound ways above and beyond the human mind's ability to comprehend. He worked steadily, pulling the feelings out of the various fragments of Scripture and giving them the power and splendor they deserved.

He breezed through one portion highlighted by the words "the trumpet shall sound." Handel was determined to produce the finest trumpet solos he'd ever created, surpassing even the trumpet work he'd written for what he now called his "Hallelujah" chorus.

He came to the final lines Jennens had provided. They took place in the throne room of God, where tens of thousands of angels rang out, "Worthy is the Lamb that was slain, and hath redeemed us to God by His blood, to receive power, and riches, and wisdom, and strength, and honour, and glory, and blessing." Entranced with the phrases, he shaped the music to bring crescendo upon crescendo, reinforcing the words and their impact.

Exhausted, he put the quill down and read the final triumphant chorus again. He sat at the harpsichord and sang the chorus. He was satisfied with it, yet he felt unfulfilled. He felt something was missing. The piece needed greater finality. An end. An exclamation mark to seal the story once and for all.

Would he dare search Scripture for another verse to fill the need? How would Jennens feel if he, Handel, stepped away from his music and added to the libretto? He picked up the final sheet of his music and stared at the final chorus. He then put it down in frustration and got up from the harpsichord.

Handel pulled the curtains aside and opened the window, poking his head out for some fresh air. He saw the night watchman pacing his way slowly down Brook Street. A carriage trundled by while two chairmen hustled across the street with an empty sedan chair. The moon shone brightly and he saw the stars shining in the clear skies above. He felt the warmth of the early September breeze but knew that the autumn and winter lay just around the corner.

He took one more breath, sighed, and closed the curtains and window.

He wandered into the composing room once again and picked up Jennens' libretto, scanning the final part once again, ensuring he had missed nothing. He came to the final verses from the fifth chapter of Revelation and noted Jennens' final approbation.

"Amen" appeared on its own line, below the verse. At first, he'd assumed that Jennens had intended it as his final comment, signifying the finish of his libretto. There was no verse annotation and therefore it had probably not been intended to be included as part of the libretto itself. He could have easily written "The end" instead of "Amen."

But as he read the script and pulled his Bible closer, Handel saw that it was indeed part of the scriptural text. The heavenly creatures had uttered the word as the elders fell down and worshipped.

Handel thought about it, chewing over the word and its meaning. It was perfect. Amen. So be it! The word summed up the entirety of the libretto. God had done what he'd said he would; Mankind was redeemed. It was over.

The word resounded in his head. He began writing the music that flooded his mind. He repeated the word over and over, rising and falling, soaring and wafting, multiple voices layered and at all levels crying out and declaring the work finished. From quiet and peaceful to exhilaration and great volume, he spun the word and music to encompass all the meanings and emotions he could. Trumpets and drums lent power and triumph to the piece, supplementing his use of the chorus voices as instruments in and of themselves.

And finally, they all came together in one majestic and overpowering final "Amen."

He was sweating as he put the quill down, having added the notation "SDG" at the bottom of the page. That notation, *Solo Deo Gloria—To God alone the glory*, was the closest he could come to his deep feeling that morning. He was finished. The oratorio was done.

He picked up the quill once again and noted the date one final time: September 12, 1741.

PART THE SECOND

*IN WHICH MR. HANDEL VISITS DUBLIN, IRELAND
AND FINDS ACCEPTANCE OF HIS MUSIC
ONCE AGAIN*

CHAPTER NINE

With a groan of frustration, Handel closed the window curtains in his room at the Golden Falcon and stalked down the stairs into the common tap room. He stumped to the table, stopped the maid, and requested a pint of ale before dropping into his seat. The anticipation of Dublin was pushed to the back of his mind. It had been a fortnight already, waiting in Chester for the tempestuous Irish Sea to calm down. Everyone in the town had told him this was one of the fiercest storms in years. He was sick of hearing it.

Back in London, friends had assured him that the fastest and most convenient route to Dublin was to take the stagecoach to Chester on the River Dee and a packet boat thence direct to Dublin. They agreed that while the shorter sea voyage was from Holyhead on the Island of Anglesey in North Wales, getting to Holyhead overland from London was a nightmare. Far better to go through Chester, the main embarkation port for Dublin, they said.

What they didn't tell him, he groused to the innkeeper and others around him, was that the Dee had silted up so badly that the packets now only sailed from Parkgate, some ten miles downstream from the town. The river was wider there, but also more prone to the contrary winds and rougher seas, meaning packets frequently had to ride out the storms in the Irish Sea close to the mouth of the Dee. As he'd found out.

"All true, Mr. Handel, sir," the innkeeper commented after a sustained bout of Handel's complaints. "But just think of those poor devils sitting on those packets, rocking and bouncing in the rough seas. Throwing up their suppers over the side of the boat regularly, no doubt. Well, them as can eat in those awful seas, anyways."

Somewhat chagrined and mollified, Handel thanked the man for his blunt honesty. He determined to concentrate on something other than his frustrations. For more than a week he spent time with local musicians and singers who, flattered by the great composer's attention, strove to impress him with their musicianship and voice.

At one of his frequent visits to the local coffeehouse, he met with Chester's preeminent organist, asking him to bring together choristers from the Chester Cathedral to rehearse some of the newer choruses from *Messiah* he intended to introduce in Dublin. He stressed to the organist how important it was that the selected choristers be able to read music by sight. The organist, Mr. Baker, agreed that there were a number in the town, including one printer named Janson, who was one of the best musicians and finest bass voices in the area.

Happy to be filling his time, Handel set the rehearsal for Tuesday night at the Golden Falcon. When the group arrived, he handed out his scores, sat at a small, rickety but still playable harpsichord, and began.

His excitement rapidly turned to agony and then anger as the rehearsal went wrong from the first notes. While a number of the singers did indeed sing with gusto and volume, he realized with a sinking feeling that their musicianship was minimal at best, reminding him of the sneering comments made by London musicians about musical ability and quality, or lack thereof, in the provinces.

After his fourth attempt to get the group to understand the pacing, sensitivity, and volume required in "And with his stripes we are healed," he slammed both hands down on the fragile instrument, shouting in anger and frustration. In particular it was a strong bass voice that constantly failed to grasp the music.

"No, no, no, no, no! How many times I have told you that it must be like this!" His fingers flew over the keys yet again, repeating the notes and increasing in volume where needed and softening where he wanted. "Ach du lieber, are you all tone deaf? Like this. Again!"

His hand lifted and began conducting the singers one more time, only to slam down once more as sour notes rang out.

"Nein," he roared. "You, sir, Mr. Janson, is it not? Step forward!"

His finger shot out, pointing at the man he considered the worst culprit. The bass singer, a lanky young man with reddening a face, stammered his acknowledgement and pushed his way to the front, head hung low in the face of the composer's fury.

After cursing him in four languages, including English, Handel poked the unfortunate man in the chest repeatedly, emphasizing each painful word. "You scoundrel. Did you not tell me you could sing at sight?"

Flustered, Janson looked away, seeking the nonexistent support of his colleagues. Seeing none, he gulped twice. "Yes, Mr. Handel. But I didn't say I could do it on *first* sight!"

A burst of laughter from the assembled singers startled Handel. He stepped back, a look of both shock and amusement playing across his face. He snorted to hold back a laugh and then turned grim again.

He next turned his ire on the organist.

"Did I not ask for your finest musicians and singers, Mr. Barker? Yet you bring me amateurs," he roared.

He glared around the assembled singers, calming himself and reminding himself that this was only a rehearsal. It was not a practice before a performance, and most certainly they were not the kind of singers he would normally use.

He shot a withering look across the group and then nodded to them. Handel sat back at the harpsichord.

"Again, gentlemen." He turned to the mortified Janson. "If you please, Mr. Janson, refrain from singing until you learn the music." He paused for effect. "By whatever means you use." Another pregnant pause. "As long as it is sometime tonight."

The rehearsals continued for several nights until Handel was reasonably satisfied, making annotations and modifying the choruses where needed to suit the voices on hand. He noted that Janson finally did catch on and, to his surprise, did indeed have an excellent voice. There might be some hope for him yet.

His stay in Chester did provide one benefit. He met, and was more than suitably impressed with, Charles McClain and his wife. He also found out that McClain was a magnificent organist in his own right, while Mrs. McClain had a better than adequate voice. He invited them to attend one of his rehearsals, and at McClain's invitation he then attended Chester Cathedral where McClain performed a recital on the cathedral's magnificent organ. Discovering they were both headed on the packet to Dublin, Handel immediately engaged them both to participate in his subscription series and to help debut his *Messiah*.

Days later, the accursed storm still prevailed. Handel looked out at the rain still beating fiercely against the inn's window.

As he delivered a pint of beer, the innkeeper stopped next to him. "Some good news for you, sir. They say the storm has finally blown itself out. The packets will be landing at Parkgate sometime on the morrow. There are at least seven packets to land and then embark Dublin passengers. With luck you might be able to leave tomorrow night, or the next day for sure."

Handel smiled and leaned back. "That is indeed good news, Mr. Farrow. It is already November 16. I had hoped to be in Dublin long before this, but I thank you for your hospitality and patience. Now then, let us celebrate with a good-sized plate of your finest roast beef, sirrah. And some wine. With potatoes and fresh bread on the side."

One hundred or so miles to the west, a disgusted Lord Dawlish rode back to the city from the tiny fishing village of Howth, which stood on a promontory of land where one could get an early sighting of any packets sailing towards Dublin. He'd rented a room in a small inn originally for a single night, but the violent storm had extended his stay nearly two weeks. Each day he'd come to the pier, waiting for the sight of the packet that his informants said would carry Handel to Ireland. Local fishermen now told him the fierce autumn gale had finally blown itself out and the packets would arrive in the next day or two. He wrapped his heavy cape tighter around him as he rode, trying to ward off the chill winds that swirled around him. He'd wasted days watching for the packets so he'd have early warning of Handel's arrival—to no avail, until now.

So far, he grumped inwardly, his Ireland visit had proved frustratingly unproductive. He'd not heard yet from Ilchester's shipping agents either. He still had no idea when the ship would arrive in Wicklow. More importantly, he'd hit solid walls as he poked around, trying to find ways to destroy Handel's upcoming arrival and visit.

To his chagrin, he'd found the man was actually extremely popular amongst the gentry and nobility of the city. More, they were excitedly looking forward to his visit. Dawlish's own scathing comments that Handel represented a bygone era of music were only met with laughter and scorn. At a dinner just before he left for Howth, one Irish lord had had the temerity to silence Dawlish in mid-rant: "Gad sir, I've never heard such balderdash." With that, the man had turned his back on Dawlish and wandered into the host's drawing room, pulling the entourage of other guests with him and leaving Dawlish mouth agape and alone.

Far from discouraging him, it made him even more determined to succeed against Handel. No man, noble or otherwise, would dismiss him so cavalierly. He was a lord, and he was from London. No provincial popinjay would speak to or treat him so rudely. Frustrations he could deal with; failure he could not. Besides, he kept reminding himself, a dukedom depended on how well he did his job.

He urged his mount to a faster pace. Partly he wanted to get out of the foul Irish weather, but also he had a potentially powerful meeting today that he'd arranged weeks ago. On a tip, he'd made contact with a man who would more than suit his purposes.

Four hours later, Dawlish paced the quayside along the north bank of the River Liffey. The quays were brimming with activity, workers loading and unloading the ships that were Dublin's lifeblood. Why Ilchester couldn't use this bustling port still eluded him, but he shrugged the thought off.

Twenty minutes passed. He couldn't pace up and down the quay much longer without attracting further attention—or worse, trouble. Suddenly, he heard a whispered "Milord." He spun and saw a small, filthy urchin. Muck smeared his face and dirty bare feet extended from his ragged and torn trousers. Dawlish peered down his hawk-like nose, unsure whether the words had indeed come from this being.

The child beckoned to him. "Milord, come. Follow me."

Unsure what to do, having expected a man to meet with him, Dawlish hesitated. By now the urchin was moving swiftly away, although he turned and beckoned with his hand.

Shrugging, Dawlish began moving towards him, his right hand gripping his sword. He hesitated to draw it, fearing it would create a scene or threaten the busy crowd of workers loading the ship next to him. Nevertheless, it paid to be cautious. He tightened his grip nevertheless and pulled slightly to ensure the sword was free in the scabbard and easy to withdraw if needed.

The urchin dipped into the shadows of a dark, narrow laneway. Even though it was only half past three, dusk was rapidly drawing in on an already dark, drizzly day.

As he approached the lane, he gripped the sword tighter. His muscles tensed and automatically he began planning his moves should this prove to be a trap. He looked into the alleyway, but the boy had disappeared. In his place, hidden in the gloom, he saw a man's shadow.

"Far enough, your lordship. No need to come further." Dawlish halted. The harsh, raspy voice spoke again. "I'm told you wish to hire some men for a special job."

The voice waited.

"I was told to meet a man named O'Toole. Is that you? If not, clear off," Dawlish snarled, knowing he needed to establish his supremacy in this conversation. He drew the sword halfway so its steel was more than visible.

"Take care, milord. I'm not playing games. I go by O'Toole and was told you wanted some brawny lads. One signal from me and the lot will descend on you before you can finish drawing that sword or take a step towards me."

Dawlish looked frantically around and saw many of the quayside workers ambling towards him.

"Look here my man, there's no need for threats. On either side." Dawlish dropped his weapon back into its scabbard. "Now, if you are O'Toole, I need some of your men to create a little disturbance tomorrow."

"It will cost you. Ten guineas in advance."

"Six. Three now and the rest when the job is done. At this laneway, if you prefer shadows."

There was a long silence. "What is the job?"

"A packet will arrive in Dublin tomorrow on the tide. A certain person, a musician named Handel, is on board. When he leaves the ship, I want your men to create a noisy demonstration around him, telling him to go home and that he's not wanted in Dublin. If you can, chase him back up the gangplank. You know, that kind of thing. I'll leave the details up to you. But he must be confronted with an angry group of citizens who want him gone."

"We can do more than that, milord," the harsh voice rasped. "We can make sure he goes home. In a box."

Dawlish shuddered. This was a rougher crowd than he'd ever dealt with in London. "No violence. Just make it extremely clear that he is not wanted."

The next silence was punctuated by a sudden snort of disgust. "Very well, Lord High and Mighty Dawlish. Three guineas now, the rest tomorrow evening. Here."

Dawlish gasped at the man's use of his name. He thought he'd taken care that his identity not be known, to ensure he wasn't connected to any disturbance.

"Yes, I know who you are," said O'Toole. "I know everything that happens on my patch, particularly when a well-dressed aristocratic fop is asking after me." He paused. "Give the boy the money."

Suddenly, the urchin popped out of the dark alley, hand extended. Dawlish reached into his pocket, drawing out three gold guineas, and placed them in the boy's outstretched hand. Quick as a flash, the boy grabbed the money and darted back into the alley. Dawlish strained his eyes, peering into the laneway to see his quarry but seeing nothing.

He suddenly felt rather than heard the presence of men behind him. He looked around and discovered that three stood within a few paces, watching him carefully. Behind them, but within calling distance, he could see four others.

Dawlish stepped forward, sweating profusely as he passed the watching men. None moved. He pushed between them and quickly walked along the quayside towards the ferryman who would take him across the river and, he hoped, safety.

As they crossed, the ferryman said nothing, merely holding out his hand for the farthing payment. When they arrived, he watched as Dawlish climbed the steps to the south bank of the river and the safety of his waiting carriage.

"Damn me, but this is a miserable job Ilchester gave me," he muttered to himself as the carriage swept through the nearly deserted streets, past the castle and towards the terrace house Ilchester had rented for him between St. Stephen's Green and Trinity College.

Inside, he was still shaking from the encounter, O'Toole's threats looming high in his thoughts. He sat and immediately began a letter to inform Ilchester of the latest news and complaining about the unexpected threats and problems facing him.

Just as suddenly, he stopped writing and tore the letter up.

I'll wait until tomorrow, he told himself, *when I have news about the way Handel's landing was thwarted.*

With excellent news to convey, he could complain even more profusely and it wouldn't jeopardize the dukedom.

The next morning, he hurried to the landing stage where passengers and mail from the packets arrived. He was surprised by the gathering crowds, most of them dressed in their finery. His sharp eyes also noted a squadron of mounted dragoons and several infantry platoons taking up positions close to the landing stage. The crowd, he observed, was in a happy, celebratory mood.

Dawlish approached one of the Irish nobility, remembering that he'd met the man at a social evening. Lifting his lace handkerchief, he bowed and greeted the man.

"Good day, Lord Dawlish," the man said, smiling. "I must say I'm truly surprised to see you here on this blustery morning."

Dawlish returned the smile and asked why his presence was so surprising. He was chagrined at the man's reply that his negative views on Handel were well known.

"None of us thought you'd show up to actually greet the renowned composer. We even took bets on it. I lost, obviously."

"Just wanted to see what the fuss was all about," Dawlish mumbled, nodding goodbye and pushing against the ever-increasing and ever-boisterous crowd.

The noise reached a frenzy as the man himself, George Frederik Handel, stepped onto Irish soil for the first time. Cheers and shouts of welcome dominated the frenzy. Dawlish found one of the few high spots on the quayside, hoisted himself onto a bollard, and scanned the throng for O'Toole's heavies. He was annoyed; they were supposed to have stopped the man from even landing.

While the cheers rang out, he heard rather than saw a commotion with shouting behind the crowd. Dawlish jumped down and began pushing his way through the crowd, trying to get closer to the disturbance. As he did, some soldiers pushed him aside, also heading towards the uproar.

The assembled throng was cheering, waving, and shouting as Handel entered a carriage adorned with the coat of arms of the Lord Lieutenant.

By God, Dawlish thought, *you'd think it was the King himself arriving, not some dried-up musical has-been.*

Dawlish glowered at the smiling throng in front of him, forcing them aside by sheer willpower. By the time he got to the back of the crowd, the disturbance was over. He saw some of the soldiers disappear around a corner.

"What happened here?" he asked a bystander. "I heard shouting. Looked like there might be some trouble."

"It was just some hooligans from the north side," the man spat out. "Shouting nasty things about Mr. Handel, they were. The rest of the crowd began shouting back and pushing them. Those northside bog-dwellers even used their clubs to take some swings at people. The soldiers stepped in pretty sharp then. Last I saw, those vermin were scattering down every lane and alley in the area, redcoats close behind."

The man moved on as Dawlish was pushed against a wall by the crowds leaving the quay. He glimpsed the carriage bearing Handel as it moved slowly through the mass of cheering, waving people, no doubt heading up to the castle. He sniffed in disgust and disappointment, then slowly slipped down one of the nearby lanes, heading towards the Temple Bar area where he could hire a sedan chair.

As he reached the end of the lane, someone grabbed him from behind. He struggled, hearing a raspy voice behind him and to his left. He tried to turn his head to see who spoke, but his assailant's substantial arm around his neck held him rigidly.

"Sure now, my lord, it's a shame our little demonstration against your man was thwarted," said the man who called himself O'Toole. "But you still owe me three guineas."

"Nonsense, O'Toole, or whoever you are. I paid for a loud, boisterous protest designed to humiliate Handel and drive him back on board the packet. All I saw— or rather heard—was a few mealy-mouthed shouts from far away. Too far away…"

A massive fist slammed into his stomach and he doubled over in pain, driven to his knees.

"Dear me, sir. T'was our agreement to create an uproar at the pier, was it not? And did you tell me about the huge crowds that would gather there? And the soldiers? No, my Lord Dawlish, you did not. But create a fuss we did anyway. So it is now time to pay. Six guineas was our agreement, three then and three now. But don't worry your pretty head about the details. I'll just take my payment."

He reached into Dawlish's huge coat pocket and drew out the money pouch. Dawlish heard him as he tipped the coins into his hand and expressed surprise at the amount.

"Well now, I give you thanks, milord, for my payment of your debt and the extra to cover additional costs brought about by the need for my people to avoid the Viceroy's men for a while." The last thing Dawlish heard was "Take his sword too."

Suddenly, the arm around his neck loosened and he felt an enormous blow to his head. Everything went black.

CHAPTER TEN

*IN WHICH MR. HANDEL ARRANGES HIS
CONCERTS AND HEARS THAT AN OLD
ACQUAINTANCE IS IN TOWN*

What a harried, happy, and fulfilling few weeks it had been since his arrival, Handel mused. He'd been the guest of honor at countless lunches and dinners, not to mention recitals and other musical events. As Matthew Dubourg had promised, the quality of musicianship was extremely high. Indeed, Dubourg had accompanied Handel on many of these occasions, sitting quietly beside him and whispering comments to him. From these instructive moments, Handel began to build his knowledge of the instrumentalists and singers who would be available to him, and in short order he began contracting them to perform at his first subscription series.

Handel was surprised by the fervent admiration the people of Dublin had for his friend the duke, now the Lord Lieutenant, though as one prominent merchant banker pointed out at an evening recital, the acclamation largely came from the wealthy and Protestant sectors of Dublin society.

"There would be far less cheering amongst the poor of Dublin, or indeed amongst the Catholics in this province," he said quietly, leaning over towards Handel and introducing him to the class and religious divides whose tendrils ran throughout the province.

While the underlying political and societal tensions fascinated him, Handel's main focus was preparing for his subscriptions. He decided there would be six concerts. The first, scheduled for December 23, would feature *L'Allegro ed il Penseroso*, as well as an organ concerto and several other concertos for various instruments. The second concert, he decided, would be *Acis and Galatea* and assorted smaller pieces, while for the third he would present his first English language oratorio, *Esther*. All three would then be repeated, totaling the six proposed performances.

His advertisements told potential ticket buyers to come to his house on Abbey Street to purchase them. The house was more than adequate for his needs. It had lots of space for him to rehearse, entertain, and conduct business. Although it was on the north side of the Liffey, the nearby Essex Street bridge gave him easy access to the critical locations he needed on the south side, such as the two main cathedrals, the music hall, and the castle.

Only two days ago he'd walked across the bridge to the new Neal's Musick Hall on Fishamble Street. At first glance, the location suited him well. It was close to both Christ Church and St. Patrick's cathedrals, where he'd tentatively arranged to use some of their singers. They would form the core of his vocal needs throughout the Dublin visit.

He was more than impressed with the new hall's interior, which was exemplary in its furnishings and decorations. The balconies formed a horseshoe facing the main stage, and despite its size and complexity the acoustics were, he proclaimed to the grinning owners and members of the musical society, "marvelous" and "wunderbar!" There was no question in his mind that the Musick Hall would be perfect for his needs. He immediately engaged the hall for all his performances.

It was a chilly, windy day as he returned to Abbey Street. The crisp winter air was made more bitter by the swirling wind up from the Liffey.

Friends had told him that Susannah Cibber was also in Dublin. He was intrigued. The humiliation she'd suffered in London mirrored his own experience, though not, he told himself gruffly, to the same extent. Nevertheless, he was curious. Just last night, he'd been told, Mrs. Cibber had performed solo numbers at a recital. Perhaps, he mused, she would be willing to re-enter musical theatre. If so, he would certainly want her to highlight one of his performances. He'd have to contact her and arrange a meeting.

He mounted the steps to the house on Abbey Road where his new manservant Tobias, hired at Devonshire's recommendation for the duration of his stay, quietly took his coat, shook it, and hung it on a hook. Tobias was short and stocky—"a true Celtic look," as Devonshire had described him, with beefy red cheeks and a constant put-upon expression on his face. Nevertheless, as Handel had found, Tobias was meticulous in looking after his house and keeping the accounts. He was also eminently capable of handling the expected crowds who would arrive at the house to purchase subscriptions, thus relieving him of one of the more tedious tasks of promoting theatrical events.

"Sir," Tobias said in his quiet but authoritative voice, "I am informed that your harpsichord has just arrived on a ship in the harbor. It will be delivered tomorrow."

"Excellent, my dear Tobias, excellent. You will have it placed in the room I chose for my rehearsals and recitals, yes?"

Tobias nodded and coughed discreetly. "You remember, sir, that today is St. Nicholas' Day? You are invited to the castle for dinner with the Lord Lieutenant."

"Ach! You are very much correct, Tobias. This is December 6, the beginning of the Christmas season, and we exchange gifts tonight, yes? My gift to the duke is a very special piece I have myself composed for him. I trust he will be pleased with it."

Handel had no sooner asked Tobias for coffee and settled into a big comfortable armchair than he heard was a loud knock on the door. Moments later, Tobias stood in the drawing room doorway.

"Sir, Mister John Putland, Dean Owen, and Dr. Wynne from the Mercer Hospital request the honor of speaking with you."

At Handel's nod, Tobias showed them into the room. Handel stood to receive them.

"Mr. Handel, sir, we are honored," said Mr. Putnam as Handel gestured for them to sit. The man then introduced himself as the treasurer, and all three as trustees of the hospital. "Sir, some months ago in an exchange of correspondence, you agreed to do a charitable service for our hospital. The famine which hit earlier this year means conditions in Dublin have grown severe over the past few months and we are caring for far more people than we expected."

Dean Owen introduced himself also as prebendary, or honorary dean, of St. Patrick's Cathedral, and John Wynne as a sub-dean of the same. "We are grateful for your interest in our humble attempts to serve the poor of our city. We are here to ask your favor, and whether you would play the organ at the Round Church as part of our fundraising service."

"Round Church?" Handel looked at them in bafflement.

"Forgive me, sir. I meant St. Andrew's Church at the corner of Suffolk Street and St. Andrew Street. It's just that everyone here refers to it colloquially as the Round Church," said Owen. "For a number of years, many of your great works, including *Te Deum*, *Jubilate*, and various anthems, have been played on the organ there as part of our attempts to increase our funding. To have the great Handel himself play would increase our fundraising potential immensely."

Handel smiled. "I would be most honored, and if you give my man your proposed date he will mark it and make sure there are no conflicting engagements." He pursed his lips. "I have one other suggestion, gentlemen. While I would most happily be at your 'round church,' as you call it, you will recall that in our correspondence we also discussed a special event for not only the hospital but for the Charitable Infirmary and the Prisoners' Debt Relief as well. With your agreement, I have in mind a special oratorio, newly composed, that I would like to suggest for that event."

The composer watched them pensively, aware that this was the first public mention he'd ever made about *Messiah*. For now, he would keep the title and subject matter under wraps, at least until he confirmed the necessary performers and date and began rehearsals.

The three men smiled and clapped.

"Most generous, sir, most generous," Mr. Putnam exclaimed. "And we accept most gratefully."

As Tobias served coffee and some sweetmeats, they began to finalize the details.

That evening, Handel celebrated the beginning of the Christmas season at the castle. His carriage drove through the main entrance on Palace Street and made its way through the lower courtyard to the main entrance in the upper courtyard. Red-coated soldiers guarded the entrance, muskets firmly at attention and eyes fixed resolutely ahead as he passed. The entryway was festooned with flickering light from huge oil lamps specially constructed for the event. Inside the castle's dazzlingly white entrance hall, he could hear the strains of a string quartet, probably led by his friend Matthew Dubourg.

Handel was greeted courteously by the Viceroy's attendants and escorted up the grand staircase by the Viceroy's private secretary. Along a sumptuously decorated corridor, they passed a procession of paintings of previous Lords Lieutenant watching guests walk by as armed soldiers stiffly stood at attention every few yards. At the end of the corridor, the ballroom entrance was guarded by two more rigid soldiers.

Inside, the ballroom was emblazoned with scarlet walls and white trim marked with fine gold leaf decorative plaster. The scarlet and gold theme extended to the great chairs lining all four walls. Against one wall, a string orchestra under Dubourg's masterful leadership entertained the slowly assembling guests. Handel smiled when he noted that, as requested, a harpsichord had been provided.

On the way up to the ballroom, the Viceroy's solemn and obsequious secretary had advised him that while the Viceroy would be involved in many such dinners and events across the month-long Christmas season, this one was special. Each guest, he explained, was either a special friend of the Lord Lieutenant's or an honored visitor to the city. To Handel's great amusement, the secretary told him that he qualified in both categories. Privately, Handel wondered if that fact perhaps explained the man's overly fawning attitude towards him.

Devonshire noticed his arrival and immediately Handel showed a leg, bowing as low as his girth would allow. The duke acknowledged him and whispered, "I can't spend much time talking with you right now, George; I have other guests to greet. But I crave your indulgence for a brief conversation in my study before you leave. My man will come and get you."

The duke then escorted Handel to a small circle of guests standing in a corner.

"George, I don't believe you've met one of our guests from north of the city, Richard Talbot from Malahide Castle."

With that, the Viceroy left to greet other guests while Talbot and his wife, along with the four other couples, expressed their pleasure at meeting the great composer and assuring him they would be purchasing subscriptions for his concerts.

Once the extensive and enjoyable dinner had finished, the group of thirty left the formal dining room and wandered back into the ballroom. As they gathered, Handel bowed toward his host and took his seat at the harpsichord.

"Ladies and gentlemen, it is the tradition on this, St. Nicholas' Day, for friends to exchange gifts," Handel announced. "I would like to offer my own special gift. It is a composition written since my arrival in this great city and dedicated to my good friend and patron, the Lord Lieutenant of Ireland, His Grace the Duke of Devonshire."

With that he began a sparkling air that rose to crescendos and dropped to soft tinklings on the keys. His gift was so well received by both the duke and the audience that Handel was requested to replay it several times, interspersed with a number of other short pieces. Two of his better-known compositions were played with the accompaniment of Dubourg and his small orchestra.

As the evening wore on, the chatter and laughter grew, wine flowed profusely, and the servants bustled around trimming lamps and exchanging candelabras with burnt candle stubs with fresh candles.

Handel was just wondering if Devonshire had forgotten his desire for a private chat when the unctuous secretary tapped him discreetly on the arm and whispered a request to follow him.

They slipped out of the room unobtrusively and proceeded back down the sumptuously carpeted corridor. At the other end of the hallway, the secretary opened a door, stepped back, and announced Handel. Once Handel was inside, the secretary discreetly closed the door behind him and Handel found himself alone with the duke, who gestured for him to sit.

Devonshire was the picture of relaxation. He stretched back on his chair, wineglass in hand, as he waited for his guest to sit.

"It is so good to see you again, George, and to see you looking so hale and hearty. I am much pleased at your recovery from your previous health and… er… other troubles. I am so glad that you accepted my invitation to come to Dublin and share your magnificent music. I can assure you we are all expecting something great to come out of your time with us."

Handel smiled and bowed his head in modesty. "Thank you, Your…" He hesitated as the duke raised a warning finger. "…William. I very much appreciate this opportunity and assure you that I will do my best. It is truly good to be here, and I am impressed with the level of musical appreciation and talent in the city."

Devonshire waved his hand dismissively. "I asked to speak to you privately, because I have heard some unsettling news I wished to share with you. Tell me, George, are you familiar with Lord Dawlish?"

Handel grimaced. "Aye, William, I am. He is a toady to the Prince of Wales and his creatures. My friends tell me he is particularly close to Lord Ilchester, who himself is a close confidante to the prince. Both of them were active in denigrating me across London. Some of my friends in the theatre even suspect that one or both of them were behind the mobs who disrupted my performances or destroyed my advertising posters and bills."

The duke nursed his wineglass. "You should know, George, that Dawlish is here in Dublin." Handel's head snapped up. "He's known to have tried disparaging you at several social occasions before you arrived." Seeing the anger begin to build on Handel's face, he hurried on. "You'll be pleased to know that his opinions were given extremely short shrift by those he spoke to. In fact, he has largely been shunned by the people who matter here in Dublin, titled though he may be."

"Can you silence him in any way, William?"

"Regrettably, my dear George, there is little or nothing I can do. He has broken no laws, and even here in Dublin people are allowed to express their own opinion." He paused. "Sometimes I think the people in Ireland—rich and poor, noble and laborers—have altogether too much freedom to express them! But that is another matter for another day and should not concern you.

"Anyway, I was informed earlier this week that the afternoon of your arrival, Dawlish was found staggering up a small alleyway not far from the quay. It was strange to find him there in the first place. Secondly, when he was found and questioned by one of my officers, he refused to give any information on what had happened to him. My men were in the area chasing down some miscreants who'd tried to create a disturbance at the pier. He refused their help and only demanded that they summon a chair or carriage for him. Originally, they thought he was just drunk. Only after he identified himself as a peer did they take action and help him, even though he was ungrateful for their help.

"Subsequently, however, we tracked down a miserable little ruffian we knew had been at the disturbance and brought him to the gaol. It took some time and some questioning, but it seems he was working for a known criminal around the port area of the city and down in the Wicklow Mountains. The gang leader is a man who goes by the name O'Toole, though God knows what his real name is. We've never been able to catch him, and he is well protected by the slum dwellers over there. He let it slip that O'Toole was responsible for Dawlish's condition. That coincided with some other information we obtained from some informants we rely on. They tell us that Dawlish had been asking after O'Toole in the days before you arrived. So there seems to be some connection between the two—perhaps a falling out—and it's interesting that all of this preceded your arrival, and the attack on his lordship happened on the day you arrived.

"Our immediate conclusion, of course, was that Dawlish hired the lowlifes to disrupt your arrival. Dawlish said nothing when we talked to him and has leaned on his royal connections to shield himself from further questioning by my men. I could, naturally, have him brought before me. He has no protection from my authority. But you see, George, I have nothing to question him about. He's not broken any laws that we can prove. He has not invoked our protection. As a nobleman visiting from England, I'm sure you appreciate we must be extra cautious when dealing with the man. We have questions and, yes, suspicions, but little to go on.

"I have nothing more than that, but I thought it best to make you aware of this. It may mean nothing, or it may mean more. You know that if you desire protection, I will of course provide whatever I can, to you personally as well as at your concerts."

Handel was silent for a moment, his face solemn. "Nein. Thank you, William, but as you say, there is nothing. But if there is no evidence…." He shrugged.

"You can see, though, why I wanted to speak to you privately."

Handel nodded, squeezing a small smile out at his host.

Devonshire lifted his glass and signaled to Handel to do the same. "A toast. To George Frederik Handel and a successful, nay triumphant, winter season in Dublin."

They drank together and smiled.

"I must return to the party, George, as must you. Don't worry, we'll continue to watch and scrutinize Lord Dawlish's intentions while he is here. That's part of the Viceroy's role—to ensure the preservation of peace and stability in this land in all ways and circumstances."

He stood, drained his glass and began walking towards the door with Handel.

"By the way, I'm sure you're aware that Mrs. Cibber is also in Dublin and has performed at a few private recitals," said Devonshire. "Have you spoken with her yet,

George? She might add a delightful component to your productions if you could persuade her. 'Twould not do for me, as the King's representative in Ireland, to be seen having deep contact with her, given the circumstances, but I certainly would approve and enjoy seeing her on stage performing in one of your operas, George."

It was gone two o'clock in the morning when Handel finally got back to Abbey Street. Tobias, as always, was waiting for him. Handel slipped off his heavy woolen overcoat, then his jacket, and unbuttoned his waistcoat, handing them all to Tobias.

As he removed his heavy wig, he asked Tobias for a quill and paper. Quickly, he wrote a short note to Mrs. Cibber, asking her to meet with him at his residence two days hence. One of the partygoers at the castle had given him her address, so once he'd sanded, folded, and sealed the letter, he instructed Tobias to ensure that the letter was delivered the next morning.

He climbed the stairs to his bedroom, his mind swirling with concerns about Dawlish's presence in the city and about how to persuade Susannah to participate in at least one of his evenings. As he thought, he realized there was one role he absolutely wanted her to take. But he knew it would be difficult to coax her.

CHAPTER ELEVEN

*IN WHICH MR. HANDEL MEETS WITH MRS. CIBBER
WHILE HIS ENEMIES STILL PLOT*

Dawlish threw the letter on the floor in exasperation.

It was easy to criticize and demand more results, he thought with a sneer, but neither the prince nor Ilchester were here in Dublin faced with the wall of obstinacy he dealt with almost daily. Dublin society had become enamored of Handel. They would not listen to criticisms of the composer and they certainly didn't agree that his music was out of date or that it represented foreign influence. If anything, this city was more old-fashioned British than Britain itself. It was, he moaned to himself over and over again, a real backwater, a place of exile. And so far his efforts to disrupt anything had been an abject failure.

Involuntarily, he shuddered again at the assault and robbery he'd suffered.

"Damme me," he shouted aloud to the empty room. "This would not have happened in London!"

Fortunately, Ilchester had sent more funds to cover his loss while remonstrating with him about hiring more trustworthy people to do the necessary work. More trustworthy people to cause riots, disrupt performances, and destroy advertising posters. He laughed. Ilchester was just as removed from reality as he was from Dublin!

Compounding his fears that he'd been exiled was the mild response from Ilchester about the ship that was supposedly coming to Wicklow. *If* there was a ship. Ilchester's letter made vague references to the hazards of ocean travel and the vagaries of weather and storms. And he'd pointedly ignored Dawlish's request for the name and address of his Dublin shipping company.

He called his servant to dress him for the day's activities and call the carriage for him. At first, he'd used hackney carriages, believing he'd be in the city only a short while. Hackneys in Dublin were not as numerous or efficient as those in London, but at least they had them. London's hackneys had, after all, started service almost a hundred years ago and London had grown immensely in that time. Dublin too had grown, but not to that extent. As the realization that his stay in Dublin would be extended, he'd rented a carriage and groom from a nearby livery stable. It was a generous arrangement—it was Ilchester's money, after all—so that the carriage was available at a moment's notice. It was a fair arrangement he reflected, since anything was better than those damned sedan chairs!

As he left the house, he noticed a slim, well-dressed man, black tricorn hat on his head, standing on the corner. He seemed to be observing the house. This was the second... no, third time he'd seen the same man somewhere along the street over the past few days. He obviously was not a neighbor, since he neither entered nor left any of the houses. Rather, he calmly leaned against a railing each time Dawlish noted him. Fortunately it wasn't one of O'Toole's hooligans, Dawlish decided, since he was too well dressed. He considered confronting the man, but since the stranger had made no moves towards him or shown any particular interest in him, Dawlish decided to forgo the pleasure. He had enough on his plate already.

The carriage came and, so far as Dawlish could tell, the man showed no interest in it or its passenger, allowing it to pass with no reaction at all.

They headed into the Temple Bar area, stopping at a hostelry that was popular with the Irish gentry on their way to and from the castle just up the way. The area's popularity had risen and it had become far more crowded since Sir William Temple had built his house there early in the previous century, thereby giving his name to the neighborhood.

Inside the inn, Dawlish spied the man he was looking, sitting off to the side at a small table. The fact that it was a cloudy, gloomy day added to the smoky, claustrophobic atmosphere in the inn even though it was just past noon.

"Thank you for responding to my invitation, Sir John," Dawlish said quietly as he approached the man. He slipped some coins to the barmaid as she passed, nodded towards his companion, and told her to bring Sir John Maitland whatever he wanted to drink or eat. Once the man made his choices, Dawlish sat and commented on the miserable day before he was quickly interrupted.

"Lord Dawlish, you didn't ask me here to discuss the weather," said Maitland. "You hinted at something else in your letter. Let's get to the point."

Dawlish was slightly taken aback by the man's comment.

The Irish penchant for blunt speaking is certainly true, he thought. *Unlike London, there will be very little dancing around before getting to the main issue.*

"Very well, Sir John. I was merely reflecting on the day, but since you wish, I will indeed get to the point. I understand that you attend St. Patrick's Cathedral and are well acquainted with some of the clergy there."

Maitland nodded cautiously, wondering what Lord Dawlish was driving at. As one of the city's leading merchants, he supplied grains to many of the city's brewers and distillers. He was anxious as ever to raise himself and his family in Dublin society, so the opportunity to meet with Lord Dawlish, an esteemed friend of the Prince of Wales, had intrigued him enough to accept the invitation.

"Having just come from London myself, I have very few contacts here, you see," Dawlish said. "I heard that you attended the cathedral and thought you could perhaps help. I am particularly interested in meeting Dean Jonathan Swift. I am a great admirer of his works and greatly esteem him." He reached into his voluminous pocket and pulled out a copy of Swift's *Gulliver's Travels* and laid it on the table. "All I ask is that you provide me with an introduction."

Flattered, Maitland preened. "Well, of course, my Lord, it's true I have a close relationship with many of the cathedral's clergy, including Dean Swift." He proceeded to regale Dawlish with anecdotes illustrating the close relationship he claimed to have.

Dawlish let him fawn, seeming attentive but his mind was already miles away planning his next steps. He was amused that Maitland never considered Dawlish might have arranged the introduction himself, due to his title; but he needed a stealthier approach in order to ingratiate himself with the dean. His inability to lure the Irish nobility to support him, or work for him, had hampered his ability to build relationships. The direct approach that worked so well in London clearly was not working for him here. If the Irish nobility would not help him, he needed to lower himself and puff up the rising merchant class, ingratiating himself in their society.

That he himself was a member of the merchant class was lost on him; he had a title now, and a potential dukedom. He felt himself to be above them all and merely sought to use them.

Meeting with this man was the first step. Handel, it seemed, was still too popular here. Everyone was excitedly talking about the composer's upcoming concert series. Word was that he'd already sold all the available tickets for that new music hall. Dawlish had heard further that Handel was going to do a charitable concert for some of the local, always begging charities. More importantly, it seemed Handel was hiring musicians and singers from both cathedrals. Dawlish's scheming mind had decided to try and subvert from inside, and that meant working on the singers, musicians, and their superiors.

For Handel, not even the gloomy morning could dampen his spirits. Dublin had proven to be a panacea to his soul, not to mention his financial stability. Even the few recitals and commissions he'd already received had been enough for him to send bank drafts back to Brook Street with instructions for John to pay off all his bills.

He was pleased to hear the bustle beyond his closed door. His first advertising in *Faulkner's Journal* had resulted in a constant stream of visitors to his premises, purchasing subscriptions to his first concert series. Tobias was busily accepting payment and writing out the necessary tickets which would allow the purchaser to attend not only the concert but also the rehearsals.

He contemplated Devonshire's concerns regarding Dawlish and, while they were a bit troubling, pushed them to the back of his mind so he could enjoy the rejuvenation of his life. His most disturbing thought was the knowledge that the prince and his followers were so determined to destroy his reputation that they would resort to sending a nobleman as far as Dublin to do their dirty work. Was it not enough that he was out of London now? He shook his head. He wouldn't deal with this now. Besides, he told himself, he had concerts to produce and they were coming up soon. There were more important things to think about.

He heard a lull in activity in the business end of the house and opened the door. Seeing Tobias free, he called the servant to come help him dress. This afternoon he was receiving Susannah Cibber and, surprisingly for Handel, wanted to be at his best.

Shortly after three, Tobias discreetly knocked on the door to his drawing room and announced Mrs. Cibber. Handel stood immediately and bowed as she slipped into the room.

"My dear Susannah, it is very good to see you again. You are looking well. Dublin must be agreeing with you."

"Mr. Handel, it was so kind of you to invite me, and yes, I do love this place. It is so… refreshing…after London."

"Is your… I mean, is Mr. Sloper here as well?"

"Alas, no. He is away in the Americas seeing to his father's business. We both agreed 'twould be better for me to come here, where I have friends, than to remain in that dreadful city."

He beckoned for her to sit and asked Tobias to bring refreshments. As he sat, he scrutinized her. While she was not a stunning beauty, he had to admit, she had pretty features and carried herself with a grace and élan most women could never carry off. Her short stature was noticeable in this room, but on stage it grew out of all proportion, so dominating was her personality. As she straightened her massive hooped skirt, she gave him a glittering smile—one he was used to seeing her use on the London stage. Unlike many actresses and performers, however, the smile was warm and genuine.

"I hear you have given one or two small recitals while you are here," said Handel.

"Yes, some kind friends, including Peggy Turncastle, have invited me to sing and I am very grateful. If only for the opportunity to exercise my voice."

"And a wonderful voice it is too," Handel said just as Tobias entered the room with refreshments. "May I inquire why you decided on Dublin, my dear?"

"Very simple, Mr. Handel. To get away from London and the horrors that city has for me now. You have no idea of the humiliation I suffered from people all over the city. I was a mockery and was ostracized. There was no work for me. No opportunities to perform." She was close to weeping, Handel realized. "My dear friend Mrs. Turncastle invited me here, telling me there was a vibrant music and theater life, so I decided to take advantage."

Through unshed tears, she smiled bravely at the man she secretly considered a genius and mentor as well as sometime employer.

"When I heard you were in Dublin, I was fearfully excited," she said. "Especially when I heard you were presenting a season of your wonderful music."

Handel grunted acknowledgement as he studied her. "I understand about London, for I too have suffered at the hands of those capricious crowds. I too have been humiliated and driven to despair." He looked at her kindly. "Though not to the levels you suffered, of course."

He stood and politely offered Mrs. Cibber another glass of wine before he began to pace the room.

"Tell me then, would you entertain the idea of perhaps performing in one of my productions?" He squinted at her, studying her reaction. He was pleased at the spark that lit in her eyes.

"I am flattered you would even consider it, Mr. Handel. I am, after all, an actress at heart."

"Ah, well. I intend to produce *Esther* during this series, and I certainly would like to hire you for that. You already know the part. But I also had something else in mind for you. Something that will test you as you have never been tested on stage before." She looked at him quizzically. "You will need your voice at its absolute best, and you will need to deliver the finest performance you have ever accomplished. But you will not do one ounce of acting. In fact, you will stand in one spot through the entire presentation, only sitting when you are not required." He smiled at her puzzled expression. "I will explain. But first let me show you this."

He reached over to the side table and picked up a bound book. Even at a glance, she guessed it was an entire score. He handed it to her.

"Take a look at this, my dear. It is the score for a new oratorio I completed just before I left London."

He watched her carefully as she scanned the material, knowing full well that she not only read music but understood the nuances and what he was trying to accomplish.

"I have the mezzo-soprano role in mind for you," he said. "It would suit your voice. And I intend to debut it here in Dublin where people appreciate great music."

She glanced up. "There is no role for the singers to play?"

"No. Unlike other oratorios and operas, in this the singers concentrate on their pieces rather than take on the personality of an individual and project it to the audience. It is different, I admit. And obviously, as an oratorio, there are no stage sets, costumes, or makeup."

He waited patiently while she read through the entire score.

"It is different, most certainly," she said quietly and hesitatingly. "This is a very religious and deeply intense subject." She looked at him piercingly. "You know my background, Mr. Handel. I am not suited for this at all. Nor do I think an audience would accept my singing it. Ever here, I have been greeted kindly and, by and large, accepted. But there are still whispers behind my back. Comments made behind la-dies' fans. People know. And they have their opinions. For me to sing in this... this particular oratorio, would be tantamount to blasphemy for many, sir." She down put the book. "No, I cannot do this. I thank you for thinking of me, but I cannot sing this work."

Tut-tutting, Handel dismissed her objections with a wave of his hand. "If I might be blunt, as you English say, your 'background' is precisely why you and you alone are the mezzo-soprano who should sing in *Messiah*."

He leaned forward, his hands waving with word as through he were conduct-ing an orchestra. It was a habit he'd suppressed during his depressions, although it returned now as his excitement grew. As he spoke, his eyes sparkled with fire. His entire body was as engaged in the discussion as much as his mind and speech.

"This is the most unusual libretto I have ever seen or worked with. It is be-yond anything I have ever composed in the past. Greater than producing anthems for coronations and royal occasions. Greater than any opera, or even one of my Bible-based oratorios like *Saul*, or even *Esther!*"

He softened his voice, aware that he was beginning to shout in his excitement. He called it his German side, whenever he found himself doing it. When he tried to coax people in this way, he could become almost overpowering. He took a deep breath and spoke more slowly. But the goal remained the same; he needed to convince her of his sincerity.

"I am not the humblest man," he began, noting the small smile that curled around her lips, "but in all humility I stand before you and declare that this is perhaps my greatest work. Not because of me or whatever talent I might have, but because I truly believe God directed me and guided my mind and quill as I wrote. It demanded my all. I need my singers and musicians to also give everything they have for this most magnificent story of stories. It is *his* music, not mine."

Handel waited a few moments, struggling to find the right words.

"You've heard of Mary Magdalene, surely?"

Susannah nodded hesitantly.

"I want you… no, I need you, to be my Mary Magdalene in this production. You know that she was the woman from whom Jesus cast out demons. Think of it. Think of what this woman endured in her life until Jesus appeared. She was tormented and jeered at. People avoided her and considered her a great sinner with no hope of redemption. She was shunned by the people in her town, including, probably, her own family. People would not speak to her. They mocked her. She was an outcast. But Jesus healed her, and she became one of his great followers. She was there at the crucifixion and knew how it felt to be mocked and scorned. She was also the first to know of the resurrection."

He stretched out his arms and picked the score out of her lap, flipping through the pages until he found the piece he wanted.

"Here, at the beginning of the second part. This, in particular, is the air you were always meant to sing."

Handel adopted a false soprano voice and began to sing it to her.

"*He was despised and rejected of man; a mand of sorrows, rejected of man…*" His voice dropped off. "You have been rejected and despised. You know the pain of your fellow man turning on you because they judged you a sinner. Remember, Jesus committed no sin. But Mary Magdalene knew what it was like to be condemned and then forgiven. She loved Jesus because he redeemed her. I know that you have a Christian faith and have fallen away. I don't know your present beliefs, but I do know you have felt the pain of human rejection and deep sorrow. So did she! I need you to be my Mary Magdalene. I need you to sing this air with all the depth of feeling you can gather so that the audience feels the loneliness, the depths of his despair. Be Magdalene for me. For the world."

He handed the opened manuscript to her. She contemplated it, reading and rereading it. In the silence, Handel could hear the hustle and bustle in the street outside. He heard the cries of street-sellers. He also heard the activity in the room next door, as Tobias continued selling subscriptions.

As he watched her intently, small tears filled her eyes and trickled down her face. Quietly he moved to his harpsichord and began playing the music. He half-turned to her and began moving his arms in time with the music, conducting her and willing her to begin singing. She lifted her head as he stopped and began the music again.

She began to sing. Quietly and hesitantly at first. Then she stood, her voice quavering and tears flowing even more abundantly, singing with passion and feeling, drawing it out of her soul and the depths of her own rejection by society.

CHAPTER TWELVE

IN WHICH OPPOSITION GROWS BUT
MR. HANDEL'S PLANS CONTINUE

The fashionably dressed O'Toole sauntered across the road and mounted the steps to the great black door, hammering on it with his gold-tipped cane. When the door opened, he told the servant that he was there at Lord Dawlish's invitation.

"But Lord Dawlish is not here, sir," the servant spluttered, "and he said nothing to me about any appointments today."

"Nonsense. Of course he's here. He's pulling one of his pranks on me."

O'Toole pushed the servant aside and stepped into the foyer, using his heel to slam the door behind him.

"I say, sir—" the servant began only to be silenced by the slash of the cane across his head. He dropped to the floor, unconscious.

O'Toole's constant surveillance of the house over the past week had assured him there were no other servants in the house. Quickly he grabbed the servant by the shoulders and dragged him down a hallway, depositing him in a small side room.

Looking around, he found some linen tablecloths and methodically tore them into strips. He had considered bringing ropes, but they just didn't suit the sartorial picture he was trying to portray. One thing he prided himself on was his ability to shift from one personality to another, one level of society to another.

Methodically he bound and gagged the man with the strips of linen. He then closed the door behind him and ran into the hallway, opening doors and shutting them until he found Dawlish's library.

Upon discovering it, O'Toole tossed his hat onto a nearby chair and began a systematic search, looking for any piece of information about Dawlish and why he had come to Ireland. He pulled books off the shelves, flipped through them, and tossed them on the floor. Drawers were opened, the contents examined and also thrown aside. Above all else, he wanted Dawlish to know he'd been there—to serve as a warning that he wasn't safe anywhere.

By the time he finished, O'Toole knew a lot about his prey as a man but little about his mission.

He was about to leave the library and rummage through rest of the house when he spied some crumpled papers that had been tossed into a corner. Not wanting to leave one iota of material uninspected, he picked them up and straightened them. Unlike many of his fellow Irishmen, O'Toole could read, and he whistled as he read the contents of this letter.

So, my Lord Dawlish, you have an interesting mission, he mused.

Dawlish was not, as O'Toole had suspected, a crown agent seeking to infiltrate groups opposed to English rule. He shook his head in both shock and amusement as he realized that Dawlish was indeed in Dublin purely to destroying that musician.

O'Toole laughed as he continued to read. The cost and effort Dawlish and his cohorts were willing to expend seemed ludicrous, given the issue. To O'Toole it was an indictment of the lunacy and pettiness of the corrupt nobility nesting in London.

You have a second mission, it seems, he thought. *To oversee the landing of goods down in Wicklow. And what might those goods be, eh? What might Lord Ilchester, friend of the heir to the throne, be smuggling into Ireland through a tiny fishing village that he must send a member of the peerage to oversee it?*

O'Toole sat down to think. Maybe Dawlish was a crown agent after all. He picked up a quill and quickly wrote only his name on a sheet of paper, leaving it prominently on the desk.

He next found Dawlish's bedroom and ransacked it, searching for corroborating material about Wicklow. Thinking about what he'd read in the discarded crumpled letter, he was puzzled by the man's insistence that Lord Ilchester provide him with the name of the agent. It seemed Dawlish was not completely informed about when the ship, which had no name O'Toole could determine, was scheduled to land.

As O'Toole's fruitless search continued, he considered that it might be worth his while to find out who normally acted as Ilchester's agent in Dublin. Paramount to him was how he could use the information he'd found so far. It seemed there were no dire threats to Ireland. Nevertheless, it was a mystifying mission that had been outlined in the cryptic letter. It required more thought.

With that thought, he took a last look around, stuffed Ilchester's letter in his pocket, picked up his hat and cane and left.

Dawlish looked around the interior of the cathedral, feeling impressed. Normally he avoided church if he could help it, content to attend only on Christmas and Easter. Like many, he called himself a Christian but did not need the folderol of attending every Sunday when one could be sleeping, fox hunting, relaxing, or nursing a massive hangover from the previous evenings' activities.

A cassocked priest walked him to the end of the brightly decorated nave and its multicoloured tiles with Celtic designs. As Maitland had promised, the stained-glass windows were remarkable in their ability to flood the building with light and colour even on this weakly sunny winter day.

The priest led Dawlish to a small room off the cathedral's chapterhouse. He knocked once on the door, opened it, announced Dawlish, then stepped back and gestured for him to enter.

Dawlish's eyes adjusted to the darkness of the dingy little room, a stark contrast from the bright cathedral. A grey-skinned and middle-sized man sat stooped over a desk covered with scattered books and papers. Candles flickered but shed little light.

The priest moved to quietly light an oil lamp sitting beside the door and provide a brighter aspect to the room. He turned, bowed, and left.

Dean Jonathan Swift looked up. "Well, who are you and what do you want?" he barked.

Dawlish had been warned that the man, acknowledged as one of Ireland's greatest writers and thinkers, was getting crotchety in his old age. This, they said, stoked his frequent anger and bouts of sarcasm.

"Lord Henry Dawlish, Your Reverence. I am from Derbyshire and late of London, now visiting Dublin and Ireland."

Swift snorted. For the first time, Dawlish noted the palsied shaking of his hand as Swift gripped the edge of the desk.

"And why do you disturb my hour of peace and contemplation your lordship," Swift snapped.

Still standing, Dawlish realized he was not going to be offered a seat. Partly because Swift obviously had no intention of prolonging this meeting, but mostly because the only chairs in the room were also covered with mounds of papers and books.

"Well, Your Reverence, I could not visit Dublin without attempting to meet you, sir. I am a great admirer of all your works, including *Tale of the Tub*, but I confess that *Gulliver's Travels* is the one I most enjoy and esteem. I wanted to express my appreciation to you personally for all the pleasure and, yes, thinking, you have provided to me." He reached into his pocked and pulled out his copy of the book to show Swift.

Swift grunted again. "Like my work, do you? Then what, sir, is the true title of this book?"

Dawlish sighed silently with relief. The hours he'd spent studying Swift's work was about to pay off. "Well, of course, the true title is *Travels into Several Remote Nations of the World in Four Parts*, but most people simply name it *Gulliver's Travels*, after your supposed author, Lemuel Gulliver. Printers in London now use that title on the book, as you can see."

For the first time, a wry smile cracked Swift's face. "Hmph. You do know something after all." He waved a feeble hand at one of the chairs. "Clear that clutter off the chair and sit down, sir. Put it all on the other chair. I will get to it eventually."

Dawlish did as he was told.

By the time Dawlish left the dean's office and began walking down the ornate nave towards the main doors, he found that he had been than a little impressed with the man. His sincerity, wit, and yes, even his sarcastic moments, had overrode the specter of a cantankerous old man he'd expected. Some, including Maitland, had said Swift could be difficult at times; others were blunter, calling the dean insane. Dawlish surprised himself, acknowledging that while he had intended to play the man like a violin, he'd actually liked the man.

Be that as it may, he thought as he reached the doors, *I will certainly use the man's conceit and pride in the cathedral and its singers against the Handel circus.*

He adjusted his fashionable short-tailed brown wig, brushed his dark blue breeches unconsciously, and stepped out into the cold morning. Signaling his carriage to follow, he turned right, wrapped his heavy cloak tightly around him, and began walking down towards Christ Church Cathedral.

As he walked along, he brushed aside impudent street-sellers and filthy children with the occasional swoop of his black Malacca cane. He began to realize how hilly this part of the city was. It was tiring to walk first down the slope, then up and then back down towards Christ Church. As short a walk as it really was, it was a challenge to a flabby man more used to the relative flatness of London.

He crossed the bustling street crammed with carts, merchants, and annoying beggars. He looked up and saw a fishmonger's sign at the top of a short street leading off towards the river. He stopped and spoke to one of the better-dressed merchants who confirmed that this was indeed Fishamble Street.

On impulse, he turned down the street and wandered around its tight curve, noting the street's unique zigzag. There, just as the street curved again, he came upon Neal's Musick Hall. For the first time, Dawlish saw with his own eyes the place where Handel would present his performances—the ones he intended to disrupt.

He stood across from the doors, watching people, some carrying instruments, enter. The elegantly decorated entrance set the hall apart from the other tightly packed and narrow-terraced buildings along the street.

Posters advertising Handel's concert in two days reminded him of his abject failure in his mission to this point.

"Damme me, why did I ever consent to coming to this miserable city?" he muttered, causing some passersby to stare at him. He must have quite the sight, a well-dressed man talking to himself. One plucky lad, thinking Dawlish mad, darted in to see if he could steal his purse only to be dissuaded by the very painful crack of the cane across his shoulder. The boy ran down the street clutching his shoulder, trying not to howl with pain. The rest of the crowd backed up to give Dawlish space.

He glanced down the otherwise grimy street and smelled rather than saw the Liffey River. Smoke from hundreds of chimneys obscured his sight, but he shivered as a cold breeze blew upriver, its tendrils snaking up the streets and alleys. He pulled the cloak even tighter, took one more glance at the dark, brooding ware-houses on the Liffey's edge, then turned and walked back up the street towards the cathedral. It was enough. He'd seen the place and involuntarily shivered again, stressing over his inability to turn Dublin against the man.

He signaled the carriage, having decided to return home.

Inside St. Patrick's Cathedral, Sub-Dean Dr. John Wynne spoke quietly to Swift. "Our chapterhouse has arranged, with your consent, to join with the choristers of Christ Church and assist Mr. Handel in the presentation of his works. Particularly those of a charitable nature. The dean and chapter at Christ Church are in agree-ment, and all we await now is your signature on this agreement."

Wynne pushed a piece of paper under Swift's nose.

"What's this all about, eh?" Swift sniffed suspiciously. "Our choir singing with theirs for this fellow Handel? Does Charles agree with this?"

Wynne, used to the peripatetic nature of Swift's mind these days, kept calm. He unconsciously ran his hand over his forehead, bending his lanky body closer to the dean so that he could speak quietly and still have Swift understand.

"We discussed this a few weeks ago," Wynne replied simply. "Charles… we, I mean, Dean Cobbe and his people are in favor. In fact, Charles told me that they were not only delighted but honored that their singers and ours were so highly esteemed by Mr. Handel."

"You think it would be good too, do you, John?" Swift paused. "Well, all right then." He signed with a flourish. "Now get me that medicine my physic told me to take, would you?"

Swift rummaged through his desk, found the document he wanted, and began to read.

The shakiness of his hands was very visible today, Wynne noticed, even to the point of moving up and impacting the arm.

Wynne quietly left, making a mental note to remind the priest on duty to replenish the oil in the dean's lamps. Two, he'd noticed, had been out, although Swift seemed oblivious.

Once outside the dean's study, Wynne hurried to the end of the nave where two men waited at the entrance to the choir portion of the building. The rather stout man with a huge white wig was deep in conversation with the second who, more fashionably, sported a smaller brown wig with a large black bow tied behind it.

As Wynne approached, they both turned expectantly toward him.

"It's all agreed, Mr. Handel," said Wynne. "You have your choirs. And you, Mr. Dubourg, can assemble your orchestra."

A grin spread across both men's faces.

Now I can properly rehearse and bring Messiah to the public, Handel thought.

Dubourg meanwhile, was relieved that Dean Swift had made good on his earlier verbal promise, something that was becoming rarer these days.

As Wynne and Handel continued to talk, Dubourg hurried away, anxious to discuss the hymn choices for Sunday's services with the presiding cleric.

As they walked, Handel expressed his thanks to Wynne, especially given the warnings he'd heard, even from the Viceroy himself, that Swift was not well.

Wynne confirmed it. "Dean Swift is Ireland's leading writer and thinker, but regrettably age is beginning to seize hold. He has a lot of… let's say conditions… which affect his mind. It's not as sharp as it was, and he has a tendency to swing back and forth. I've learned to be patient and approach him on serious matters only when the signs are right. Today, apart from a touch of the palsy, was a good day."

They arrived at the foot of the stairs to the organ loft.

"I wonder, Mr. Handel, if you would care to play our magnificent organ. One of the best in all Ireland, we've been told, although we do hope to add a second organ in the chapel very soon."

"A very kind offer, Your Reverence, and I would indeed love to play," Handel replied. "I do, however, have one more matter to lay before you."

Handel hesitated. He was excited about *Messiah*, but lately he'd had qualms about how the established church would receive it when performed in a public hall rather than a church setting. Added to that, he was a non-cleric and German, and Charles Jennens was equally an outsider; together they were creating a piece of sacred music in English for the edification of the masses. Handel could imagine some of the stuffed shirts of the church raging about it, especially given the negative feelings towards him in London, his reception in Dublin notwithstanding. He knew the church hierarchy took its lead from London and those in leadership of the Church of England.

As the probability of *Messiah*'s debut had grown more and more likely, especially with the recent addition of the fine singers and musicians of both cathedrals, doubts had begun to gnaw at him.

He shared with Wynne the gist of his concerns and watched the cleric's face intently to measure both his visual and vocal responses.

"And you think it would be unseemly, Mr. Handel, for church choirs to sing about a religious subject?" Wynne said. "Is Bach a cleric? Really, sir, the whole thrust of the gospel is to reach out to people who never go to church and tell them the good news, is it not? It sounds to me that that is what you are planning to do. If so, I can only commend you and purpose you to disregard those fuddy-duddies in the church who say other!"

"Actually, I was more concerned about the actual location," Handel said. "I am planning to use Neal's Musick Hall."

"Mr. Neal is a fine Christian man and music publisher. His hall is a great addition to the city. I've heard that it can hold more than six hundred people and that the sound is excellent in there." Wynne smiled as a relieved Handel shook his hand. "I have a meeting with some of our local clergy, so I cannot stay with you, sir. But I most definitely will be listening."

With that, the sub-dean walked off while Handel ascended the steps to the organ.

From the loft, Handel began softly, playing familiar church music, including some Bach. As he played, a smile broke out over his face. God was good. He had pulled him out of the depths of despair and penury, lifted Handel's mind above and beyond his trials, and allowed him to glimpse a more powerful story than his own. Handel knew he struggled with his ego, but even then God had granted him peace and affirmation.

As his spirit soared with the music, he decided to end with one final piece— his new composition, the Hallelujah Chorus.

When he ended with the final thundering chords, he noticed that the cathedral was silent. It took him a few seconds to realize that he heard nobody speaking or moving about. Looking down, he was astonished to see that everyone—cassocked priests, well-dressed individuals, even one or two children—stood stock still as they look up at him, most of them smiling and nodding appreciatively. This reaction to what they didn't realize was the first public performance of the piece, was heartening. None of them knew who was playing or what the music was, yet it had moved them. That fact alone encouraged him. It was enough.

An hour later, he returned to his house feeling uplifted. The details were dropping into place for the first public performance of *Messiah*. He had the heart of his musicians and singers lined up. Susannah Cibber was considering the role as mezzo-soprano, while Christina Avolio had already been engaged to perform the soprano part; James Bailey, tenor; and John Hill, bass. Mr. McClain was agreed to serve as the organist and Matthew Dubourg would lead the orchestra as first violin.

Pleased, he settled down to a hearty roast beef dinner with lots of red wine.

CHAPTER THIRTEEN

IN WHICH PLANS FOR MESSIAH MOVE FORWARD

"**D**olt! Imbecile! Cretin!"

Dawlish raged at his servant, who sat before him with a bloodied head. He'd arrived home to be greeted only by silence—and when he'd seen the chaos in his library, panic had set in, especially when he'd seen the piece of paper and its signature on the desk. He'd raced down the hall, shouting frantically for his servant, throwing doors open until he arrived at a small pantry cupboard and found the bound and gagged man bleeding profusely from a head wound, his eyes wide from shock and fright.

After Dawlish angrily freed the man, he grabbed him roughly by the arm, complaining bitterly about the man's inability to stop the robbery. He pushed the man into the drawing room.

All along, the frightened man stammered and stuttered as he tried to explain.

"You *let* him in?!" Dawlish's anger reached a crescendo.

"No, sir," the man gulped. "He pushed his way in and before I could do anything. He coshed me on me'ead. Nothing I could do, sir. On me honor!"

In his panic, the man had slipped back into the vernacular of his youth, dropping the fastidious language and tones his employment demanded.

"Stop bleeding on my chair, dammit man." Dawlish paced up and down. "Did he take anything?"

"Don't know, sir. I was out cold like a block of ice. Never 'eard anything till I 'eard you shouting."

"Does the name O'Toole mean anyhing to you?" Dawlish bent down and gripped the arms of the chair. He glared intently into the man's face but received only a blank look in response.

"Nothing, sir. Nothing at all. Who is it?"

"Gads! You're either a good actor or a good liar. O'Toole is the name of your collaborator, isn't it? Come on, man, confess. Empty your pockets." He pulled the man to his feet and began to rifle through his clothes.

"Bless me, sir," the servant stammered. "If I was in league with him, 'ow could I have coshed meself on the 'ead and tie meself up?"

"Your accomplice did that, I'm sure. And got away with what he wanted."

Despite the man's protestations, his empty pockets produced only one dirty handkerchief, a few pennies, and the household keys.

Dawlish stopped pacing, snapped his fingers, and pushed his servant back into the chair with more shouts to stop bleeding. He grabbed some of the linen strips and quickly tied his servant up again.

"There. That'll hold you until I can summon the parish watch."

It took nearly an hour before a burly man hammered his staff against the door, shouting out for the occupant to open in the name of the parish watch.

Dawlish had used the intervening time to scour the house, going through every room to determine what was missing only to be baffled. Nothing, so far as he could determine, was gone. Not money. Not his dueling pistols. Not even the small stash of jewelry he'd brought with him. Nothing! Which was even more frightening to Dawlish. If the motive for the attack hadn't been robbery, it must have been a warning or threat. The elusiveness of the man frightened him. In the alleyway, O'Toole had surely stolen more than enough money to satisfy him. Why was O'Toole hounding him and tormenting him? Why did he not just crawl back into his stinking lair and leave well enough alone?

The watch, for all his bluster, asked very few questions and released the servant who had begun to screech that Dawlish was a madman. A monster!

Outside, a small but growing crowd had been drawn to the front steps by the appearance of the watch. They listened to the shouting through the open front door and enjoyed the street theatre that resulted. It was a break from their normal monotonous grind.

Finally, supporting the servant who clutched a large white cloth to his head, the watch led the man down the stone steps. Dawlish was close behind, calling the servant a Judas and a betrayer of the worst kind, screaming that the man was dismissed and swearing revenge. He took out his sword and began flailing it about, trying to disperse the crowd.

Giving up, he at last stepped back inside and slammed the door behind him.

In the sudden quietness, he dropped into a visitor's chair placed in the front hall. He held his head in his hands, bemoaning all that had befallen him since his arrival. His mind swirled with a myriad of questions and a fair dose of fear. He shouted out his whys to God and called his curses upon Ilchester and even the prince for their foolhardy quest and pettiness. He raged that his own house had been violated for the sole purpose of scaring him.

His anger turned to determination. He snatched his tricorn and stormed out, failing to notice a bun-seller watching him intently, his eyes following discretely while Dawlish sought his carriage. Nor did he see that same bun-seller flash some coins at a Hackney man and tell him to follow.

Dawlish's first stop would be to the castle. Second, he would seek new lodgings, something that befit a lord of the realm, a step above what Ilchester had provided. Third, he would demand more funds to cover the expenses he'd incurred. Fourth, he would insist—no, demand—that Ilchester provide him with the name of his Dublin shipping agency.

As his carriage forced its way through the busy street, he seethed with resentment at his lot. Although he couldn't rationalize it, he laid most of the blame on Handel, the man who stood between Dawlish and his dukedom. That the suggestion of a dukedom had come from Ilchester rather than the prince himself mattered little to Dawlish; his greed and ambition had caused him to fixate on it.

If it hadn't been for that cursed composer and the prince's obsession with him, Dawlish would even now be at home in Derbyshire enjoying the lush green countryside around his estate, collecting the profits from his tobacco and slave-trading interests. Instead he'd been exiled to this miserable place.

Dawlish's confrontation with the general in charge of the castle guard was exceedingly frustrating. While the general couldn't be faulted for his solicitous care of the angry guest standing in his office, he repeatedly explained that he couldn't help. The troops barracked at the castle and outside the city were intended for the protection of the city and the Viceroy; they would only involve themselves in a civilian situation if and when civil disorder and riots arose. The army was there to protect the nation and the crown, not individuals, not even a peer. The general suggested instead that Dawlish utilize the services of the local parish watch. Or, if he really wanted bodily protection, hire a personal guard.

All of Dawlish's protests fell on deaf ears, as did his threats to report the general to both the Viceroy and the Prince of Wales. The angrier Dawlish became, the more polite and intransigent the general got.

Finally, Dawlish slammed his fist on the desk. "You'll regret this!" He then stomped out, making sure to slam the door behind him in disgust.

The bemused general and his aide looked at each other.

The aide sniffed. "He would have been more temperate and respectful had he known he was speaking to the son of a duke, while he is only a lord, sir."

"There are pompous twits at all level of society, God help us," said the general. "They're in business, the church, politics, and even the military. Look at that idiot Colonel Fotheringham over in the Third Brigade! No, Edgar, there are times to pull rank and use your position and there are times to wipe the muck off your boots and move on. Unfortunately, his lordship hasn't learned that yet. I have, so I wipe his muck off and move on."

The general stared at the door, half-expecting Dawlish to come bursting in again.

"Nevertheless, His Excellency has somehow taken an interest in his lordship, especially after that incident near the docks." The general sighed. "Make sure this meeting is in the weekly report to His Excellency."

Dawlish didn't look back as he left the castle precincts, instead turning and heading immediately for the city's administrative offices. The glower in his face was enough to part his way through the crowds, helped by the aggressive manner in which he wielded the cane in his left hand. He kept his right hand across his stomach, ready to whip out his sword at a moment's notice.

Cursing the incompetence of the Irish in general, and the military in particular, he strode into the offices demanding to see the city constable.

An hour later, he left, somewhat mollified but still frustrated. At least he now had two hired bodyguards and the assurance that the authorities were all too familiar with O'Toole. The solicitous constable had admitted, however, that the man was more like a ghost than mortal.

"My own opinion, my lord, is that the man himself is actually two, perhaps even three, people. How else can he be everywhere at the same time, committing crimes, stirring up trouble, and provoking the people? One minute he's a well-dressed gentleman, the next he's an honest craftsman. The next he's a poor beggar! He's slippery as an eel, that one. But mark my words, sir, this time he's gone too far, assaulting and robbing a fine London lord like yourself. We will get him, sir. And he will hang."

Dawlish's carriage was turning back towards his lodgings when he suddenly asked the driver to take a different route, past St. Stephen's Green and as far as Fitzwilliam Square to see a house the constable had recommend he might rent. According to the constable, the finely furnished abode might be available immediately given that the master of the house had dropped dead suddenly, leaving the family destitute.

"No doubt the widow would be appreciative of a fair lodging price," the constable had said, suggesting an amount.

Dawlish didn't care. Ilchester would be paying, not he.

As they entered the square, Dawlish wasn't so sure of the location. It seemed too far removed from the heart of the city to be of much interest. However, as they drove around, the wide square and beautifully presented red brick terraced houses with fashionable fan lights matched what he'd seen in London's newest and finest areas.

The carriage stopped at the designated house and Dawlish ordered the guards Charles and Ezra to remain. He proceeded up the stairs.

Inside, he was pleasantly surprised at how spacious and stylish it was. He was angry with himself for not having searched for a house like this when he'd first arrived, instead of taking Ilchester's meagre offering. He haggled for a few minutes with the widow and wound up paying a bit more than the constable had suggested, but he was granted permission to move in within three days.

As he got back in the carriage, he looked back and admired the house again, pleased that he'd secured it and given his patron another bill to swallow. Once he'd moved in—and hired a butler, cook, and maid, as well as other luxuries he'd avoided in the previous residence—he would set one of his burly new men the task of tracking down O'Toole while he himself worked on Dean Swift to undermine Handel.

St. Michan's Church had occupied consecrated soil, since a Norse church had been built there in the days of William the Conqueror. The building Handel gazed at, however, was a bit more modern, dating only from 1686. He sat in the carriage alongside Patrick Delaney, who'd turned out to be a wonderful and gracious host. He was also, in fact, chancellor to both Dublin's cathedrals and therefore had a big say in the ongoing life of both, as well as the activities of their clergy and choirs.

On the ride to St. Michan's, Delaney had explained that while he was a friend and admirer of Dean Swift, he too was deeply disturbed by the old man's increasing slide into poor physical as well as mental health.

"I, along with many of my colleagues, are in fact worried this might be the beginning of the end," Delaney had said after detailing some of Swift's more irrational actions and proclamations. "Such a great man and so sad to see."

Two evenings previously, Handel had enjoyed a bounteous feast at Delaney's table. The good fellowship and spirit had seemed even more remarkable to Handel when one of the other guests was heard explaining the proliferation of black ribbons and décor was due to Delaney being in mourning for his recently departed wife. Despite the loss, Delaney was solicitous to all his guests.

When Handed had privately expressed his condolences, the minister had been solemn. "My good fellow, while I grieve for my immediate loss, I know with certainty that I will see her again. So my sadness is also coupled with expectation. It is the sure hope of Christianity, isn't it, that we will live eternally? While I mourn her loss, I must also continue in the life I lead now, waiting for that day when we'll be reunited."

Handel, a bachelor, had been puzzled by this reaction. He liked many people, and many were very close to him, but he had never truly loved anyone to this extent and therefore he'd never considered either the practical or theological repercussions of the death of a loved one. He determined to think further on this intriguing matter.

Over a glass of wine later in the evening, he'd carefully discussed the matter of *Messiah* with the respected minister, broaching the idea of using biblical stories in musical and theatrical presentations. Delaney himself had brought up the issue, praising Handel for the production of *Saul*.

"I had the honor of being in London and attended a performance," Delaney had said. "Excellent, my dear fellow. Marvelous!"

Hearing this, Handel had told Delaney of his concerns about playing religious music in theatres.

After listening carefully, Delaney had scratched his chin. "My good man, it is most unseemly to attend the theatre for what I might call 'profane' stories. But it is most certainly different if the story is one of faith. Religious truth must be movingly conveyed." He had leaned forward, using his half-empty glass to punctuate his points. "Not just movingly conveyed, but with the warmth of piety, ardor of benevolence, and zeal of Christian charity. And your *Saul* did exactly that!"

Handel had then revealed his plans to debut *Messiah* in Dublin at the charitable evening. Patiently, but with passion, he had told Delaney about the libretto and its total reliance on words taken directly from the Bible. He'd related his worry that some in the church might object to it being performed in a theatre rather than a church. Delaney had listened carefully, smiling and nodding the entire time.

"Well, 'pon my word, sir, you absolutely must allow us Dubliners to be the first to hear it." Delaney had wagged his finger at Handel. "My ecclesiastical side would say that it should be debuted at one of the cathedrals. My present-the-gospel-to-all side, however, says it unquestionably must be done at Mr. Neal's Musick

Hall. Let those who are superficial about their Christianity come face to face with it in a new way. The fact that you're planning it as a charitable event should mollify many who might harbor doubts, one would hope."

The conversation had continued for more than an hour, interrupted only when Delaney had needed to say goodbye to his other guests. When Handel had mentioned his need for a place where he and his musicians could rehearse *Messiah* given the limited amount of time available at Neal's Musick Hall, Delaney had immediately suggested St. Michan's for its resonance and availability.

It was a chilly but sunny day, and from the street, even through the overlay of smoke, Handel could see the Wicklow Mountains standing stark against the sky. Prominent was the peak that locals called Sugar Loaf, seeming ghost-like as the haze and clouds wafted around it. It reminded him of how small this city was compared to the vastness of London. For all he had been enjoying his visit and felt rewarded by the reception of this warm and generous people, he still missed London and its challenges.

As they stepped down from the carriage and into the church, Delaney extolled the virtues of the building as well as the superb new pipe organ that had been installed in recent years.

Inside, they were met by the vicar, who escorted them around. After many minutes contemplating, Handel turned to the vicar and arranged times and donations in return for using the space during the week.

At Delany's and the vicar's urgings, Handel accepted the invitation to test the new organ as it has never been tested before. With a pleased grin, he spent a good ten minutes playing a variety of numbers. He ended, as at St. Patrick's Cathedral, with a powerful rendition of his Hallelujah Chorus. He nodded to the vicar when he was finished.

"It is good," Handel said, nodding up to the organ. "Very good!"

"And now, my friend, I think a good lunch is in order," said Delaney. "Have you ever tried The Old Sot at the Essex Street Bridge?" Handel shook his head. "Then, sirrah, you are in for a treat!"

With that, Delaney hustled Handel out of the church.

The beefsteak feast they enjoyed was just as good as Delaney had promised, despite the somewhat crude-sounding name of the establishment.

"I am pleased that Dean Swift has agreed to allow both choirs to participate in Messiah," Delaney remarked as he forked another slice of meat into his mouth. "With Matthew Dubourg there as well, I think you are assembling a most admirable and proficient group for what you tell me will be a real treat for the ear. And your subscription series is a very real success. I enjoyed every one of the performances. Tell me, now that they're finished, when do you propose to stage your new work. What was it you called it? *Messiah?*"

"Ah." Handel leaned back, hands folded over his very full and protruding stomach. A contented grin crossed his face. "I was planning for it to be soon, but now it seems it will have to wait. The Viceroy wrote to me this very week and suggested—and you know a suggestion from him is as much as an order—that I offer a second series of subscriptions. So great was the approbation and appreciation of the first series that he feels the people of Dublin deserve a second." He took a sip of wine. "I am glad. It will give me time to properly rehearse the choirs and orchestras together. I am not proposing to present *Messiah* until the first week or so of April. Anyway, it would seem to best fit the Lenten season, would it not?"

Both men sat back, satisfied and full at the end of the meal.

CHAPTER FOURTEEN

IN WHICH SOME PEOPLE BEGIN TO HAVE DOUBTS

Susannah Cibber sat on an elaborately embroidered green and gold sofa, using a fire screen to shield her face from the hot flames melting her substantial makeup. The roaring fire was necessary on this cold winter evening. As requested by her friend Peggy, she had earlier sung a number of songs ranging from those made popular in the London theatres to some of Mr. Handel's own music, including *Lascia ch'io pianga* from *Rinaldo* and ending with her own brother's popular *Rule Britannia*.

Yet now, not even half an hour later, she saw the faces of other women hidden behind their wooden-slatted fans. She heard their whispering and the occasional titter. Oh, they'd all applauded and congratulated her to her face, but some—a small number, she had to admit—had taken to the fans or stepped out into the hall for their little discussions.

Peggy sat on the sofa beside her. "You were marvelous, my dear. Simply marvelous." She saw Susannah's eyes, pointing at the tittering, gossiping women. "Pay no heed to those three, my dear. They aren't worth worrying about. They are silly, petty women who have no position in society. I invited them only because I felt sorry for them. Their husbands are provincial merchants trying to enter society in the city." She sniffed. "Well, that's the last time they'll be invited to any of my evenings and I'll make sure they will not have entry to any other gatherings of my acquaintances, you may be sure!" She signaled a footman to come over with a hot chocolate drink for each of them. "So, tell me. You met with that wonderful Mr. Handel. Are you going to sing in any of his concerts?"

She nodded. "He's asked me to be in *Esther* in his next series of concerts. He's doing a second, you know."

Peggy smiled. "Yes, my dear, I heard just this week. I will, of course, buy the whole subscription and I would love to hear you sing *Esther* again." She looked at

Susannah carefully. "Were I you, I would be over the moon about it. It's what you wanted, isn't it? Yet you seem so glum."

Susannah sighed. "It is, of course, and I am delighted that Mr. Handel invited me to participate. But those women—"

"Pshaw! Ignore those jealous and petty harridans. Pay them no heed. They have no culture, no class."

"Thank you, Peggy. I really appreciate all your support and what you're doing for me. But those women… how many more of them are there even in Dublin? How many more will mock or scorn me?"

"La, my dear, don't give any of them one iota of your thoughts. Look around you at the others here, many of them wives of the city's leading citizens. Did they not applaud vociferously? Did they not surround you with their heartfelt congratulations and appreciation? What are those three fishwives against the cream of Dublin society, eh? The real women here adored you, and you received many invitations to perform recitals in their homes, did you not, my dear?"

Peggy glared over at the three still-gossiping women and sniffed loudly. The women gradually dispersed.

"You cannot even compare that reception against a few who gossip behind their fans," Peggy continued. "No, my dear, those who applauded you and asked you for recitals are the genuine heart of our society here. Do you think for one moment that they don't know of your, shall we say, troubles? Or that they haven't read the London papers talking about Cibber's lawsuit? Of course they have. Pshaw! I say again, pshaw! They know exactly who you are and what your history is, m'dear. And they loved you and your music anyway." She beckoned a footman over and asked for a glass of wine for both of them. "I don't doubt some of them have the same kind of marital problems too. It's just that they aren't brayed about in public."

Susannah hesitated. She was grateful to Peggy for her unswerving support and encouragement, both in London and here. Truth be told, she was still struggling with Handel's request for her to participate in the oratorio.

While Handel had not sworn her to secrecy, he had not as yet been very public about his new project. Although she'd given him a tentative yes, he'd given her time to think about it. The salary was certainly generous enough, but she felt ill at ease with the subject matter. Not, she scolded herself, that she didn't believe even a repentant sinner like her would be rejected by God. The issue was whether the public would accept her singing the pieces. Gad, it was a difficult situation.

She finally decided to test Peggy's opinion. But not now. Not here. As they enjoyed the wine, Susannah broached the idea of a private lunch the next day.

"You have something on your mind, something troubling you, don't you, m'dear?" Peggy asked perceptively. "You must come here and we'll talk about it. I will arrange everything. Shall we say around one of the clock?"

Dawlish was shown into Swift's study yet again. He'd become a regular visitor, building a relationship with the old prelate.

"I brought you this bottle of the finest French brandy, Your Reverence." Dawlish placed the bottle on Swift's desk. "They do say this is a fine vintage."

A twinkle lit up Swift's eyes. "And I'm sure it passed legally from France to England and thence to Ireland, eh, my lord?"

Dawlish shrugged. "All I know is the origin of the bottle. How it made its way here is less of my concern. Now, sir, if you have some glasses, shall we enjoy?"

The next hour passed quickly, the discussions ranging from topics of theology, during which Dawlish merely let Swift talk and occasionally grunted agreement, to societal trends in London. They got into a mild disagreement over the political aspirations of the Irish people, with Dawlish agreeing to read more of Swift's writings on the subject. He also agreed to meet with Charles Forbes, a leading writer on Irish issues in London, as well as Sir Henry Carmichael, a Member of Parliament who had strong views on the issue.

As they sipped their brandy, Dawlish carefully steered the conversation towards music. "You're aware, of course, that the German composer George Handel is in Dublin…"

"Yes, met the fellow twice so far. Excellent music and he's doing concerts here as well."

Dawlish let the favorable reference pass. "I heard he proposes to use some of your choir members for various performances as well."

"Anything we can do to help improve the cultural offerings, we will do, so long as it does not interfere with their church duties," Swift replied. "Of course, we personally scrutinize the proposed concerts to make certain there are no profane or worldly situations or even references in the works. Mind you, my sub-dean and others assure me that Mr. Handel's music is most acceptable."

"Well, he has been known to tackle religious subjects, Your Reverence, and in theatres as well. All well and good, but do you think you should allow your choir to engage in theological performances in worldly places?" Dawlish hesitated, then waved his hand airily. "But sir, you are the theologian and I am a mere landowner. I bow to your discretion on the matter. If you approve, so will I."

Swift sniffed. "Well, sir, it all depends upon the particular issue and particular circumstances, doesn't it? I make no blanket declarations."

"I hear his operas and performances take considerable liberties with the Bible stories."

Swift glared at him and shook his head. "Never, sir. That will never be allowed."

Having planted a seed, Dawlish skillfully steered the discussion to other topics. When Swift dismissed him, Dawlish walked back up the nave with a smug grin on his face. For once he seemed to be making progress. Slow progress, but progress nevertheless.

Outside the cathedral, he jumped into his waiting carriage. His guard Ezra, who'd been waiting outside, helped him in and then stood in the carriage door watching his master expectantly.

"You have news?" Dawlish asked.

"Not exactly, milord. We've noticed a particular breadman hawking his wares around the square over the last few days. Doesn't seem to sell much, or even try. Rather he pays a fair amount of interest to the houses on your side of the square. This morning, Charles decided to see exactly what was up. As soon as you left, the baker whistled up a hackney and set out. He seemed to be following you. Charles then followed him and wound up here. Charles saw your carriage and assumed you were inside, but the baker then took off. We suspect he met with someone and left someone else to keep an eye on you. We're trying to determine just who that is."

"And you let the baker go?"

"Yes, sir. Whoever he was, his job for the day was done. We suspect he'll be in place tomorrow in the square once again. We suggest that unless you have other plans, you take a carriage ride around the city with no particular destination. We'll follow him as he follows you. After an hour, stop at any particular place, like the cathedral here, and go inside. Then exit at another door and hire a carriage to take you home from there. We, meanwhile, will follow him after he hands off, and have a little chat with him in private."

Ezra pounded a fist into his hand to emphasize his meaning.

Dawlish's good mood of the day dissipated. His anger was such that he had been getting ready to shout at his guard. But as Ezra spoke, he saw a glimmer of sense in the proposal. He eventually nodded his approval and told Ezra to stay with him for the rest of the day. He then gave the driver an address and sat back, huddled into a corner, remaining silent as Ezra shut the door and jumped up beside the driver.

His mind spun. For a while he'd thought he had escaped O'Toole's notice. Apparently not. The realization struck him like a kick in the stomach.

Dawlish's next stop was at the home of Sir John Maitland. There, he was fawned over by the man and his wife. Dawlish spent a casual few hours pumping Maitland for more information about Swift.

During the conversation, a casual remark caught Dawlish's attention. "What do you mean, Handel's sacred oratorio?"

"I don't know much, milord, but I was speaking with Matthew Dubourg the other day and he says he and the choir members are looking forward to performing a sacred oratorio at Mr. Handel's charitable concert next month."

Dawlish tucked the information away. Before he raised the matter with Swift, he must cultivate Dubourg. That would provide the perfect excuse for him to return to the cathedral the following day.

That evening, dressed in his finest, Dawlish arrived at one of the grand homes on the extreme southeastern border of the city, near the village of Dundrum. It was the Dublin residence of the Earl of Foyles. He'd received the invitation to dinner due to his status as a friend of the heir to the throne. It seem fitting that his connection to the prince was finally becoming known.

As the evening progressed, Dawlish found he was enjoying himself for one of the first times since he'd set foot in the city. He flirted with a few women, took part in the dancing, and reveled in the massive twelve-course meal. Throughout dinner, he admired the great candelabras hanging above the enormous room. Gold-plated cutlery glistened from the long, white-clothed table, along with scads of crystal glasses. A roaring fire added to the already overheated atmosphere. He barely noticed the carved plaster moldings and gold leaf furnishings, not even the heavy tapestry curtains and striking yellow paint that outlined the massive dining room.

He estimated more than fifty of the city's society were present. As he participated in small talk, inhaled snuff, and regaled the women with the latest stories and gossip from London, he noticed a tall, thin man glancing his way on occasion. The man looked vaguely familiar, even though Dawlish was certain they'd never met. He stared at the man until the man eventually turned away.

The man's identity niggled away at him as the meal progressed. He couldn't see the man clearly, since they were placed on opposites sides of the table, along the same side of the table. The man was seated considerably closer to the host.

As everyone rose following the meal and the women began moving towards their own drawing room, Dawlish turned to the lady he'd been chatting with.

"Excuse me, Lady Arabella, but could you tell me who that man is?" Dawlish pointed at the intriguing fellow. "The one in that dark blue embroidered ensemble. With his back to us."

Lady Arabella scrutinized the man carefully. "Why, that's Lord William, the Duke of Ennis. He's often in town but rarely attends parties such as this. He largely prefers his own company, it seems."

Dawlish hastily excused himself and strode over to Ennis.

"Excuse me, sir, I believe you are the Duke of Ennis. I am Lord Dawlish, from London and Derbyshire. I can't help but think we've met somewhere before. Probably in a different place or circumstance? London perhaps?"

Ennis coolly looked him over head to toe, then answered in a frosty tone of voice. "I don't think so, sir. If we had, I'm sure I'd remember it."

That voice too sounded familiar to Dawlish. He nodded to the man, thanked him for his time, and moved away. As he departed, he stopped one of the footmen, received a glass of wine, then wandered to a part of the room where he could quietly observe Ennis. He tried not to stare, but the more he studied the man the surer he became that he knew him.

Dawlish moved closer, trying to be unobtrusive yet eavesdrop on the duke's conversations. As he heard the man's voice again and its intonations, his imagination ran wild.

As Ennis leaned against a wall speaking with a bishop, Dawlish's mind clicked. A cold smile came over his face.

He approached the two men, excused himself, and asked for a private conversation with Ennis. At a nod, the bishop wandered off to find another victim to hear about his successful flower garden.

"And what can I do for you, sir," said Ennis wearily. "Lord... um, Darvish, is it?"

"Dawlish. And I wonder if we could speak out there." Dawlish pointed towards the prominent glass doors that led onto the stone balcony.

Ennis, an amused smile on his face, turned immediately and led the way.

Out on the terrace, Ennis turned and leaned against the balustrade.

"You don't fool me, whoever you are," Dawlish hissed. "I don't know what lies you spun to gain entrance here, but you, sir, are a fraud. You are O'Toole, and you are wanted by the constabulary, and no doubt by the Viceroy himself." He shook with anger, his voice quavering at the end.

To his shock, Ennis laughed out loud and slapped his knee. "Sure now, that's the best story I've heard all night. Whatever possessed you to say that, sir? I am who I say I am, the Duke of Ennis. I have no idea who this creature O'Toole is, I assure you!"

"Your voice. Your mannerisms. You were prowling around my house. You even broke in. It all adds up. You, sir, are a fraud and I demand satisfaction. I will have my second speak to yours on the morrow and we will set a date and time."

Dawlish could barely contain his mixture of anger, excitement, and fear. He'd found his Irish nemesis!

Ennis merely laughed, which further enraged him.

"Do you understand, sir?" Dawlish demanded. "I am challenging you to a duel."

"My good fellow, you have certainly provided me with amusement for the night, but again, you are making a false claim." His smile disappeared and he leaned into Dawlish's face. "I suggest, sir, that you refrain from making wild accusations without solid evidence to enforce them. We Irish have a particular dislike for you English who accuse us of all kinds of falsehoods, seize our lands, and even our lives. Be very careful what you say and who you say it to, sir, or I will indeed have satisfaction."

Before either could speak further, the doors flew open and the Earl of Foyles himself stepped out.

"Needed a bit of air too, I see. You are enjoying yourselves?"

The Earl slurred his words. His enjoyment of the evening had certainly involved ample amounts of the wine, port, and brandy he'd made available. The half-empty glass he waved about confirmed it.

Ennis straightened himself. "Thank you, Henry, I am indeed enjoying myself. This poor fellow has mistaken me for some churlish individual named O'Toole."

Foyles roared with laughter, spilling his wine. "Best one I've heard yet, William."

"I denied his charge, of course, but it seems the deluded fellow has challenged me to a duel." Ennis laughed again. "I'd rather not waste my time on a drunken fool, lord or no."

Foyles turned to Dawlish, his tipsiness vanishing. "I've known this wee lad since he was a babe in arms," he said sternly to Dawlish. "His father served with me in the regiment. And he's been the Duke of Ennis since he was seventeen." The earl wiped his mouth with his voluminous coat sleeve. "I think, sir, you would do me a favor if you would leave our little ball now. Perhaps you've had a mite too much to drink and need to sleep it off instead of insulting my guests. There will be no talk of duels in this house. Nor will you attack, verbally or otherwise, my very good friend."

The earl turned away, seized Ennis by the elbow, and led him back into the room.

A furious Dawlish trembled with anger, unable to either speak or move. He'd been humiliated in front of one of the province's greatest earls—and this would surely get back to the Viceroy, and no doubt from him to the prince. He could not think of a bigger disaster to befall him and he kicked himself for acting so impulsively. Dublin's doors would close on him now and further undermine his efforts.

Before he could move, a liveried footman appeared. "My lord, the Earl of Foyles has asked me to escort you to your carriage. I have taken the liberty of summoning it for you."

In silence, a humiliated and seething Dawlish was led along the terrace, through another set of doors into an antechamber, and then into the hall. Before he knew it, he was being assisted into a carriage and, without further ado, sent off.

Just before dawn, a shadowy figure banged on a door in the heart of Dublin's slums. Finally, a candle-holding man opened the door, still rubbing sleep from his eyes. He listened to his instructions and then closed the door immediately.

An hour later, the reasonably dressed slum dweller stood in the cold on the steps of the Custom House beside the Liffey, bracing himself against the biting winds roaring in off the Irish Sea to the east. He pulled his cloak around him and stuffed his half-gloved hands into the overwide sleeves. He watched as the Custom House clerks arrived for the day's work, nodding at some he recognized, waiting for the one he wanted.

Finally, the man he wanted showed up. The two spoke quietly, exchanged coins, and then parted—one to his work, the other back to his slum.

Lunch with Peggy that afternoon was indeed private. A portrait of her illustrious naval father hung over the ornately decorated fireplace and a roaring fire warmed the room. Extra lamps had been lit to compensate for the sunless and smoke-draped day that spilled its gloom into the room through the large windows.

Peggy dismissed the maid and footman once the sweet had been delivered to the table. She waited until the door clicked closed behind her, then laid her spoon down and watched Susannah for a moment or two.

"So what troubles you so much?" Peggy asked, putting her elbows on the table and cupping her chin on her folded hands. "I know it's not those dastardly women."

Susannah flashed a quick, wan smile. "It's Mr. Handel. Or rather, it's not Mr. Handel so much as what he's asked me to do."

Peggy looked up in horror.

"No, no. Nothing like that!" Susannah blurted, equally horrified. "It's a new oratorio he's asked me to be in. It sounds wonderful. It is wonderful. But I don't think I should do it." She hurriedly stammered on before Peggy could get a word in. "I mean, he's shown me the book and I've read some of the music. In fact, I even sang one piece for him, but it's just not right for me. I cannot do this, but I truly am ever so grateful to Mr. Handel for asking me. I just fear that he's asking me out of pity."

Peggy looked at her sternly. "That doesn't sound like him at all. He has often written music especially for you, and even changed the score to suit your range. He's a genius composer and has a great grasp of the abilities of the singers and musicians he employs. If he asked you to sing an oratorio, he did it because he knows you and knows your talent."

Give her a script or libretto, and Susannah was as eloquent as they came. But as she'd shown in her days testifying at the London court, she found it very difficult to express herself when dealing with intensely personal issues and thoughts.

She was silent for a moment, then struggled to explain. "It's not even that, Peggy. It's the subject matter. I don't think it's suitable for me. I should not, must not, do it. I just don't know how to let him know. I fear he will be dreadfully disappointed. He wanted me especially for this."

Peggy stood up, announcing that this was likely to be a long discussion and better served if they sat in comfortable chairs in the drawing room rather than at the table. She led Susannah into the drawing room, stopping only to instruct the footman to bring brandy.

They settled into the chairs and waited until the drinks were served and the door closed.

"Now then, m'dear, I cannot think what kind of theme Mr. Handel would work on that would so upset you," Peggy said. "It doesn't sound like him at all."

Susannah shook her head and flashed an embarrassed smile at the older woman. "Actually, it's not that there's anything wrong with Mr. Handel's subject, it's that it would be wrong of me to do it. It's that the subject is so holy, and I am so full of sin. It would be blasphemy for me to participate, much as I might want to. That's what has me sore troubled."

Peggy sat back and nodded to Susannah, waiting for her to explain. Twenty minutes later, amidst a lot of sobbing and tears, Peggy leaned back in her chair.

"Do you really want my advice?" Peggy asked.

Susannah nodded, still sniffing into her kerchief.

"You're telling me that Mr. Handel is presenting a sacred oratorio that has never been heard before, that it is a brilliant piece of music, and that you feel unworthy of the role he has offered you."

Susannah nodded again.

"Stuff and nonsense, Susannah. Mr. Handel was eminently right to choose you and you would be foolish beyond belief to refuse."

Susannah's head snapped up. She'd expected Peggy to agree with her and commiserate, not support Handel.

"What is this story about, eh?" Peggy asked, her voice stern. "You tell me it's about the age-old story of the redemption of man. Redemption from sin, is it not? And who can most identify with sin other than a sinner? Yes, you are a sinner. So am I. But your sins, if I may be so bold, are much more in the public eye than ever mine will be. If that's what the story is about, then of course you must do it."

Susannah was stunned.

Peggy paused a moment, then continued in a softer, kinder voice. "You are being offered a chance to redeem yourself in a very public way. Your talent is beyond question, as is your stage presence. Now you've been given the opportunity to show yourself as an example of the very thing this oratorio is speaking of. No, my dear Susannah. I agree with Mr. Handel. You cannot refuse this. You must do it. And you must do it with the deep awareness of who you are and what you have done and, I trust, with an even deeper awareness of what you need. Not just from the audience, but from the hands of God himself."

CHAPTER FIFTEEN

IN WHICH MR. HANDEL FACES DEFEAT
AND DISAPPOINTMENT

The dreariness of the morning was nothing compared to the funk Dawlish had fallen into. A hangover, compounded by humiliation and topped with a feeling of failure yet again, circulated in his brain. His short temper had already roasted his servant and the maid-cum-cook he'd secured along with the house. His surliness became even more prominent once he found out that the breadman had not appeared on the street that morning, and the plan to follow him and find his leader vanished along with him.

He forced himself up and allowed his frightened servant to dress him. After a quick breakfast of kippers and oatmeal, he stalked into the entrance hall, calling for Charles and ordering him to accompany him to St. Patrick's Cathedral. It was time, he decided, to stop playing fancy games with Dean Swift and maneuver him into stopping Handel.

The bits and pieces of gossip he'd picked up at the earl's last night had confirmed what Maitland had told him: Handel was planning a sacred work and would present it in a theatre. That, he knew, would be enough to get Swift's blood boiling. It would be a simple matter to persuade Swift to spoil the plan. It would be a partial victory at least.

At the cathedral, Swift reacted to the news just as Dawlish had expected, particularly when he recalled that he'd authorized the choirs of both cathedrals to participate in the production.

"God in heaven," Swift stormed. "That a sacred play should be performed within a common theatre, open to the dregs of society, is scandalous." He thumped his fist down on his desk. "It cannot be allowed. No, sir, it will not be allowed!"

A smug grin crossed Dawlish's face. "And, Your Reverence, I'm sure if it is held here, he will do the same in London. Perhaps you should contact the church authorities at Lambeth Palace and express your horror that sacred materials should be so profaned. It's blasphemy, sir, and I felt I had to bring it to your attention." He leaned forward and offered snuff to the cleric who waved it off.

"Yes, yes, of course, Dawlish. You did the right thing, man. Thank you for bringing it to my attention."

Swift wandered off into a session of remonstrating with himself, wondering why nobody at either cathedral had spoken to him about this and why Handel, a good composer and churchman, from all accounts, would perpetrate such a blasphemy.

"As to the latter, Your Reverence," Dawlish interrupted, "I can perhaps shed some light. Mr. Handel, it would seem, is not as proficient as he perhaps once was. The fact of the matter is that he was run out of London, such was the poor quality of his work. Perhaps he's hoping to use this travesty to regain his standing?"

Another seed planted, Dawlish thought. This was turning out better than he'd hoped.

"Thank you, Lord Dawlish, for your kind consideration in coming to me with this abomination rather than telling others. It will be stopped, mark you. It will be stopped."

With that, Dawlish showed a leg and swept his hat in a low bow. "My pleasure, Dean Swift. Anything I can do, I will."

He left the cathedral in a much better mood than he'd arrived and directed his carriage to return immediately home. Inside, he found Ezra waiting for him. The servant handed him a letter.

"It was delivered soon after you left, milord."

Dawlish ripped it open and scanned the contents. As he finished, he called for Charles and Ezra and issued new orders. He told them little except that he was leaving Dublin on a short journey south. He left Charles in charge of the house, to keep his eyes peeled for the breadman. In the meantime, Ezra would accompany him by carriage.

He retreated into the large drawing room he'd repurposed into a private study and reread the letter. Ilchester's agent was concise, he had to admit: the ship he was waiting for would arrive at Wicklow in the next two days, and would his lordship favor the agent with a meeting outside the Custom House this afternoon? To ensure the secrecy of the ship and merchandise, the agent, a man named Liam Flannery, would meet Dawlish on the Custom House stairs.

This was all well and good, Dawlish decided, relieved that the day had finally come, but he'd have his guard Ezra with him. There would be no more forays on the quayside with louts and urchins. And no more of this man O'Toole.

Two hours later, the carriage pulled up on the quay. It was without doubt one of the noisiest and smelliest places on God's great earth, Dawlish decided. The sounds and smells of the river, at this stage more sewer than river, combined with the noise of the ships and their crews combined to assault his ears and nose. He'd not noticed it as much the last time he was there, but he'd other things on his mind at the time.

He stepped down from the carriage. When Ezra left the driver's side and joined him, Dawlish looked over at the Custom House. Men were busy going in and out of the building, but he spied a man standing at the foot of the steps, leaning against the balustrade and watching him intently. Quietly he told Ezra to wait but be prepared to come to his master's defense if needed.

Dawlish strode over to the Custom House.

"Lord Dawlish?" The man stepped forward and bowed. "My name is Liam Flannery. I have the honor to be Lord Ilchester's Dublin agent."

Dawlish took in the prosperous-looking man with his fashionable wig and sturdy chocolate brown jacket and breeches, covered by a black cloak. Even the man's black-buckled shoes were polished to a high shine, speaking to the fact that its owner spent more time inside an office than outside in the harbor.

"If you don't mind, your lordship, Lord Ilchester suggested that I discuss this matter with you outside rather than in our offices." Flannery's hand swept discreetly around the quayside. "Not as much chance for ever-prying ears to overhear something they shouldn't. Whereas in there…" He gestured towards the building and shrugged.

Dawlish nodded to him. "Yes, yes. Get on with it man. What news?"

"As I said, sir, the ship—her name is the *Swallow*—is expected to make landfall tomorrow or the day after, God- and weather-permitting. She will sail into Wicklow Bay and anchor off the harbor, close to the village. You will see her name painted on the transom. The captain will meet with you on the shore and the transaction will take place there. He will hand over the merchandise and a packet of documents you are to bring back to me. I will certify the documents as landed and legal and arrange for shipping to London. Your part, Lord Ilchester tells me, will then be done."

"And what of the merchandise itself. What is it?"

"I'm afraid, your lordship, I am not at liberty to state the nature of the shipment. However, you would be wise to use a covered coach and take a few sturdy men to Wicklow and have it brought to the city. The documents must be in my hands as quickly as possible. Once you get here and the documents are taken care of, I will let you know by the next day what your share of the settlement will be and ensure that a draft in that amount is credited to you."

"If the ship is due tomorrow, that leaves little time for me to get to Wicklow," Dawlish said. "It's forty miles or so south of here, isn't it? Why wasn't I informed earlier that the ship was arriving. I could've made my arrangements and been there when she arrives. I've been trying to find you all this while, since Ilchester neglected to give me your name."

Flannery shrugged his shoulders. He obviously cared little for Dawlish's concerns. "I am only passing along Lord Ilchester's instructions, my lord. I was made aware of the ship's potential arrival this morning. She was sighted passing Dunlough Bay the day before yesterday. Fast couriers brought the news. I wrote to you immediately."

Flannery waited impassively while Dawlish digested the information.

"Do you have any papers or anything I need to pass along to the captain, to prove that I act on Ilchester's behalf?"

The man shrugged again. "That was not in my instructions, sir. Now, if you don't mind, I need to return to the office."

Flannery stepped back, bowed, and left a baffled Dawlish standing on the quayside.

"Blast! Damn and blast." Dawlish spun and jumped back into the carriage, ordering a return to the house and barely giving Ezra time to clamber up beside the driver.

Along the way, they stopped at a stable attached to a prosperous inn. There, Dawlish haggled over the price of hiring a coach, two horses, and two men ordering that they follow as quickly as possible to his house.

As it was, he'd barely been in the house thirty minutes before the coach arrived. In consultation with his two guards, Dawlish decided to leave immediately and stay in the seaside village of Bray overnight. An early start in the morning would see him arrive in Wicklow no later than early afternoon, provided the roads were in decent condition and bad weather or other catastrophes did not delay him.

After the debacle that had hit his house earlier, he decided to leave both Ezra and Charles behind. This was, after all, just a quick trip to Wicklow and back, and he could foresee no particular danger from the likes of O'Toole. A quick scan of the square showed no sign of the breadman or any other lurkers. To be safe, he even had Ezra and Charles check the neighboring streets while he packed his satchel.

In less than an hour, Dawlish was riding south. Although it was a clear day, a brisk wind cut through the door cracks, chilling him. The streets were bustling with activity, though most of the heavier traffic was headed into the city while he was leaving. He grumbled to himself that he should have had earlier notice, and every so often he glanced out the small window at the rear, trying to see if anyone was following.

As planned, he stayed the night in the coastal village of Bray.

A pre-dawn start the next day meant Dawlish arrived in Wicklow just before noon. They stopped on the dirt track beside the rough-hewn stone jetty, sighting no ships other than a small fishing smack unloading its catch.

Dawlish sought out the local inn, seeking a meal. The ride had been uneventful albeit physically exhausting. His tension level increased as he worried about how he and the captain would identify each other. His curiosity had been piqued. What was this merchandise that must be so secretly imported? Had Ilchester cornered the market on some new product? Would he, Dawlish, see great financial gains as a result?

Exhausted and angry with Ilchester for the ridiculous situation, Dawlish finished his meal and arranged stabling services for the coach and horses, leaving the two hired men to fend for themselves.

All morning, a menacing dark cloud had hovered over the horizon. Even a landsman such as he could see it was bringing bad weather. Sure enough, a heavy drizzle began to fall when he left the inn. Against his better judgment, he walked down towards the small and unremarkable harbor.

Rain dripped off his hat and down his collar despite the heavy cloak he wrapped around himself. Somehow, he promised, as God was his witness, Ilchester would pay for this whole exercise. He'd been assaulted, robbed, humiliated, and endured a grueling ride south. Added to that, he'd suffered uncountable misery and attacks on his dignity throughout his time in Ireland.

And now he found that the ship he'd waited months for so patiently still had not arrived.

Damme, what a horrible venture this Irish trip was turning into.

Sub-Dean John Wynne read the note from Swift in horror. It had been handed to him by one of the dean's assistants, who had informed him that Swift had taken ill and retired to his rooms where he did not wish to be disturbed.

Wynne read the first part of the letter again:

I do hereby require and request the Very Reverend Sub-Dean not to permit any of the Vicar Chorals, choristers or organist to attend or assist in any public musical performances without his consent…

He read further down the missive.

And whereas it has been reported that I gave a license to certain vicars to assist at a club of fiddlers in Fishamble Street, I do hereby declare that I remember no such license.

Wynne dropped into a nearby pew, resting his head in his left hand, which in turn rested on his knee. He shook his head again. Of all things! And now! Only a couple of days earlier he had told the governors at the Mercer Hospital of the dean's approval and shown them his signed agreement. It was recorded in the governor's minutes.

This was devastating. It was a mighty blow to the hospital's hopes. It was nothing short of betrayal, and yet Wynne couldn't help but be charitable: the dean probably did not understand the implications. Certainly he must have been led by someone who opposed the charities, but did Swift understand that he was being manipulated? Wynne didn't think so.

The event was essential to all three organizations, and Wynne knew the concert had great promise and hopes attached to it. Last year's famine alone had severely depleted the hospital's funds. The other charities were equally hoping Handel's concert would help, he knew.

They were not the only ones who'd be disappointed. Almost the whole of Dublin society had wonderfully supported Handel's triumphant series of concerts. Already there was talk all over town that Handel would debut a new composition. Excitement for it had been growing tremendously. He'd heard from a number of those involved in the rehearsals that the music was beyond magnificent, even inspiring.

And then there was the great composer Handel himself. It would be an enormous blow to his prestige and blight his Dublin sojourn markedly, not to mention, probably, his own soul.

Wynne found himself in a dilemma. He knew Swift was in failing health and Wynne loved and respected the dean and tried as much as possible to cover up Swift's mistakes and failings. But this was something he could not hide. It would have very public repercussions and, if the concert was cancelled it had the potential to turn the city, perhaps even Ireland itself, against one of the land's greatest writers and beacons.

The concert had to go on. Wynne had no doubts about that. But how to handle it?

He called a group of the clerics and servants in the church to him. Without explaining, he dispatched them to find Handel, Patrick Delaney, Charles Cobbe, and Matthew Dubourg and insisted that they return with them immediately for an urgent meeting at the cathedral.

Within the hour, all had arrived at Wynne's workroom except Handel. He showed Swift's letter to each of the three clerics and saw from their white-faced expressions that they shared his reaction. Wynne quelled a lot of the outraged discussion, particularly from the passionate Delaney, and suggested they wait until the composer arrived.

When Handel finally walked into the room, he saw four grim-looking men sitting around a table. Wynne greeted him, gestured for him to sit, and then explained that he had some bad news. He handed him Swift's letter without comment.

Handel read it. Then read it again.

"But he cannot!" Handel shouted. "He agreed already, has he not? We are in rehearsals. The charities are advertising the concert. This is the beginning of April. I have hired the hall and soloists. It is only two weeks away!"

Handel's frustrated reaction emboldened the rest, who echoed his cries.

"Ach du Lieber," Handel groaned as he sank into his chair and cradled his head in his hands. "What am I going to do? I am finished. This will destroy my reputation yet again."

Dubourg got up and came behind Handel. He placed his hands on the composer's shoulder and squeezed slightly in comfort. "We will fight this, George. Never fear."

"Matthew is right," Wynne added. "Dean Swift is in the grip of a softening of the brain. It's a form of acute mania, which causes him to be both forgetful and impetuous. We have his signed agreement. I have no idea where his negative view of the musicians or the Musick Hall came from, unless somebody has given him those thoughts."

"Could we not go ahead without the singers from St. Patrick's?" Handel blurted. "Just use the ones from Christ Church and perhaps one or two others from other churches in the city!"

"Alas, no," said Wynne. "Many of the Vicar Chorals are in fact joint between the two cathedrals. If we remove the ones from St. Patrick's, Christ Church does not have enough choristers left to carry on. That's why we had to have both cathedrals agree; if one refused, or in this case changed their mind, it would not be possible to continue. As for people from other churches, none of them are trained or proficient enough to match the standards of the cathedrals, and therefore certainly not enough to do justice to *Messiah*." A quick grin crossed Wynne's face. "As you told me you'd found out in Chester!"

Handel cradled his head in despair.

"Gentlemen, we have work to do." Wynne's eyes swept around the room. "I believe God has gifted this man with a magnificent talent and I believe that his creation of *Messiah* is God-given. I know you agree with me, Patrick." He strode to the end of the table, all eyes following him. "Our first step is prayer, for the dean and his mental condition and that we can persuade him to change this directive." He waved the letter in the air. "And prayer for Mr. Handel and those who've worked so hard on this presentation, as well as for our charities that will benefit. I ask myself who would like to prevent this evening from happening, and I can think of a few earthly and one unearthly who would benefit. Gentlemen, prayer is our first step!"

He signaled Dubourg to continue comforting Handel.

"After we pray," Wynne continued, "I suggest that you and I, Patrick, are the ones who should garner all our strength to wrestle with the dean and with his demons."

When the prayers were finished, and with a word to Charles Cobbe not to mention the letter to anyone at Christ Church, Wynne, Delaney, and Cobbe left, leaving Dubourg and Handel to commiserate.

"I feel destroyed, Matthew," Handel said. "Simply destroyed. All the joy I felt as I composed, and as I heard the choruses and soloists out loud, is gone. I have a huge empty hole in me." He paused, his mind wandering. "I feared this might happen, that the church would turn against the thought of presenting *Messiah*."

"Nonsense, George. The church has not turned against you or *Messiah* at all. Did you not just meet with three leading clerics of the church in Ireland who are determined to see it move forward? Don't blame the whole church for the ill-considered actions of one sick man."

Handel tried to smile but couldn't. "Thank you, Matthew. But a blackness I thought I had defeated is creeping upon on me yet again."

CHAPTER SIXTEEN

IN WHICH MRS. CIBBER DECIDES AND
LORD DAWLISH IS CONFOUNDED

Handel sat despondent in his drawing room on Abbey Street, the news from Swift having hit him hard. Despite Dubourg's words of comfort, he was convinced that Swift's actions confirmed his worst fears, that the church hierarchy would undermine any efforts to present *Messiah*.

He could, of course, make arrangements to bring *Messiah* to one of the two main cathedrals. Or indeed, he could wait and present it at one of London's great churches, St. Paul's or possibly Westminster Abbey. Surely here in Ireland, however, Swift would have no objection to his people singing in church.

But Handel foresaw problems, problems he would not compromise on. First, in all likelihood the church would not allow the use of a full orchestra. The score had been written for strings and winds, including trumpets and horns, as well as timpani. No, they would insist on organ only, such was their aversion to any so-called worldly influences. It was ironic, he thought, that less than a hundred years earlier even the organ had been considered a worldly instrument. Such had been the Puritan stranglehold on England after Charles I lost his head to Cromwell.

Not that Handel minded the organ, of course. It was his favorite instrument. It gave him deep satisfaction and peace. But *Messiah* had not been written for organ alone; it demanded a full orchestra.

He also doubted that at least one of his projected soloists, Susannah Cibber, would be welcomed in a cathedral setting, given her history. For all their parroted talk of saving sinners, people of Mrs. Cibber's ilk would not be allowed a place in any presentation. Which probably, he thought, also left out several of his instrumentalists, and possibly even one or two of the extra singers in the chorus, if their stories were as publicly knowns as Mrs. Cibber's.

And if held in a church, the concept of the oratorio would be demolished by those petty clerics who would want to add a church service element to it, including probably a sermon.

He shuddered at the thought. No, it was very unlikely he would ever present *Messiah* in a church setting.

As he mourned the news, another thought hit him. The charities were counting on a filled theatre of paying audience members. The nobility and people of Dublin society were expecting also something new. They'd already sold out the first subscription of Handel concerts, and most of the tickets for the second series had also been sold. He couldn't suddenly exchange the program for the evening and replace it with some tried and true Handelian music. They'd already heard the best. They would not turn out for the charity event, and the charities, who'd been extremely supportive of him, would suffer.

The success he'd enjoyed so far would dissipate. He would have to leave Dublin on a sour note.

His hopes, what little they were, hung on John Wynne and Patrick Delaney. The trouble was, he realized, his volcanic temper was beginning to boil, and he was sorely tempted to march right into the cathedral give Swift a piece of his mind, if not a kick in the rear—a swift kick!

Holding him back was the thought that it would undermine what Wynne and Delaney might accomplish, and it would reflect badly on Handel, no matter how justified he might feel, if he castigated a sick old man who also happened to be one of Ireland's heroes. Hard as it would be, he had to keep his anger in check. This, he also knew, was when he really needed to pray.

But he found it difficult to find the heart to do so, let alone the words.

He was still contemplating matters when Tobias quietly announced that Mrs. Cibber was in the entry hall, desiring words with Mr. Handel. At Handel's nod, he ushered her in.

Up to this point, rehearsals had not included Mrs. Cibber's solos, since he had been waiting for her response to his invitation. He had, however, been quietly looking for alternative contraltos with talent. So far he had been unsuccessful. He feared he would have to send to London and hire someone from the theatres there, thus incurring greater expense. And that decision would have to be taken no later than today. Whatever expenses he suffered on this performance, would come directly out of his pocket. All the costs for the fundraiser were his, as all revenue from ticket sales would be equally distributed amongst the three charities.

"Mr. Handel, I pray you forgive me for arriving without an invitation and without notice," Susannah began.

He smiled at her and assured her she was welcome, inviting her to sit.

"You asked me about singing in *Messiah* and I shared with you my doubts and fears." Her faint smile began to stretch wider. "I have thought long and hard about this, Mr. Handel, and I believe now that you are right. I need to sing this oratorio, come what may. People may change their impression of me, or they may not. I cannot change that. But this *Messiah* you've composed, sir, is as moving a piece of music as I have ever been asked to take part in. If I turn down this opportunity, it is one I will regret for the rest of my life. Even if no one other than you knows that I turned it down, *I* would still know. And it would haunt me forever. I am honored and grateful that you asked me and, if you have not changed your mind, I would humbly accept."

Although he'd hoped for it, he was surprised. Even when asking her, he'd anticipated the very real possibility of rejection, despite all his persuasive powers. He thought for a moment, realizing that she knew nothing of how perilously close to cancellation the oratorio's performance had come. Conflict arose in his mind even as she spoke. To be fair to her, he should let her know that Swift had destabilized everything. But at the same time, Wynne had specifically requested that nothing be said until he'd had a chance to confront Swift. Handel had protested, shouting that he'd already booked the hall and paid for advertising as well as the musicians and singers who expected payments after the performance. Reluctantly, he had agreed to keep quiet and not mention a word to those involved. He had, however, on Wynne's advice, secured a second date for a possible performance one week later. The advertising could be easily changed. Nobody would make a fuss, and if the first evening really did have to be cancelled, it gave the prelates more time to change Swift's mind.

No. He could say nothing to her.

He thanked Susannah for her acceptance. "I cannot think of anyone who can sing this with more emotion and conviction than you, my dear. You have made this old man's heart glad and I know that people will not only accept you in this oratorio, they will rave about you and your performance."

He took her into the room he was using as his music room and office. There, he gave her a full copy of the score with admonitions to read the words carefully and feel them in her heart.

"I also recommend that you read the particular verses in the Bible that you will be singing," he advised, "so that you can understand their setting. It's like understanding a character. You read the story of Esther in preparation for that oratorio, didn't you? Well, this is the same."

They then discussed rehearsal times and location and disagreed on her performance fee—at her insistence.

"I am grateful for the opportunity, Mr. Handel, but as this is for charity I would be churlish to accept money for this appearance," she said.

He sat down at the harpsichord and began playing some of the music so that she could become acquainted with some of the choruses as well as the three other soloists' parts, particularly the soprano's.

All the time, his mind churned with questions, doubts, worries, and fears.

If there was any beauty looking out on Wicklow Head or along the Murroughs, the grassy seacoast wetlands leading north from the town, it was lost on Dawlish. All he could see through the rain and mist was murky water and surf crashing ashore. The sea disappeared into a vast, uninteresting grey mist that hid the horizon.

The one thing he was sure of was the cold.

Rain soaked through his heavy woolen cloak. Standing alone on the shore, he watched impatiently for a sight of the *Swallow*. He shivered as rain dripped off his fashionable brown felt hat and down his collar, getting worse each minute he was out there. He thought about taking his snuff but rejected it, worried that his sneezing would grow more monstrous if he caught the ague. He promised himself he would consult with an apothecary as soon as he returned to Dublin.

Darkness set in, made worse by the low black clouds. When he could see no more in the gloom, he splashed through puddles back to the inn where he negotiated a room for himself and arranged for the two hired coachmen to sleep in the stables with the horses. Resentfully, he paid for a cheap supper and breakfast for them as well.

Upstairs he took one look at the dingy straw mattress and flicked a threadbare woolen blanket onto the rough oak floor with his sword. He dropped fully clothed, even to his boots, onto the hard wooden bed and wisp-thin down mattress.

Angrily, he wrapped himself in his soaked cloak. If he was going to have a rough, uncomfortable night, he would do it in his own clothes and not risk the fleas, lice, and diseases that might lurk in the blanket. He pulled his leather satchel up and used it as a pillow.

Feeling miserable, he cursed Ilchester for the thousandth time.

As Dawlish stumbled down for breakfast the next morning, he saw that the sky had cleared. He'd hardly slept. Howling winds, the sounds of rain lashing against the wooden shutters, and chills permeating every corner of the room robbed him of sleep. He'd have been better, he grumbled, to have curled up on a bench in the taproom beside the roaring fire and saved himself the cost of the room.

He was leaning over a steaming bowl of oatmeal with a mug of what these people laughingly called coffee when a shadow loomed over him. He looked up to see a crusty red face covered with several days' growth of grizzled beard staring down at him. The stocky man's clothing was well-worn, patched in places, and he wore no hat or wig. Wild strands of white hair flew in every direction from his balding head as he plunked himself down on the bench across from Dawlish, unannounced and uninvited.

"Do I have the honor of speaking with Lord Dawlish?" the man asked, leaning forward and whispering.

Carefully, Dawlish put his spoon down and stared at the man. It flashed through his mind that he should have brought one of his own men.

At first he didn't acknowledge the question. His hand slid under the table to his sword grip.

"And who are you, sir, that you accost me in the middle of my meal?" Dawlish asked.

The man grinned and bowed his head. "Thaddeus Spike, milord, mate aboard the good ship *Swallow*. I pray you will forgive me rough ways, milord, as I was ordered not to bow or in any way identify you as a lord. Me orders is to bring ye to where we have her laying offshore, just around the headland." He jerked his head to the right. "Finish your meal, milord. I will wait outside the door."

Before he could move, Dawlish reached out and clamped Spike's right hand to the table.

"I was told the captain would meet me here," Dawlish said. "Not a deckhand."

The mate winced at the grip. "Don't know about that, sir. I was just given me orders and I obeys the cap'n. He said go to the inn and meet with your lordship and lead you to the ship."

"How did you know to approach me, eh?"

Despite the pain, Spike grimaced and nodded around the room. "Any of these others around look like a lord, milord? Gimme some credit for brains, milord."

Dawlish glared at him for a few moments, then slowly released the mate's arm. "I will speak to your captain about your boorish attitude, my man. Mark my words."

As the mate stood up to leave, Dawlish jumped up too, knocking over the unstable bench he'd been sitting on.

"I've had enough of this foul mess they call food here. I'll go with you now."

Dawlish had the landlord rouse his men and, at Spike's suggestion, order them to bring the coach along the coast road.

"Up over the headland, sir landlord," Spike said. "Tell 'em to takes the road to the crest, then tell 'em to abide by the stone wall on the downhill side. There's a small footpath where they must wait."

They set out, with Spike leading the way with his rollicking seaman's walk. They only had to pass a few small cottages before they made it out onto the grassy hill leading over the headland. While Dawlish climbed in silence, Spike chattered.

"That there's St. Brides 'ead and beyond that is Wicklow 'ead, sir." Spike pointed southwards. "We anchored in a small bay 'tween the two. They got a small beach down there."

The wind on the headland strengthened with each step upwards. Dawlish finally succumbed to the indignity of clamping his hand atop his hat to keep both the hat and probably his wig from flying off.

At the top of the hill, he glimpsed back. He could see the tiny village curving around the end of Wicklow Bay. Beyond he made out the Wicklow Mountains. Below, as promised, a schooner swayed at anchor in the gently rolling surf.

It took fifteen minutes to reach the beach. Four sailors waited by a boat as Spike jumped in and asked Dawlish to join him.

"I would have thought the captain would at least meet me here," Dawlish said.

"Know nothing about that, milord. Only knows the captain is aboard and sent me to fetch ye."

Dawlish pulled his cloak around him and stepped in. Before he could seat himself, the three sailors had already jumped in and were locking oars into the oarlocks while the fourth pushed the boat off the shingle beach and then jumped in himself to pick up the fourth oar. They crashed over the surf and were soon in calmer water pulling hard for the ship.

Dawlish clambered up the ship's dangerous-looking rope ladder. Moment after he climbed aboard, Spike jumped to the deck and led him down to the captain's cabin.

After a short time, Dawlish emerged clutching a satchel of papers. He looked across the deck where Spike was already supervising the offloading of four large, padlocked boxes.

The captain came behind him and led him to the boxes. "You will see, milord, that there is a seal placed upon each lock. That seal is to be broken only by the agent in Dublin. We have not touched the boxes."

Dawlish knelt and examined the seals. "I don't recognize this seal. Where does it come from?"

"Don't know, sir. They was sealed when they came on board and we was ordered not to touch them while they was in our care. And we haven't."

"See that they are taken ashore quickly," Dawlish said.

Without another word, the crew lifted the boxes and struggled to lower them into the waiting boat. When two boxes were loaded, a second boat pulled alongside while the first was rowed toward the shore.

"As soon as my men and boats are back on board, we weigh anchor," the captain declared, turning his back on the nobleman.

Ignorant buffoon, Dawlish thought. *I'll be complaining about you and your high-handed treatment of a British nobleman to the agent and to Ilchester himself.*

He lowered himself into the second boat once the final box was secured.

When he got to the beach, he found the sailors had commandeered the two hired coachmen to help them carry the heavy boxes up the cliff path from the beach and onto the waiting coach.

Once aboard, Dawlish ordered the coach to make all possible haste for Dublin. They bounced and jostled down the rough road into Wicklow Town. From there, the fastest route was the coast road up to Bray and then inland.

At a sharp turn in the road, a mile or so outside the town, Dawlish was idly staring out one of the windows when the coachman suddenly pulled sharply on the reins, bringing the horses to a sudden halt. Dawlish stuck his head out of the window and was shocked to see some red-coated soldiers flagging down his coach. Before he could fully comprehend what was happening, an officer stepped up to the coach door, opened it, and coldly told him to step out. The man looked vaguely familiar.

"Colonel Somerfield, Sixth Irish Dragoons, sir," said the officer as he opened the door. "Would you please get out of the carriage and step to the side?"

"This is an outrage, Colonel, an absolute outrage. I am Lord Dawlish and I am on urgent business. How dare you stop me and my coach. You may be sure, sir, that I will protest to His Excellency the Lord Lieutenant most strongly about this. Be assured that not only will the Viceroy hear about it, but so too will the Prince of Wales."

Dawlish continued his volley of protests as he reluctantly emerged from the coach. Ignoring him, the colonel ordered the coachmen to alight. He then sent his soldiers to pull the boxes down. Despite Dawlish's increasingly loud and agitated protests, the soldiers used their musket butts to smash the padlocks and seals and open the boxes.

"My Lord Dawlish, sir, may I enquire where you got these?" Somerfield pointed down to the four boxes tightly packed with bottles of brandy. "And why you are transporting them to Dublin?"

Shocked, Dawlish dropped to his knees, reaching to touch them before the officer restrained him. Flustered, he looked up at the man, suddenly recognizing him as the aide to the general he complained to at the castle.

"But these aren't mine," Dawlish blurted out, flustered. "I mean, this is not what I was doing... this is preposterous... I have no idea what these are or how... how did they..."

He stopped suddenly, baffled. His hands and voice shuddered.

"Sergeant, put these boxes back in the coach and escort it to Dublin." Somerfield beckoned to two previously unnoticed officers. "Lieutenant Smythe, you're in command of the troop. You'll move more slowly, but I expect you at the castle no later than tomorrow afternoon." He then turned to Dawlish and the second officer. "I have a fast coach waiting. You, milord, will sit inside with the captain. Consider yourself under arrest. I will ride beside you."

Spluttering and objecting all the while, Dawlish resisted until Somerfield threatened to tie him in the carriage. Spurning dignity, Dawlish savagely kicked the carriage door, hurting his foot in the process, and vociferously and loudly alternated between complaints and threats. The captain sat stone-faced facing him as the nobleman cursed and called down the wrath of God upon all the imbeciles who made up the military in Ireland.

They rode through the afternoon and night without stopping, arriving finally at Dublin Castle in the early hours of the next morning. The two officers escorted a tired and subdued Dawlish into a spartan office in the castle.

God in heaven, Dawlish thought. *This is an absolute disaster.*

He still couldn't make head nor tail of the events of the past twenty-four hours. The taciturn officer sitting across from him gave no information, speaking only to ascertain Dawlish's physical needs during the trip. Bread and cheese provided by the captain had been his only sustenance. The stops they'd made for Dawlish to relieve himself had been humiliating, as both officers stood watching and waiting while he went behind trees or bushes.

He sat inside a sparsely furnished room, the only light coming from three small, foul-smelling oil lamps on side tables and a fire in the room's only fireplace.

Finally, the door opened. General Fitzherbert, commander of the garrison, strode in and took the chair across from Dawlish. He put up a hand to silence the man's immediate complaints.

"Lord Dawlish, can you explain your actions over the past while, the past two days in particular, and explain how you came into possession of those boxes?"

Dawlish regained his composure and, with a menacing sneer, reminded the general that he was a friend of the prince.

Fitzherbert cut him off icily. "And I, sir, am the son and heir of the Duke of Rutland, who is himself the cousin of both His Majesty and His Royal Highness. So do not try to threaten or intimidate me, sir."

Dawlish flopped back onto his chair, realizing he'd overreached. A sweat broke out on his forehead.

"Now, sir, your story."

The brief interrogation provided very little information. Dawlish reluctantly turned over the package of sealed documents he said had been given to him by the captain. He then declared that they'd been intended for Lord Ilchester's shipping agent.

Fitzherbert looked thoughtfully at the nobleman, then weighed the package in his hands. As Dawlish watched and protested, he broke the seal and drew out the papers. He studied each one of the enclosed sheets.

"Perhaps you'd care to explain this then."

Fitzherbert spread out the papers and laid them on the table. Each was blank.

Shocked, Dawlish picked up each one, examining them carefully and blustering as he did so. "I cannot. The captain merely gave these to me and told me to deliver it all to Mr. Flannery, along with the boxes, when I arrived back in Dublin. I was never privy to any information about the merchandise itself. I was kept totally uninformed about this whole business, and you can be sure I will raise this matter with Lord Ilchester when I get back to London."

"As to London, milord, it may be some time before you will be seeing that city. And Lord Ilchester will be the least of your problems." Fitzherbert watched as a red flush of anger swept up Dawlish's face. Before the nobleman had an opportunity to open his mouth, the general continued. "You need to understand, sir, that you are facing a very precarious situation. Either this is a matter of smuggling, which is serious enough in and of itself, or far worse, this is a case of treason. Perhaps this was a trial run to beat the revenue officers with a view to running guns to criminals and those who oppose the Crown on this island." He glared at Dawlish. "That a nobleman of our country should find himself in this predicament is frankly shocking. One expects it of other nations, of course. But our own? Unthinkable."

Dawlish went pale as the blood rushed from his face. He gripped the edge of the table until his knuckles turned white.

"But I am innocent," he said, slumping back into the chair. "I've done nothing except travel to Wicklow for a package as instructed and attempt to bring it back here to Dublin and deliver it to the rightful agent." He floundered, desperate to make Fitzherbert understand. "I wanted nothing to do with smuggling. I told Ilchester that when we were in London—"

"You admit then that it was a smuggling operation."

"No. No. That's not what I meant. I meant…well, um, I was telling his lordship only that I was concerned about the secrecy I was forced to work under… that it might be considered smuggling. But I had his lordship's assurance that it was nothing of the kind. He was adamant about that."

Beads of cold sweat broke out on Dawlish's forehead. Unthinking, he whipped his wig off and wiped it across his face.

Silence dropped over the room as Fitzherbert gathered the papers and placed them back in the envelope, watching Dawlish carefully all the while. He stood suddenly and called for an officer to escort Dawlish to the guest quarters.

CHAPTER SEVENTEEN

IN WHICH A DECISION IS REACHED

The day after reading Swift's missive, Wynne finally arranged a private and extended meeting with the dean.

"Stop immediately! How dare either of you presume to question my decisions." Red-faced, Dean Swift glared fiery daggers at the two men in front of him. "That you, John, my sub-dean, should have the temerity, it is… it is beyond belief. It's monstrous!"

"Dean Swift we fully recognize your authority in making such decisions," Wynne said. From the other side of the table, Delaney added a hearty "Aye." Wynne struggled to find the words. "Our desire is not to question, Dean Swift, it is to understand." He waved his hands around, beating the air in frustrated confusion before raising them in supplication. "We know you love the church and want to protect it. But we also know that a key element of your own long service here has been to ensure that the poor and sick in our nation be dealt with fairly and provided for when sick. That is what you have taught us all, Dean. That is why we do not understand this order."

Delaney added his own observations, reminding Swift that the past two years had been particularly harsh as famine had driven many into the heart of Dublin city.

"There are many, many more sick from fevers and hunger crowding into our hospitals," Delaney said. "And we are hard-stretched to take care of them."

Wynne nodded. "Our funds are running out rapidly. A charitable affair would help us replenish our ability to meet their needs. Not to mention helping prisoners who are in jail only for breaking the law to feed their families. It is a Christian thing we are seeking to do, Dean."

Swift cradled his head in his hands, shaking both with anger and stress. "I need my physic, gentlemen. I must needs rest."

Solicitous, Wynne agreed that Swift did not seem at all himself. "While we wait for the man to come, we do need to understand. I'll send for him now."

Quickly, Swift grabbed Wynne's arm. "Hold. I am not myself, as you say. I don't want that moldy-breathed fraud to see me. Just let me rest. I will talk to you tomorrow."

Wynne cradled Swift's shoulders. "We understand that, Dean. But we also need to understand why you are cancelling this charitable event. Time will not allow us to wait until tomorrow. People have to be told; those buying tickets will have to be refunded. It will cause great havoc in accounting for monies in and out of our various funds. To do that, we must comprehend your decision now. Today. So we can explain to our charitable agencies why this money is being refused them suddenly."

Swift kept his head in his hands, mumbling to himself the arguments pro and con. "I need to think, gentlemen."

"Yes, you do, Dean, and we want to help you clarify your judgement. How do we convey your decision while also confirming your deep desire to help the poor, the hungry, and the invalids?"

"I do want to help them, John. I do. I just… I just want it to be done rightly."

"And it shall be done rightly, Dean. I promise." Wynne glanced up at Delaney.

"Perhaps if you could help us understand your antipathy to Mr. Handel and his desire to stage Messiah?" Delaney jumped in. "Do you dislike the man and his music? I have heard portions of this work, sir. I believe it is sublime!"

"No, Patrick, it's not the man or his music. I too like it. But this work sounds strange and unchurchly. I was told it was blasphemous."

"Perhaps it would help if I read some of the words to you," Wynne said calmly as he laid a copy of Messiah before him. "Tell me, Dean Swift, what is so objectionable about this work and its words that you would not want the people of Dublin to hear?"

When Swift didn't answer, Wynne went on to quote the Bible first, and the words of the libretto second. Swift closed his eyes as Wynne quietly recited the verses and references, nodding frequently.

"A few weeks ago, you commented to me about the marvelous music you'd heard on the organ," Wynne continued. "Beautiful and moving were your words. That music was Mr. Handel playing on our organ. And he was playing one of the pieces in this work. It *is* moving, Dean Swift. It *is* inspiring. And it is only one of a series of similarly moving and inspiring pieces that will touch the souls of all who hear. That is the work called Messiah which is to be presented at the Musick Hall for the benefit of Mercer's, the prisoners, and the sick and poor of our city. It is the Christian message. In short, Dean Swift, this is a species of music different from any other anyone has ever heard."

He waited for Swift's response but all he got was a low grunt.

Swift rubbed his eyes and looked up. "Good words, of course. But it's where they are being used that's at issue."

Calmly, Wynne continued. "Yes, I notice that you made a remark about a club of fiddlers in Fishamble Street. To be honest, I can think of a number of things you could say about Mr. Neal's hall, but a club of fiddlers is far from the truth and certainly does not describe what is planned."

Patiently he and Delaney went over the situation again, reminding Swift how much he loved Handel's music and describing the proposed concert and the elegance of the hall.

"I remind you, this performance will bring in the scoffers among our highest society," said Delaney, "those who live selfish, self-indulgent, greedy lives all week and who never darken a church door except for the highest occasions. I must add too, Dean Swift, that the description of Mr. Neal's hall as a club of fiddlers is, frankly, not an honest one." Delaney spoke quickly before Swift could interrupt. "As you know, Mr. Neal himself is a firm and devout member of this cathedral and has been very generous to various appeals in the past. His hall is designed only for the finest cultural and musical performances to enhance the reputation and civility of our fine city, sir. He would have nothing to do with a common taproom, and neither would we!"

Delaney stood, paced a few moments, then turned and placed his rigid arms on the table, leaning towards Swift, willing him to hear his words.

"Dean Swift, you have spent many years demanding the best from the choir and musicians of this parish. You have worked unceasingly, pushing them weekly to raise the quality of their music to the highest possible level. Now they finally have a piece of music truly worthy of their best. It's music that transcends earthly hopes and pleasures and instead takes us from the depths of despair to the highest glory of heaven. The choir is worthy of this music, Dean Swift. And the music is worthy of the finest choir."

Quietly, Wynne slipped a chair next to Swift, reached out and held his hands. "I know, Dean Swift, that your heart is well-disposed to the less fortunate in this land. You yearn to help them and show the love of Christ and his followers to them." He looked deep into Swift's face as a warming smile came over it. "Allowing the choirs to participate in this event will confirm that love, that Christian charity, to all who attend. And when they hear of it and experience the physical results of the funds we raise, the less fortunate will understand that charity and its source as well."

Swift nodded affirmation. "Yes," he whispered. "They must see that we care and experience it."

Delaney slipped a chair to the other side of Swift. "Remember, Dean, the Lord Lieutenant has approved and supports this event. He has indicated that he himself plans to attend. What better way to show the true scope of Christian love than to let him see it in action as well? And he will ensure that a report of this fine action of the heart of the Church of Ireland reaches His Majesty himself."

"We Irish may have difficulties with the Crown and the way they govern this island," Wynne said, "but I believe our Viceroy is a man of honor, charity, and good principle."

Swift began to waver. "But Lord Dawlish said it was idolatrous to allow our church musicians to participate in raucous and unseemly palaces of sin. He said the concert would be profane in that regard."

Wynne and Delaney looked searchingly at each other, Wynne's eyebrows raised in surprise. He thought for a moment.

"And since when did this London dandy decide theological issues for Ireland's greatest theological thinker and writer, eh?" Wynne cajoled. "And what credentials does he bestow to justify his claims? Has he seen or heard the manuscript of this performance, as you have? How many times in the past few months has he been in the cathedral, or indeed any church, for a service? He is very bold to say what he says, but I wonder about his motivation."

It took another fifteen minutes before Swift finally agreed to rescind his order.

"Who else has seen my order?" Swift asked quietly, feeling very tired.

"Only the two of us," Wynne said, indicating himself and Delaney, "along with Charles Cobbe, Matthew Dubourg, and Mr. Handel." Anticipating his next question, he added "And with your permission, we will not inform any others, so there will be no fears that you are dithering. You made a decision and wisely came to us first. On reflection and in full command of the facts, you have modified that decision."

Swift nodded. "I am tired, John. I fear sometimes this is becoming too large a job for me." He looked up and held Wynne's gaze. "Thank you for standing beside me, helping me and taking some of the burden."

"Dean Swift, we all know and understand that your concern... your love is for the church and the people," Wynne said. "Of that, we have no doubt. This will be for the betterment of our people, I assure you, as well as the betterment of mankind all over. It is a good decision."

He and Delaney then chatted with the dean about other official church business before leading him to his residence where his house servants ensured he was taken care of.

As the pair walked back towards the church, they looked at one another, a soft smile spreading across their faces.

"That was a near run thing, John," Delaney said. "We must let the others know immediately."

A pensive Wynne nodded in agreement. "I want to know more about this Lord Dawlish and why he was trying so hard to sabotage our concert. I have seen him ensconced with the dean several times, but I had no idea of the kind of influence he had on him."

"I can tell you that society has a very poor impression of the man," Delaney noted. "He has been an unwelcome visitor in many Dublin homes. He's considered a boorish poltroon with visions of himself far above his standing." He thought about the man for a moment. "I do recall hearing that a number of months ago he made some very disparaging remarks about Handel at one of Sir Ronald Baker's soirees, but I thought nothing of it. Typical London popinjay, I thought. But now…"

He let the statement die away.

When they arrived in the nave of the church, Wynne immediately sent messengers to both Handel and Charles Cobbe. After expressing his thanks to Delaney for his support in the meeting, and saying goodbye, he set off himself in search of Dubourg.

Dawlish was taken to a pair of small rooms used for visiting guests. After ensuring that Dawlish was fed and checking that the man's bed was properly prepared and a fire lit, Fitzherbert left, warning Dawlish that there would be a guard outside the door.

On the way back to his own rooms, Fitzherbert struggled to understand what was going on. If it was smuggling or treason, it was the most irrational, ludicrously handled plot he'd ever heard of. Only a group of amateurs and poltroons would have created such a stupid scheme.

That Dawlish was a poltroon and egotistical buffoon, he had no doubts. But somehow he didn't seem like a smuggler or traitor. He cared more for his own luxury and status than for devious schemes.

Even if it was smuggling, the items were petty in consideration. Yes, brandy was subject to high duties. And yes, smugglers tried to evade customs officers with these products. But it was only three boxes. Ilchester, and even Dawlish, could have purchased most of the brandy for the cost of the boxes, let alone the cost of hiring a ship and crew to deliver it.

Fitzherbert scratched his head. There was also the troubling issue of the warning they'd received, telling of a major weapon smuggling operation in Wicklow. They'd never found the one who delivered that letter, but it had smacked of authority and knowledge. Loath to miss any opportunity to plug a hole in the island's security, he had ordered Somerfield and a troop into action. As for the ship? Well, Fitzherbert counted on his naval counterparts to find and, if necessary, sink it.

The whole thing baffled him. It made no sense. But there it was, suspicious activity and illicit goods. He retired for the night, still churning the mystery over and over in his mind before sleep finally engulfed him.

On Abbey Road, there was quiet rejoicing as Handel received Wynne's message. His heart jumped with happiness while his outward visage remained calm. He merely thanked the messenger and calmly turned to Tobias.

"Be pleased to send a message to Mrs. Cibber immediately, and to Mr. Dubourg as well, asking them to gather at St. Michan's. We need to increase the frequency and length of rehearsals if we are to do this." He paused a moment, then added, "Oh, and ask the bill posters to get to work and let the *Journal* know that I want the advertising to begin immediately."

With the door to his private area closed, Handel did a little jig, his hands waving and a huge grin on his face. He then flopped down eagerly on an elegant yet comfortable sofa that had been sent over on loan from Devonshire. He propped his head in his hands and offered a quick prayer of thanks for the news he held in his hand.

The excitement returned in a flood. Messiah would indeed be produced. While he'd come to peace with the cancellation and accepted that if nobody other than he and God heard it he would be content, he knew that deep down, sharing *Messiah* with the masses had become a deep passion for him.

Now that *Messiah* was on, there was much to be done.

Apart from a few sessions with either Fitzherbert or Somerfield, Dawlish had been left alone in isolation. Simple food was served to him, and when servants brought it through the open door he could see the armed guard outside. Most of the time he just sat on one of the chairs or lay on his bed. He requested some books and they were promptly delivered, though he had difficulty concentrating long enough to even grasp what the authors were writing about.

More often than not, he merely played with the food they provided. He pushed it around on the plate, eating only a few mouthfuls. He was served tea and wine, but nothing stronger. He'd demanded someone to deal with the legalities of his situation, only to be told that should he be arrested, he would indeed receive legal help. Until then, however, he was to consider himself merely a guest of the castle under guard for his protection.

A black cloud descended on him. Raging thunderstorms of thoughts bounced back and forth, spinning around in his head.

On the morning of the third day, the door opened and an officer stepped in, telling Dawlish to accompany him. They walked down the long corridor and up some stone steps. He realized he was being taken back to Fitzherbert's office and was soon ushered in through the door. Fitzherbert sat at his desk and Somerfield stood beside him. Somerfield gestured for him to be seated.

A large mullioned window let in a blaze of light. It was, Dawlish saw, a fine sunny day.

Fitzherbert stared at him without speaking for a few moments. "I find this a most difficult issue, Lord Dawlish. At worst, as I have told you, you face possible charges of smuggling, or perhaps even treason. Both have severe penalties up to and including death. Yet there are some peculiar aspects of your story, some you already know about and others you do not."

The general flicked his hand at Somerfield, who immediately handed over a piece of paper.

"For example, you may not be aware that the night you were brought to the castle, the boxes of smuggled brandy were also being brought to Dublin," Fitzherbert continued. "In the middle of the night, my men were passing Enniskerry just outside Bray when they were accosted by a gang of brigands. Our men were tied up, stuffed into the coach, and the goods taken. Just before they left, the leader of the gang leaned into the carriage and jammed a note into the lieutenant's uniform." He shoved the piece of paper across to Dawlish. "Read it."

Dawlish glanced at the note. It was brief, but its message stabbed him in the gut: "With thanks, O'Toole."

He swore, drawing down a voluminous series of curses on O'Toole's head. His mouth went dry, and at the same time he began to sweat again, his heart pounding so loud that he believed the two officers could hear it.

Dawlish flung the paper back at Fitzherbert suddenly as if its very touch would harm him.

The general was unperturbed. "We also interviewed Lord Ilchester's shipping agent, Mr. Dumfries, who told us he's never heard of a Liam Flannery, never employed anyone of that name, and most certainly would not conduct business on the steps of the Custom House."

Fitzherbert shifted his weight in the chair, pursed his lips, and templed his hands against his chin.

"In fact, he assured us that Lord Ilchester has never instructed him to deal with you. He has given us a signed statement that he knows nothing of a ship called the *Swallow* and certainly never chartered it. He says too that he knows nothing of a special shipment to be delivered under such surreptitious circumstances. I have, of course, reported all this to His Excellency."

Dawlish was hit by a flash of conflicting feelings, from rage to fear to confusion to nauseating tremors. His mouth went drier than an Egyptian desert.

"But I told you, this O'Toole has been threatening me," Dawlish protested. "He broke into my rooms where he assaulted my manservant. He must be behind this whole fiasco."

Fitzherbert grunted again. "We also received this with the letter." He pushed some pieces of crumpled paper across the table.

Dawlish grabbed at them and scanned them quickly. "O'Toole sent these? One is Lord Ilchester's letter to me and the other is a draft of my letter to him."

A relieved look crossed Dawlish's face. He stared back at Fitzherbert as he shoved the papers back at the officer.

"You see, they prove my innocence," he said with a triumphant grin. "This correspondence must have been taken from my house and O'Toole used the information to set up this entire charade."

"And why would he want to do that, sir?" Fitzherbert asked. "What immense grudge does he have against you that he would go to these extremes, eh, my lord? I would remind you that while these letters might cloud the issue, they most certainly do not explain Mr. Dumfries' statements—and he is a respected shipping manager whose honesty has never been in question. Indeed, in this letter Lord Ilchester never responds to your questions about the agent, does he? Perhaps he too was confounded by your letter and did not understand what you were talking about."

The general collected the papers in his hands and tapped the table with them.

"All any of this does is add confusion to the entire matter, Lord Dawlish. They prove neither guilt nor innocence. They obscure." He slapped the papers down sharply. "The one complicating factor in all this, which neither you nor your letters explain, is why you are in Dublin at all. Why did you leave for Dublin in the high season and our admittedly foul winter weather on the dubious promise of a very flimsy and nonsensical business arrangement?" Fitzherbert flashed a cold smile at Dawlish. "A man who delights in his acquaintance with the high and noble of our land, who enjoys the dalliance with lovely ladies, a man who ponces around in the highest state of fashion, left all that in London, for this?"

Fitzherbert waved his hand towards the window, pointing at the Dublin roof-tops and chimneys belching smoke from peat and wood fires.

"There are so many holes in your story, I could drive two coach and fours parallel through them, 'pon my word! You've lied to me consistently, sir, and nobleman or not I will see you brought down and imprisoned if but one more lie escapes your lips. There is enough evidence to show that you consorted with known criminals and were in Dublin on a flimsy premise. It's all been a thin fabric of lies. You pranced around town like a stiff rump, but I think perhaps you're nothing more than an egotistical lout outclassed by those around you! Let me be blunt, sir. If I do not hear satisfactory answers to my questions, your quarters will be changed from guest rooms to a cell inside this castle. You will be charged with treason, since the smuggling was of a minor character. You are on the brink of ruin, my lord, and your relationships, real or imagined, with Lord Ilchester and His Royal Highness will not save you."

He glared at the blanched, quivering man in front of him. Dawlish's eyes looked frantically around, panic setting in.

"Now, I want answers, sir, and no more prattle," said the general. "I want to know why you came to Dublin at this time. How did you know about O'Toole and his brigands? What is your connection to this criminal? I will have no more fantasies about Lord Ilchester and phantom shipping agents. No nonsense about merely wanting to visit this city. I don't believe a word of it."

Fitzherbert crossed his arms and leaned back in his chair. Somerfield crossed the room and took a chair behind Dawlish, close to the door.

"I will have the truth this day, sir. The truth, mark you, and quickly."

CHAPTER EIGHTEEN

IN WHICH THERE ARE RISES AND FALLS

In three separate locations, Handel, Wynne, and Delaney each bought a copy of *Faulkner's Dublin Journal*. Each turned excitedly to the advertisement they were looking for:

For relief of the Prisoners in several Gaols, and for the support of Mercer's Hospital in St. Stephen's Green and of the Charitable Infirmary on the Inns Quay, on Monday 12th April will be performed at the Musick Hall in Fishamble Street, Mr. Handel's new Grand Oratorio call'd Messiah, in which the Gentlemen of the Choirs of both Cathedrals will assist, with some concertos on the organ by Mr. Handel. Tickets will be had at the Musick Hall, and at Mr. Neal's in Christ-Church Yard at Half a Guinea each. N.B. No Person will be admitted to the Rehearsal without a Rehearsal Ticket, which will be given gratis with the Ticket for the Performance when pay'd for.

If Handel had not been entering St. Michan's with a large crowd of people walking past the church, he would have danced another jig.

A satisfied grin was all Wynne would allow as he put the paper down and readied himself for a meeting with some of the lower-level clerics at the cathedral.

Delaney merely nodded with gratification, then put the paper aside while he enjoyed a small snack of bread and cheese.

Inside St. Michan's, Handel gathered his people around him and greeted them. "Ladies," he said, nodding towards Mrs. Cibber and Signora Avolio, "and gentlemen." He took in the chorus and musicians. "This is a special day. We have all been practicing *Messiah* in different groups and in different forms, but today is a great day. Today, for the first time, we will rehearse it together and, in its entirety, from the Sinfonia through to the final Amen chorus. We will have one more rehearsal on Monday afternoon and then on Thursday we will do our public rehearsal at the Musick Hall. This will be followed by our formal debut in honor of the three charitable institutions the following Wednesday. You have all worked hard. You all know your parts. Let us then bring it all together."

In short order, all had scrambled around the chairs and found their precise spots. Handel sat at the harpsichord placed in front of both the orchestra and chorus while the four soloists took their spots between the groups, women to one side and the men to the other.

Handel waited until they were all set, then raised his right hand and began the slow, gentle Sinfonia.

When they finished the entire work, Handel dismissed them and was surprised to find the Viceroy sitting quietly in one of the back pews.

Handel rushed up the aisle, stopped, and showed a leg to the Viceroy. "Your Grace, I had no idea."

"I thought we were George and William when together?" Devonshire reminded him. "Congratulations, by the way. This truly is a most wonderful and inspiring work."

Handel had the grace to blush and bow again.

Devonshire stood. "I took a moment or two to meet with Dean Swift on another matter. Dr. Wynne told me where you were, so I thought I would take the opportunity to come over here and listen, since I was already out of the castle. I only caught the last little bit, but, George, you have surpassed yourself. I think this might be considered one of your finest compositions." He gestured outside. "Come out to my carriage and let's go along to your rooms. I have a small matter to discuss with you."

Although the streets were jammed with people, animals, carts, and carriages of all sizes and descriptions, the Viceroy's carriage made good time across the streets of the city, due in no small part to the dragoons providing escort and clearing the way before him. The large, ornately decorated carriage moved serenely along, pulled by its four matching greys. People parted as the procession neared them, with many standing aside to applaud, bow, or curtsey as they passed. A few stood silent, watching but showing no reaction as the King's representative trotted by.

Inside the padded red velvet of the luxury coach, Devonshire again remarked on the music he'd just heard.

"But I wondered, are you sure of the choice of Mrs. Cibber to sing in such a sacred oratorio?" he asked. "I have no personal animosity to the woman, but her story is well known here, George. Some may question her… suitability."

"That may be true, Your... uh, William... but I will tell you this: Mrs. Cibber understands, perhaps more than most of us, the great depths of rejection and sorrow. It is at least closer to what Christ must have felt than many might feel. She has a way of conveying that directly to the heart of the listener."

The Viceroy nodded sagely. "Now, I have an important question. Have you met or spoken with Lord Dawlish since he's been in Dublin?"

Puzzled, Handel searched his memory for any recollection. After a few moments, he shook his head. "I haven't met him at any dinners or balls. I'm sure I would have remembered it." He chuckled. "After all, there aren't that many lords in Dublin that I would let one drop through the holes, as you English say,.

"Not quite the expression, George, but close enough." Devonshire smiled and rubbed his chin. "It's just that we have this little problem."

The Viceroy went on to explain the circumstances by which Dawlish had come to the garrison's attention.

"So Lord Dawlish has been smuggling, or involved in something deeper?" Handel asked. "I am, of course, curious about such a strange story, but I have to ask, what has that to do with me now?"

"That's the odd thing. General Fitzherbert finally got the man to confess that his main purpose in coming to Dublin was to disrupt your season here, much as was done in London. He claims it was at the behest of the Prince of Wales and Lord Ilchester."

"Mein Gott! This is fantastic!" Handel exclaimed. "This is abominable. Why does the prince hate me so? I cannot escape these vermin." Suddenly cognizant of his friend's position, he glanced up and began stammering an apology. "I do not mean to disparage the prince so bluntly, Your Grace."

The Viceroy dismissed the thought with a wave of his hand. "Vermin is just about the right word, George. I think His Majesty would most heartily concur. So, to be clear, you've not run into Dawlish or spoken with him here and he has not acted against you in any way in Dublin that you're aware of?"

Handel shook his head. "You warned me he was around, but other than that I was not bothered at all by his presence. It has had no impact on me."

Devonshire pursed his lips. "Well, I promised General Fitzherbert I'd at least ask you. Don't worry, the man is our guest at the castle for the next little while until we get to the bottom of this. He won't be able to cause any problems and I cannot imagine him finding anyone to help upset your productions now."

As they arrived, the footman jumped off the carriage and rushed to open the door.

"Well, my friend, I wish you well next week with the concert," said Devonshire. "I may see you briefly afterwards, but I am leaving for London within the next month and I have a lot to do yet."

Handel stepped down, bowed, and expressed his thanks to the Viceroy for all he had done to smooth his entry into Dublin society and music culture.

Devonshire lifted a finger into the air. "One more thing, George, before we part. From what I've just heard in person and from the reports of others involved in *Messiah*, I have no doubts about how triumphant it will be, so I strongly urge you to consider presenting it again within a week or two." A twinkle alit in his eyes. "I know you're footing the cost of the charitable affair and taking no fee, and I believe a second performance will be joyfully received by the people of the city. It would mean that you can recoup the costs and perhaps even turn a profit on it, eh?"

The Viceroy signaled to the footman who closed the door quickly and joined the driver as they rode off down Abbey Street towards the Essex bridge.

Handel was pensive as he entered his lodgings. He was pleased by the Viceroy's support and knew that if he recommended a second performance it was tantamount to a command. But the other news bothered him. He'd thought, naively perhaps, that his problems with the prince's opposition had been left behind in London. Now, it seemed, the difficulties had crossed the Irish Sea with him.

He was at least relieved to hear that their plans had been foiled, but the prince's antagonism obviously remained. He would have to consider this carefully as he prepared to return to England.

Dawlish was brought into the office once again, this time thinner and more disheveled, a far cry from the fashion dandy image he'd portrayed before. Bereft of a wig, his hair was pepper and salt exploding in all directions while his facial hair tried frantically to catch up. His eyes were red with worry and lack of sleep.

He stepped in and bowed to General Fitzherbert, who gestured for him to take a seat.

"Lord Dawlish, over these last few days we've tried to confirm and understand your motivations and actions during your time in Ireland. We have not yet found absolute proof of treason or even smuggling, although the circumstances are such that even the Viceroy was confounded by your behavior." He rubbed his hand over his eyes, then stared directly at Dawlish. "As garrison commander I am deeply concerned with treason. Your connection with that well-known and elusive brigand O'Toole raises all manner of suspicions. I am bothered by it, sir. Greatly bothered."

Wearily, Dawlish returned his look. "I've explained that, General. I represented myself as a merchant and went to very disreputable establishments. I was seeking someone who would help me disrupt Handel's visit."

"And you did this at the behest of the Prince of Wales, correct?"

"Yes. Well, His Royal Highness' request as given to me by Lord Ilchester."

Fitzherbert drummed his fingers on the table before him. He picked up a signed document from Dawlish and laid it in front of him. "I have laid before the Viceroy the facts as we know them, plus these, your own words. We have also increased our efforts to find this man O'Toole."

Dawlish wondered about relaying his suspicions about the Irish Lord Ennis but decided against it. The humiliation of that episode at the Duke of Foyle's still rankled and was best left in the chamberpot where it belonged.

There was a knock on the door and Somerfield entered, handing the General an envelope.

"Everything is arranged, sir, and all the belongings are on board," said Somerfield.

Fitzherbert nodded. "Well, milord, the Viceroy has made a decision regarding you. A decision, I might add, that I find very charitable and one I do not fully agree with. Please stand, your lordship."

He and Somerfield stood to attention, while Dawlish, with a sinking feeling in the pit of his stomach, pried himself up from the hard chair and stood warily, searching their stern faces.

"Lord Dawlish, it is the order of the Lord Lieutenant of Ireland that in the absence of firm evidence of treasonous activity, and the absence of solid evidence connecting you with O'Toole's smuggling ventures, you are to be released from custody. However, also by order of the Lord Lieutenant, you are to be removed immediately from Ireland and returned to England. In this envelope is an order for your passage on the packet weighing anchor on this afternoon's tide. It is the Lord Lieutenant's strong suggestion that once in England you immediately remove yourself to Derbyshire. I am to inform you that it is his intention to report this entire matter in the fullest detail to His Majesty in person within the month. It will be, sir, a damning report. It is therefore his added suggestion that you consider leaving England for the foreseeable future and visit your plantations in the colonies." He then turned to Somerfield. "You have the officer and troop that will accompany his lordship to the quay and ensure he gets on board the ship?"

Somerfield saluted. "Yes, sir. All ready. His lordship's belongings were collected from Fitzwilliam Square and placed aboard."

Dawlish stared wildly at both officers, searching their faces for an indication of what was really happening.

"You jest, sir?" Dawlish's voice quavered, then grew steely. "This is nothing more than exile and only the King himself or the courts may do that."

Fitzherbert responded icily. "As the King's Viceroy, the Lord Lieutenant has the power to exile you from Ireland and he has done so. What the King does upon receipt of the verbal report is, of course, up to His Majesty. The Lord Lieutenant was merely making a suggestion to you, sir, given that your position in court and in London society will be severely compromised. Make no mistake, milord. This enquiry is not over. It will continue and, if we find proof that you were complicit in any of these charges, His Majesty's government reserves the right to prosecute."

"You've ruined me with this judgement," Dawlish lashed out. "If my friends… if Lord Ilchester and the prince find out, they will destroy you."

Unperturbed, Fitzherbert glared at the broken nobleman. "As to your ruination, that, sir, is the fault of none other than yourself and your blind determination to scurry for Ilchester and His Royal Highness' approval. I doubt either will have the power or fortitude to counter His Majesty's ruling, which will, I am sure, sanction the Viceroy's judgement in this matter. Now, sir, if you please."

Fitzherbert signaled Somerfield, who opened the door to reveal an officer and a company of armed troops. He gestured for Dawlish to step outside. As he did, two smartly uniformed men stepped behind him and led him out of the room and down the hall.

Outside, the officer and Dawlish entered the carriage. A small escort of dragoons swung into place behind and the entourage trotted out of the inner courtyard.

Fitzherbert stood by the window, watching as Dawlish's carriage wheeled out from the entrance and made its way under the clocktower into the outer courtyard.

"He got off light, sir," said Somerfield. "The Viceroy was most generous."

"Aye, he was."

"I am still puzzled by the O'Toole connection though, sir. How did O'Toole know about the ship and its cargo and why would he tip us off to the fact?"

Fitzgibbon rubbed his chin. "We'll never know unless we actually catch the blackguard," he growled. "My best guess is that he enjoys playing cat and mouse with us. That letter from Ilchester to Dawlish gave him the information to let him thumb his nose at us, the Viceroy, and the King."

The general swung away from the window and poured a drink from a decanter on the sideboard.

"It's possible he actually provided the brandy, hired the ship, and set up the entire farce." He wagged a finger at Somerfield. "All of us—Dawlish, you, me, the Viceroy—were pawns in his little joke. The best laugh, for O'Toole, was that he even got his brandy back! He took down a lord or two in London without setting foot in the city and showed our vulnerability. Yes, Somerfield, I imagine we're the laughingstock across the city and, in a few months, probably the entire island." He slammed his fist on the table. "But we will get him, sirrah. Eventually, he'll slip up and by God we'll have him. Then we'll see who has the last laugh!"

A subdued Dawlish allowed himself to be led up the gangplank. He watched as the army officer handed the Viceroy's letter to the ship's captain, saluted, then turned without a word and strode back down the gangplank. As soon as he hit dry land, one of the mates began bellowing orders. The gangplank was removed and lines holding the packet fast, were let go.

Stunned by the swiftness of his removal and still muddled by the events of the past week, Dawlish leaned against the ship's rails. The reversal of his fortunes began to hit home. No matter how he tried to justify his actions, he'd failed and had indeed ruined his prospects. There would be no rewards. There would be no dukedom. Nor would he gain financial redress from Ilchester, if indeed Ilchester would even acknowledge him.

A black rage tore at him, but it was an anger even more bitter because he had nobody to lash out at.

The little ship slipped out into the middle of the river as the current seized her. As Dawlish looked back at the pier, he gasped; a knife-like pain slashed through his gut. Standing on the pier, looking right at him, was Lord Ennis. A smile creased Ennis' face when he made eye contact with Dawlish. The smile grew, then he tipped his hat and bowed towards Dawlish.

Dawlish felt a sudden rush of nausea as he realized how incredibly stupid he'd been through the whole affair, and how Ennis—or rather, O'Toole—had played him so superbly.

He threw up into the river.

CHAPTER NINETEEN

IN WHICH MR. HANDEL IS PLEASED

Handel had expected a good turnout for the rehearsal, since those purchasing tickets for a concert were also given a free ticket to attend the rehearsal, but it was packed. Fishamble Street was jammed with horse-drawn transports battling with sedan chairs arriving and attempting to deposit their passengers while others tried to pull out of the melee. Dublin had never seen anything quite like it.

If anything, it was worse inside. The balconies were filled to overflowing. Men and women shoved and elbowed each other to try and gain the best possible vantage point.

In the seated section of the hall, it was only slightly less chaotic.

Before the performance, a stressed and beleaguered Mr. Neale and his staff had tried to bring some semblance of order so the performance could start on time. Two of his men had a difficult time sorting rehearsal ticket holders from hangers-on and those who merely hoped to buy entry at the door.

The next morning, an exhausted but exhilarated Handel awoke later than normal and sent Tobias to pick up the Friday, April 8 edition of *Faulkner's Dublin Journal*. Anxiously he turned the pages until he found the report he was looking for. He knew the rehearsal had surpassed his expectations, and *Messiah*'s reception had exceeded anything he'd ever seen before, but it *was* just a rehearsal, and it *was* just his personal—and yes, prejudiced—perception. What was more important was how greater Dublin would react.

Yesterday, Mr. Handel's Grand New Sacred Oratorio was rehearsed at the Musick Hall in Fishamble Street, to a Grand, Polite and Crowded Audience; and was performed so well, that it gave universal Satisfaction to all present; and was allowed by the Greatest Judges to be the finest Composition of Musick that ever was heard and the sacred Words as properly adapted for the occasion.

Handel already knew that the audience had enjoyed the performance, but this public affirmation meant a huge amount. He must write Jennens, he decided, and inform him how well the performance had gone.

He eagerly picked up a copy of the *Dublin News-Leader* that Tobias also brought to him. He skipped a few lines then read,

Mr. Handel's new sacred Oratorio, which in the opinion of the best Judges, far surpasses anything of that Nature which has been performed in any other Kingdom.

He put the papers down, his delight overflowing. Even at this early hour, he asked Tobias to bring a bottle of the finest claret to celebrate. It was vindication for both of him as a composer and in his belief in this particular composition.

Yes, he would assuredly write to Jennens, but probably not after a mere rehearsal. He would wait until after the formal debut Wednesday.

In the meantime, he wrote notes to all his performers, detailing minor changes in how he wanted them to project or play, and adding extra notations for them to write into their own music sheets. For Handel, no matter how excellent or well received a performance was, it could always be better; there were always little changes to bring improvement, and *Messiah* was no different.

Just before lunch, Tobias handed him a letter from the Viceroy. In it, Devonshire noted that he'd already heard excellent reports from those who'd attended the public rehearsal—"as I had no doubt there would be," he wrote—and informed him that His Excellency would attend the performance in person on Wednesday, before leaving for London. Devonshire hoped Handel would consider presenting *Messiah* in London in the next season. The Viceroy concluded:

I will make all efforts to assure His Majesty how excellent the new composition is and how His Majesty would appreciate and enjoy attending such an evening.

In all likelihood, Handel told himself, the Viceroy had sent one of his close aides to attend the rehearsal and report back to him. At the very least, there would have been officers of the garrison keeping an eye on the chaotic crowd. One spark on that dry tinder could have turned a triumph into catastrophe.

Handel shuddered. If Dawlish had been there carrying out his mischief, catastrophe might indeed have been the word.

By Monday, the city was buzzing with talk about the upcoming debut of *Messiah*. Those who'd attended the rehearsal relished the fact that they would hear it a second time. Those who'd not previously bought tickets struggled to find a way to purchase the very few still remaining.

Hopes for some were raised when a note in *Faulkner's Dublin Journal* that morning pleaded,

> The Stewards of the Charitable Music Society request The Favour of Ladies not to come with hoops this day to the Musick Hall in Fishamble Street. The Gentlemen are requested to come without their swords.

At the rehearsal, Neal had proposed an idea to alleviate some of the press inside the theatre and perhaps even sell a few more tickets for the charity concert itself. His plan was to limit the space each individual man or woman took up, with hoops and swords gone. He estimated it would allow some fifty to sixty extra people to crowd into the hall. With a capacity of around six hundred, that would mean an almost ten percent increase in attendance, and therefore revenue.

The Viceroy's earlier suggestion of a second performance of *Messiah* was looking to be a profoundly wise piece of advice. And for Handel, a profoundly lucrative one.

For all the furor and excitement, Handel spent the next two days in seclusion. He knew he must prepare himself mentally, physically, and emotionally. He realized deep inside that this wasn't just another performance; he felt this work would define him.

In the aftermath of the rehearsal's reception, his mind churned with conflicting emotions. On the one hand, there was the joy and exhilaration about what had happened so far, but on the other, he still had the worries and fears of every artist, that people wouldn't like or appreciate his work. A free rehearsal was one thing; the reality of the performance before the height of Dublin society was yet another.

Across the city, Dean Swift and Dr. Wynne sat in an almost empty cathedral, Matthew Dubourg waiting with his violin and Charles McClain sitting in the organ loft. A number of the choir members stood at the ready.

"I want you to hear how some of the music so wonderfully underscores the words of Scripture, Dean Swift," said Wynne. "You will hear how they blend and make the words all the more powerful. I wish you would change your mind and attend the entire performance on Wednesday."

Swift shook his head. "No, I fear I cannot, even though it is so near. You know it is difficult for me to stand or even sit for that long. 'Tis best I forgo it. Now let me hear what you have for me."

Dr. Wynne signaled for the two musicians to begin. Swift listened and read as Wynne pointed to the pertinent Bible verses as each selected piece of music was sung and played. He noticed that Swift's hands kept time with the music.

When they ended with McClain playing the Hallelujah Chorus, Swift looked at Wynne with a wide smile on his face. The dean applauded the singers and musicians.

"Thank you, John, for being patient with me," Swift said. "I see now that I was wrong to listen to that blackguard from London. I still have reservations about this being done in a secular theater but am willing to abide by your wisdom. It is for Christian charity, after all."

With appreciation and apologies, Swift headed back to his private quarters, assisted by Wynne.

The choir dispersed to their other duties while McClain walked up to Dubourg.

"He seemed to like it," McClain remarked, nodding in the disappearing Swift's direction. "He is too ill to attend the premier?" It was more a question than statement.

Dubourg nodded. "It's a shame in a way that he will miss it. But he seems content."

Wednesday evening was just as chaotic as the previous week's rehearsal in terms of the massive crowds and crush of wheeled vehicles. Neal arranged guides to move carriages in and out of Fishamble Street. He insisted, with the support of the parish watch and some troops from the garrison, on enforcing a one-way passage through the crooked street, blocking the end of the street at the Essex Quay and refusing to allow carriages to turn up it. Thus, the only way to the theatre was a circuitous route through the streets to enter Fishamble next to Christ Church Cathedral. They could drop their occupants there and allow them to walk down to the theatre or join an orderly but slow-moving line of carriages and sedan chairs heading down the street. Only the shortest stops were allowed at the theatre entrance, in order to allow passengers to disembark. Once that was completed, they were forced to move on. Drivers were told they could use the quayside to wait until after the performance when the whole procedure would be repeated.

Oil lamps blazed at the Musick Hall entrance. The crowd noise rose to a crescendo as attendees—without hoops and swords, as requested—pushed through the crowds to find their assigned seats. Others, the ones not fortunate or rich enough to get seated tickets, jostled for position in the main section of the hall.

Inside, Matthew Dubourg, as first violin, patiently tuned the orchestra as the choir and soloists entered and took their positions. Stage boys scurried about and began turning the flames up on the footlights. The lights themselves drenched the entire theatre in the deep red of the velvet curtains that hung over the stage. The gold thread trimmings sparked in the light.

A special box, prepared for the Viceroy, was draped with the Union flag.

The soloists took their place on stage and McClain took his seat at the portable organ, especially installed in the Musick Hall for this occasion.

Handel entered to great applause and seated himself at the harpsichord.

At a signal, Handel stood, as did the orchestra, as the Viceroy entered his box. Dubourg conducted as the orchestra played "God Save the King." As the final notes died away, Handel bowed deeply towards the Viceroy's box.

Silence then descended over the audience as the crowd settled. Handel raised his arms and the strings began the dramatic slow notes of the Sinfonia.

If there was one thing that subconsciously impressed itself upon Handel as he led, it was the absolute hush that descended on the audience as they worked deeper and deeper into the oratorio. He was so intent on conducting and playing that he couldn't look around and gauge the audience reaction. All he knew was that, apart from a few stifled coughs, the prevailing mood was silence. Was it a silence of dislike or disapproval? Or was it a silence of appreciation? He could not tell.

So far there had been no reaction, positive or negative, to Mrs. Cibber's participation. But soon the performance came to the beginning of part two and the air he had written especially for her voice; the chorus "Behold the Lamb" was in its final notes. Handel glanced up at her and smiled encouragement as she stepped forward and looked around at the audience, and then him.

The strings quietly led in with the somber orchestration. Then Susannah Cibber opened her mouth and the solemn words flowed, *"He was despised, rejected…"*

It was a performance such as Handel had never heard from her before, not even in the rehearsal last week. He chanced a quick glance at the audience to his right and saw them mesmerized. The orchestra's final notes slowly and quietly ended.

Before she could take her seat and the choir stand for the next chorus, a visibly moved Patrick Delaney, tears streaming down his face, suddenly jumped to his feet in the balcony and shouted, "Woman! For this, all thy sins be forgiven you!" He gripped the balcony rail and applause quickly broke out around the hall.

Susannah, unsure what to do, flashed a quick and appreciative smile at Handel, and then took her seat as the choir and orchestra began the next piece, *"Surely, he has borne our grief."*

The applause died away and Delaney sat.

Handel smiled as he played. His gamble on using her had paid off. She had indeed portrayed the depths of grief, humiliation, and rejection he had yearned for his audience to feel. She had profoundly touched their hearts.

As the final amens of the Amen chorus rang around the hall, thunderous applause and calls rained down on Handel and the performers. Flowers, handkerchiefs, even hats were tossed onto the stage. Broad grins appeared on all the soloists' faces, especially Susannah's, as well as those amongst choir and orchestra.

Handel turned to the royal box and smiled, bowing in thanks a number of times to the wildly applauding Viceroy who, in turn, honored Handel with a deep bow of his own. Handel turned towards the audience and signaled all the performers to stand and bow, as did he.

When he gestured to the choir and soloists to leave, loud cries of "No, no, again!" and "More! More!" resounded from throughout the hall, from the pits in front to the highest, remotest corners of the balconies. The audience was refusing to let them leave.

Finally, gesturing again for the performers to leave, Handel walked over to the organ, took his seat, and began playing the first of the two concertos he'd put into the programme at the charities' request. The clapping and shouting slowly began to dribble away.

It took hours for Handel to escape the hall. He had to thank the performers, especially the soloists and Susannah, and then make his way gradually through the admiring throngs before he finally made it back to his rooms.

Sleep eluded him.

On both Thursday and Friday, he received many notes of appreciation and congratulations from some of Dublin society's greatest leaders. There were so many invitations to dinner that he'd be forced to stay another year if he accepted them all, he thought with a chuckle. He especially treasured a note from Devonshire filled with warm appreciation and wishes for the future. A Mr. Laurence Whyte even sent along a poem extolling Handel's virtues and music.

Even so, it was not a time to relax and drink in the accolades. The second presentation of *Messiah* was confirmed with Neal and the performers, and he had finished approving advertising and posters.

An official thank you from the Mercer Hospital and other charities told him that more than seven hundred people had jammed into the theater Wednesday night. It meant that each charity would receive the princely sum of approximately four hundred pounds, enough to set them on a firm footing for this year and others to come.

Early Saturday morning, while finishing his breakfast and reflecting on the week ahead, he began to think about his return to London later in the year.

Tobias quietly entered and informed him that Mrs. Cibber was outside. She was ushered in. For the first time in a long while, Handel saw a fully relaxed and happy woman standing before him.

"Forgive me again, Mr. Handel," she said. "I seem to have developed a habit of dropping in on you without an appointment."

Smiling, he bowed and waved off her apology.

"I thought first that you should see this."

She handed him a copy of *Faulkner's Dublin Journal* for that morning, folded so that he could see the report on *Messiah*.

He accepted the newspaper and read it.

Words are wanting to express the exquisite Delight afforded to the admiring, crowded Audience. The Sublime, the Grand and the Tender adapted to the most elevated, majestic and moving Words, conspired to transport and charm the ravished Heart and Ear.

He scanned the rest of the article, which commended him for the event and the massive donation the charities received.

He jabbed at the article looking up at her, speaking seriously but with a grin creasing his face. "You, my dear Susannah, were an essential partner in this triumph. Your performance was absolutely magnificent, and I could not have been more humbled by anyone's performance than I was by your sublime effort."

"I, more than anyone, appreciate what you did for me, Mr. Handel. You had faith in me when I did not. You convinced me despite my feelings." Tears began streaming down her face. "I am forever in your debt. You rescued me out of a mire of shame and gave me my career and my pride again."

"I did not expect Mr. Delaney to interrupt so vociferously, my dear, but I can tell you that while Delaney is impulsive, he is also a man of true heart. You moved him. And many others with him. Your sins are indeed forgiven, Susannah. But not by Delaney or the audience. You needed to forgive yourself and be forgiven by the one of whom you sang. That was your real triumph Wednesday."

As they sat, they discussed the upcoming second performance. When pressed on the idea of returning to London with him and performing *Messiah* there, she balked.

"I have all the gratitude in the world and appreciate your kind offer, Mr. Handel, but there is nothing in London for me now," Susannah said. "William is abroad. My brother Thomas is here in Dublin and will be for the foreseeable future. Only Mr. Cibber is left in London and I would not care to be in the same place as he. I can perform in Dublin quite cheerfully now because they have accepted me, and indeed forgiven me. I am not the target of shame and disapproval that I would be should I return to London." A beaming smile lit her face. "You have given me my career and my life. But it is here in Dublin now. I regret that I cannot return."

He nodded sympathetically. "I accept that decision, my dear, and respect it. But know this: as long as I produce *Messiah*, there is a place reserved for you in it."

Handel was surprised by the even more fervent acceptance during *Messiah*'s second Dublin performance. Letters and flattering newspaper coverage showered him with acclaim. It didn't hurt that the proceeds from that concert turned a great profit as well.

He was happy.

PART THE THIRD

In which Mr. Handel rejoices and returns to London

CHAPTER TWENTY

IN WHICH MR. HANDEL MEETS NEW CHALLENGES

Unlike his delay-strewn journey to Dublin, Handel's return to the capital was entirely uneventful. After a round of wonderful and entertaining soirees and dinners at the homes of Ireland's elite, he'd finally embarked on a packet that took him swiftly back to Parkgate. Even the stagecoach from Chester to London was without fuss or bother and they arrived in decent time.

He was touched by the number of well-wishers who either dropped by his house on Brook Street to welcome him home or sent notes of welcome. He was even more surprised by the large number who remarked on his success in Dublin, many of whom asked about the new oratorio they'd heard so many good things about. News may travel slowly, but they'd read the reports from Dublin newspapers or heard from those who'd preceded Handel on the trip back to London.

John was also happy to see him home again, not least of all because he was no longer fending off merchants and lenders who were owed money. At John's urging, Handel rested for a week after his arrival. His only excursion was to St. George's one morning to pray and sit once again at the church's organ.

John, meanwhile, ran interference on visitors, letting in only those closest to Handel while keeping hangers-on from intruding on his master's rest. He merely took their names and promised that Handel would respond to their good wishes in the fullness of time.

One quiet afternoon, following a delicious and abundant lunch, Handel retired to his study. The exhilaration of Dublin added to the exhaustion of his travels, which had so far delayed something he had promised himself to do. He could no longer put it off.

He sat and pulled a quill and paper toward him. The long-postponed letter to Jennens was underway.

My dear sir,

It was indeed your humble Servant, which intended you a Visit in my way from Ireland to London, for I certainly would have given you a better account by word of Mouth, as by writing, how well your Messiah was received in that country. Yet a Noble Lord and not less than the Bishop of Elphin (a Nobleman very learned in Musick) has given his observations in writing on this Oratorio. I send you here annexed, the contents of it in his own words. As for my success in general in that generous and polite Nation, I reserve the account of it till I have the Honour to see you in London.

When he finished the letter with enquiries about Jennens' health and well being, he began to copy portions of the bishop's review. He'd met with and enjoyed Edward Synge's erudite knowledge of music early in his Irish stay, delighting in his lively and knowledgeable observations about Bach, Telemann, and others. The two had enjoyed deep dialogue on the present state of music in Britain and Europe. Handel had appreciated the depths of Synge's knowledge and so was both honored and humbled by the bishop's written comments on *Messiah*.

He appended those comments to his letter:

As Mr. Handel in his oratorios greatly excels all other Composers I am acquainted with, So in the famous one called Messiah he seems to have excelled himself. The whole is beyond anything I had a notion of till I read and heard it. It seems to be a species of Musick differently from any other. The composition is very Masterful and artificial, yet the harmony is so great and open, as to please all who have Ears and will hear, learned and unlearn'd. Without doubt this Superior Excellence is owing in some measure to the great care and exactness which Mr. Handel seems to have used in preparing this Piece. One is the Subject which is the greatest and most interesting. It seems to have inspired him. Another is the Words which are all Sublime and affecting in the greatest degree. A third reason for the Superior Excellence, Tis that there is no dialogue In this piece the attention of the Audience is engag'd from one end to the other.

By the time Handel had finished copying much of the bishop's praise, he had added another three pages to his letter, adding finally,

I send you this, sir, only to show you how zealous they are in Ireland for oratorios. I could send you a number of Instances more from others in Print and writing. I am sir, your most obliged and humble servant.

His final comment to Jennens was a promise that they would meet in London and he would tell him all about the trip, especially since he felt badly that he'd not stopped to visit him once he'd landed back in England.

The one thing he did not comment on, was the possibility of staging *Messiah* in London. Part of the reason was that his initial enthusiasm, fired by Devonshire's fervent persuasion, was diminishing. Dublin had not been safe from the machinations of the prince and his cohorts and obviously nothing had changed the way they perceived him. Which could only mean continued opposition to anything he attempted in London.

After Swift's initial antagonism to *Messiah*, Handel was particularly wary of the negative response the church hierarchy in London might have. And he had no powerful and influential prelates here like Wynne or Delaney to count on.

No, he thought, he must be very careful and wise about his music. He would employ information and strategy rather than simply charge ahead as was his wont.

Even as those thoughts crossed his mind, he marveled at how he'd changed in the past few years. Being a smidge away from debtors' prison and finding out who your friends really were had a way of doing that. His monumental ego and drive for success had been modified despite his changed circumstances. Grateful as he was for the Irish reception, he realized that his creative genius still danced on a thin rope dangling between public adoration and public censure.

If he did produce *Messiah* in London, it must only be the result of a well-considered and strategic decision. Nothing less.

Despite his agreement to rest, Handel still spent time considering an upcoming season of concerts. He realized now that oratorios were the things currently in demand by audiences; Italianate operas were finished as entertainments.

Always *Messiah* lurked in the back of his mind. He could not ignore the overwhelming reception it had received in Ireland. It buoyed his confidence, not to mention his financial future. London, though, was a different kettle of fish, as the English said. London was a fickle but discerning audience. They considered themselves trend-setters and a step above what they considered their lesser cultured provincial counterparts.

London was also the feasting ground of people like the prince and his followers. It was their city and they still influenced a lot of people. The open defiance of the King and his wishes divided the nobility. Truth be known, though, the bulk of them merely sat on the fence, caring only for their own entertainment and pleasures while the political drama played out. They largely ignored the hatred between King and prince, father and son, waiting for a clear victor to be declared. Then they would hop off the fence in grand support of the winner.

It was on Handel's fourth weekday visit to St. Georges that the rector approached him following his time on the organ.

"My dear sir, you have yet again graced us with your talent on this wonderful instrument and I am grateful, as are these." The rector waved his hand around the small crowd seated in various pews. "They come every Tuesday, ostensibly to pray but I don't wonder they're also hoping the great Mr. Handel will be playing and thus add a great musical voice to their prayers."

The man's deep brown eyes twinkled, a small smile cracking the stern visage he believed a rector should present in church.

"So we are indeed most thankful that you are back in London," the rector added. "Though I fear the Bishop of London is not so well inclined."

Handel's eyebrows arched in surprise and curiosity. "He dislikes the idea of my playing your organ, sir?"

"No, Mr. Handel. Not that. I hear that he is not happy that you have returned to London."

"Ah. He supports the prince against my music, does he?"

The rector paused, trying to be delicate. "It's more that he heard you presented a concert of sacred music while in Dublin and that you did so in a tavern setting. He was livid when he heard the news."

Handel gripped a pew back in shock and anger. "Then my lord bishop is completely wrong in what he has heard, my dear rector. I did not present sacred music at a tavern, and I'd be obliged if you would tell him so. In fact, sir, you can tell him that I would be happy to meet with him face to face and explain that his information is monstrously wrong and insulting." Handel snorted. "To think I would do such a thing is unbelievable. This lie must be stopped in its path."

The rector shook his head. "I'm afraid I don't have the Bishop's ear, Mr. Handel. I opposed him on certain matters of faith and principle and he has refused to speak to me since, other than for the most formal or ecclesiastical needs. Bishop Gibson is a headstrong man who cannot see other than his own truths. He has even defied both the King and the prince on matters he considered vital. My speaking to him would only make things worse. And I doubt, sir, that you would be welcome at the bishop's palace for an audience, I regret to say."

Handel's good mood dissipated. A scowl darkened his face. "I will fight this monstrous falsehood, sir. I will find a way to face this bishop of yours and show him the absolute error of his information. And if he will not listen to me, then I shall see that he listens to the Duke of Devonshire, who knows the truth of the situation."

He thanked the rector for giving him the freedom of the church and organ yet again and dismissed the man's apologies for hitting what obviously was a raw nerve.

"My fault, sir, for being overly sensitive on the matter," Handel said.

The conversation troubled Handel all the way back to Brook Street. He walked rather than take a sedan chair because it gave him time to think in the fresh warmth of the late summer.

If the rector was correct, Bishop Gibson had been given, and was spreading, sheer lies about the Dublin performance. Whether the lies had been deliberately set or merely the result of misinformation was scarcely the issue. Lies were lies, and incredibly damaging. Regrettably, it seemed that the bishop was an intransigent individual who would not be swayed once his mind was determined on a path. Setting the truth alone before him might not be enough.

He brooded over the matter for a number of days, which soon stretched into weeks. It did not stop him, however, from reworking other music he'd written since finishing *Messiah* last autumn. Through September and October, he'd composed around Newburgh Hamilton's libretto for *Samson*. He'd planned to work on it in Dublin, but events had overtaken him and he'd put it aside. Now, back in London, he took it out and instantly realized it needed a complete rework. He flung himself into it, planning to use it in his upcoming season.

As he worked, he realized that he had a perfect role for Mrs. Cibber. She'd rejected the concept of a return to London but, he thought, if there was another major role for her, there was a possibility she would return to London for the season. Slim perhaps, but possible.

Even as he wrote the music, he penned a very persuasive letter to her. He laid out his rationale once again for her to at least consider a London season, and sent her a copy of the music for the oratorio so she could see the role he had in mind for her.

More importantly, he told her, he had been reliably informed that even Theo Cibber would not oppose her performing in London again, as long as it was not at his theatre. Other theatre managers, missing one of their favorite actresses and singers, and therefore revenue, had apparently pressured him into an agreement. Theo, he was told, was now facing ruin as impresarios, actors, and musicians all refused to play his theater. He had even agreed not to contact her and ensure he staged no competing productions while she was performing. It was, Handel told her, complete redemption for her.

Lastly, he assured her that many London society members were aware of her performance in *Messiah* and the success she'd achieved. Even in London, he told her, the moving story of Delaney's reaction was a topic of conversation.

He sent the letter, hopeful that she would respond positively.

Disappointment, however, came in letters from Jennens. While congratulating Handel on his triumphant success in Ireland, Jennens also let it be known he was less than happy with the music that accompanied the libretto. There were times, he wrote, when he thought Handel had not used all his genius. He explained that he would have preferred different pacing and moods to be prevalent in some of the pieces. The grumbling tone of his letter irked Handel, who tried to rationalize the complaints, realizing that, as well versed in music as the man was, nothing compared to hearing the music performed in all its power with both choruses and soloists. Simply reading the music was bound to be a letdown.

As he wondered about Jennens' response, he began to understand that his friend's petulant complaints were actually less about the music but rather that the debut had occurred in Ireland and not London, where Jennens had always hoped it would be performed.

With that realization, Handel understood that it was one more item amongst all the other pressing issue and obstacles he now faced.

He listed the problems mentally.

Jennens he could not satisfy without making major changes and performing *Messiah* in London.

Bishop Gibson he could not satisfy unless he never performed *Messiah*.

The Prince of Wales, Lord Ilchester, and their followers he could not satisfy unless he left Britain.

It was a dilemma. He did not know how to solve it.

CHAPTER TWENTY-ONE

IN WHICH LORD ILCHESTER IS CONFRONTED

"The Duke of Devonshire to see you, sir, on an urgent matter," the butler spoke quietly as he stood in the doorway to Lord Ilchester's study.

Ilchester's head snapped up from the reports he was reading. A quizzical look flashed across his face as his mind raced to determine what Devonshire could possibly want with him. And what did he mean by an "urgent matter"?

Ilchester knew the duke was firmly in the King's camp. There was nothing new in that situation, urgent or otherwise. Devonshire had never communicated with him before except for innocuous greetings and small talk at social gatherings or royal occasions.

Puzzled, he signaled the butler to escort the duke into the study.

"Your Grace, what an unexpected pleasure," Ilchester greeted.

Both men bowed, with Devonshire tipping his hat to the side.

Ilchester beckoned him to take a seat on one of his finest Chippendale chairs. "I'm delighted of course to have you in my home, but you have come on urgent business?"

The grim-faced duke sat, his tall stature enhanced by his rigid upright posture. He surveyed the room, noticing works of art but very few books. A Greek-looking sculpture took center stage on a side table near the desk his host sat behind, probably from Ilchester's grand tour of Europe when he was younger, the duke mused.

Ilchester's eyes narrowed. He could see from Devonshire's posture that this was not a friendly visit.

"Thank you for seeing me, Lord Ilchester. I felt it only fair to come and see you first before I present this report to His Majesty later this afternoon." The duke handed over a thick package of papers. "As you know, I am the Lord Lieutenant of Ireland, acting in His Majesty's place on that island. The report deals with matters... disturbing matters with potentially difficult consequences, and I need to discuss them with you. I regret, sir, that they touch upon you and your possible activities in Ireland. Particularly as they involve Lord Dawlish."

Devonshire's intent gaze was rewarded by a sudden intake of breath on Ilchester's part, and a twitch of the eyes as Dawlish's name and Ireland were connected practically in the same sentence. Nevertheless, Ilchester quickly regained his composure.

"I have no idea what you mean, Your Grace, nor how it might impact me at all sir. 'Pon m' word!"

"You are acquainted with Lord Dawlish, are you not, sir? And you did send him to Ireland to handle some business on your behalf?"

Ilchester waved his hand dismissively as if swatting an annoying fly. "He is known to me obviously, and yes, I have engaged him from time to time to assist with certain trading and business matters. I fail to see why this is of interest to you. Or why my connection with him is so urgent!"

"So you did instruct him to await a shipment you were expecting, and that the shipment was to be met outside the port of Dublin away from the attention of revenue officers?"

Ilchester merely stared at the Duke unfazed.

Devonshire continued. "Indeed, it seems you engaged him to arrive in Ireland around the beginning of November last and sent him funds, including renting quarters for him until the middle of April. Is that not correct?"

Ilchester flushed and spoke sharply. "I will not discuss my business affairs with you or any other, sir, be you a duke or not."

Devonshire looked down at the papers clutched in Ilchester's hands. "Before we go any further, milord, it might be gainful if you were to read the report in its entirety. It is from myself to His Majesty concerning certain affairs in Ireland that rose up recently. You will note, sir, that your name is mentioned frequently in that report. It remarks on some very strange and troubling activities that might range anywhere from mere smuggling to treason. Please read it now. If there are any errors in it, I would seek your explanation so that it can be modified."

Ilchester glared at him, then moved to a chair near a window to catch the strong afternoon sunlight. He began to read.

Finally, Ilchester flung the report on the table beside him. "This is calumny, sir, outright calumny. That a person of my position and honor should be insulted in this…." he gestured to the report "…this monstrous fabrication! I will be speaking to the prince about this, you may be assured."

"I assure you, milord, this is no fabrication," Devonshire said coldly but calmly. "This has been attested to, as you can see, by General Fitzherbert, who I am assured is a cousin to the prince and commander of His Majesty's forces in Ireland. It has also been attested by Colonel Somerfield, his second in command. I also have a sworn and attested testimony from Dean Jonathan Swift of St. Patrick's Cathedral which confirms some of Lord Dawlish's actions. And lastly, we have accounts made by Dawlish himself to my officers and signed by him." He leaned forward. "Now sir, can you tell me specifically what were the fabrications and calumny in the report? Was it Lord Dawlish's statements that you asked him to meet with a ship carrying some unknown goods in an out-of-the-way anchorage south of Dublin? As you can see, the goods were confiscated but later stolen by a notorious brigand named O'Toole. Or was it that you used Lord Dawlish to provide materials to O'Toole? Be assured, milord, I seek only to ascertain the truth of the matter. I am not interested in your overall business dealings, just with this one that, if I may be so bold, smells like a fishmonger's wife."

The conversation, heated at times, rolled back and forth. Ilchester alternated between anger, shock, and a growing nausea in his stomach. Devonshire was persistent, firmly dealing with each miniscule item in his report, deliberately and calmly moving point by point, questioning and confirming each one.

"As you will see, by the powers given to me as Lord Lieutenant of Ireland, I banished Lord Dawlish and had him returned to England," said Devonshire. "Where he went after he arrived in Chester, I do not know, although I strongly suggested to him that he avoid London and repair to Derbyshire, perhaps even contemplate a lengthy sojourn in some other nation or colony."

Ilchester finished storming around the room and sat back down. Bluster was getting him nowhere. He would now try cajoling and casting blame. A calm resignation took hold.

"Dawlish is and was a fool," Ilchester mused. "A lapdog with no brains and no abilities, but with a burning desire to promote himself above his position and seek a higher place in society than he deserved. He was easily led and used. So yes, I did use Dawlish. But not for smuggling and not for treason. There was no ship. There were no goods. I did not give him the name of my agent there. His function lay elsewhere."

"You did not promise him a title on behalf of the prince then?"

Ilchester snorted with disgust. "I might have mentioned that the prince is always grateful to those who support him and that, in time, when he ascends the throne, he might appropriately reward his friends. If Dawlish took that as a promise of a dukedom, well, sir, it only speaks to what an incompetent and foolish fellow he truly is."

Devonshire nodded. "It is as I thought. I did not believe that you, milord, or indeed the prince himself, would be so imprudent to make such promises. I am aware, sir, that there are... shall we say, tensions... between His Majesty and His Royal Highness. But I do not see such a wild offer being made, because it is not within his purview to give until His Majesty dies and the prince inherits the throne. Which, God willing, will be many years yet!"

Ilchester gratefully smiled, wiped his brow, and began to relax.

Devonshire continued unfazed. "General Fitzherbert was rightly concerned with the strange maneuvers Lord Dawlish went to in order to collect the goods in question, and his motivations. Although those goods were not weapons, he was correct to treat this event as a major smuggling ring with ramifications for the overall stability of Ireland. When your name surfaced in context with Lord Dawlish's strange behavior, it was imperative that I discuss this with you before speaking with His Majesty."

Ilchester protested that he knew nothing of a real ship and real boxes of brandy. "It was all a fabrication to persuade him to go to Ireland. I have no idea how my flimsy deceits turned into reality." He wiped sweat from his upper lip.

Devonshire methodically walked through the report once again, stressing inconsistencies. "Frankly, milord, there are many questions without answers. I had hoped to determine some truths with you this morning."

The duke then retrieved his report from Ilchester's grasp and flipped through a number of pages until he found the one he wanted.

"For example, sir, Dawlish reports that you sent him to Ireland in part to disrupt performances by the composer Handel." Devonshire scanned two of the pages again. "Yes, here it is. You asked him—no, required him 'to arrange the usual disruptions and see that none of the performances are successful.' He told us that he assumed this to mean destroying advertising bills and posters and causing verbal and physical disturbances at performances and so on." He watched Ilchester carefully. "You do realize, sir, that such activity is tantamount to fostering civil unrest. In a place like Ireland, that is like sparking a small fire in a tinder-dry forest. The general had every reason to consider treason as the motivation behind all this and that Handel was the excuse, not the subject."

Ilchester blanched and stammered. "But... but... it... it was no such thing, Your Grace. It was pranks. Nothing more. An expression of disapproval of the man's music and presence in our country. The prince is concerned that good British culture was limited by the public's approval of Handel's foreign birth and continental music. I assure you that while I support the prince in many ways and on many issues, I am His Majesty's most loyal subject and I'd be obliged if you would convey that to him."

"I will, sir, but it seems to me that if the public does not like a particular method of entertainment or a particular performer, the public will stay away and avoid it. They don't need external activities or groups to decide for them." Devonshire leaned forward. "When physical and verbal unrest occur, it can just as easily slide into chaos. That's what Fitzherbert was concerned about. I'm sure he will speak to his cousin the prince about it the next time he's on leave. Which, I believe, is later this year."

Ilchester's discomfort was vivid. He squirmed in his seat and wrung his hands when he wasn't wiping them across his face.

"I have heard nothing from you or your reading of my report to the King that indicates there are errors with the facts as I report them," the duke continued. "You may dislike what you heard, but it seems there are no mistakes or false statements. You did engage Dawlish to create civil chaos in Dublin. You did engage Dawlish on a surreptitious and apparently meaningless, perhaps even non-existent plot, which, in fact, turned into a real smuggling operation. You did intimate to him that a reward would be forthcoming from the prince upon his successful completion of whatever it was you instructed him to do."

Devonshire folded the papers and stood, moving towards the door.

"I will, out of courtesy, ensure that His Royal Highness also receives a copy of the report." The duke bowed once again to Ilchester. "I bid you good day."

Ilchester's flush grew deeper and redder. He stood along with Devonshire, protesting vociferously as they passed through the entry hall toward the front door.

The duke stopped suddenly at the door. "One final word, sir. I made a suggestion to Dawlish about becoming scarce for a while. A suggestion I believe would be worthwhile, and hopefully heeded, I should think, by anyone else caught up in this strange circumstance."

With that, he tipped his hat and Ilchester bowed deeply. He watched as the duke stepped into his carriage and rode off, his stomach churning all the while.

Ilchester raced immediately to his study, barking at the servants that he did not want to be disturbed. He flopped into a chair, head cradled in his hands, his mind a whirlwind of emotion and thought.

He knew the prince would react badly once he read the report. He was already angry that Handel had returned triumphant. That he had not communicated with

Ilchester in the intervening weeks demonstrated just how displeased he was. The report would only give him more ammunition. He'd be livid and lash out at anyone he considered to be at fault, particularly if they were at hand.

Ilchester pressed a fist harder into his forehead as if to shake loose some thoughts. He had to think. He had to protect his position. Devonshire was to meet with the King this day, but he'd said he'd merely send a copy of the report to the prince. Perhaps an aggressive strike beforehand might alleviate some of the prince's anger.

He pulled paper out of a drawer. The first step would be to formulate his own report and get it to the prince before Devonshire's report reached him. It took him almost an hour of feverish writing, rewriting, and copying before he was satisfied with the finished letter. His carefully phrased missive commiserated with the prince that although Handel had not been forced out of Britain his success in Dublin might be a blessing in disguise. It could, he suggested, actually be a catalyst to send the composer on an extended tour of Europe.

He boldly ventured the idea that the prince use his own contacts on the continent to increase interest in Handel's music and invite him to places like Germany, Italy, the Austro-Hungarian Empire and other remote spots, thus drawing him away. A honey approach rather than vinegar. Let Dublin be the start of a grand tour to take Handel offshore and keep him occupied elsewhere for years to come. He slyly noted that Dublin had proven valuable in this regard and might even be considered a success. Out of sight, out of mind, he reminded the prince.

Secondly, Ilchester accepted responsibility for using Dawlish, a man he consistently called a dupe and incompetent. He begged the prince's forgiveness for trying to use such a failure in such an important task. Dawlish, he said, had been dismissed as soon as it had become apparent that the moves against the composer had failed. His understanding was that Dawlish remained on the island for a period of time after the dismissal and then abruptly left. Where the man had gone now was a mystery, he wrote cunningly.

Finally, he apologized to the prince that unforeseen and urgent problems demanded his presence back at his estate in Yorkshire. He would regrettably have to miss much of the upcoming season in London but would of course keep regular correspondence with the prince. Until he was able to clear things up in Yorkshire and return, he would remain the His Royal Highness' most humble and loyal servant.

He read the letter once more before sealing it and calling the butler to have it delivered immediately to Cliveden. He sat back, frustrated, but congratulating himself on hopefully pulling at least some of the fat out of the fire. Once he confirmed the letter had been sent, he instructed the butler to begin the process of moving north. Ilchester made it clear he wanted to be out of London by week's end.

As his carriage trundled away through the capital's crowded streets, Devonshire leaned back against the deep blue velvet upholstery. He allowed a grim smile as he reflected on the meeting with Ilchester. He'd deliberately arrived unannounced, ready to see the man's face and gauge his reaction as he went through the bizarre events of the past few months. The ease with which the entire operation had been conducted pointed to severe lapses in the island's security.

"Today it is brandy," Fitzherbert had argued. "Tomorrow it would be weapons for an insurgency."

O'Toole, who made his base in Wicklow and Dublin, had been a thorn in Devonshire's side. It irked him that the brigand portrayed himself as an Irish Robin Hood, attacking the English authorities while championing the underdog Irish. There was a contemptuous teasing about many of O'Toole's escapades underneath which operated a serious threat to the security of Ireland. It was masked by O'Toole's sometimes playful approach to his dealings with the guards and authority.

Both he and Fitzherbert feared that others with more violent and murderous thoughts would soon emulate him with disastrous results. O'Toole had to be stopped.

Dawlish and Ilchester, he considered, were absolute fools, ignorant about politics and the situation in Ireland. He could see that they merely dallied with petty issues, such as the state of British music, turning the miniscule into mighty volcanoes while ignoring enormous matters of importance to the growth of the nation and the colonies.

"Damn them both to hell!" Devonshire blurted, causing his footman to jump down from the seat outside and come running up to the carriage door, a worried look on his face.

The carriage pulled to a halt.

"Ignore me, Alfred. I'm just speaking out loud," Devonshire said, leaning out the door.

The carriage rolled on and he returned to his thoughts. While the nation itself desperately needed strong leadership from the nobility, Ilchester and his kind, even the Prince of Wales, lost themselves instead in the search for sensory pleasures and petty disputes.

This nation would be imperiled when Frederick became king, Devonshire realized with a shudder. The man had no talent for statesmanship and no ability to do anything other than preen, spend money outrageously, womanize, gamble, and drink. The only thing he seemed to be good at was to hate and lash out.

Which is why I am a coward, Devonshire told himself. *I'm willing to meet personally with the King, but I will merely send a copy of the report to His Royal Highness. I've no desire for a useless fight with the prince.*

Besides, he tried to console himself, he was Viceroy to the King and therefore reported to him and him alone. It would be up to the King to castigate his son and heir. He doubted the King would do that, and even if he did he doubted the prince would pay one iota of attention.

Their hatred was palpable. It was not good for the country, but Devonshire saw no end to the war between them. As long as George was King, the prince was kept in check. On George's death, however, Frederick would be King.

God save the king, he thought. *And with Frederick as king, God save the nation.*

The thought put him in a deep funk.

CHAPTER TWENTY-TWO

IN WHICH A DECISION IS MADE

Handel intended to throw himself into revising *Samson*, a decision that had been met with confusion in recent days when he'd thought about, and then reluctantly refused, an offer of a thousand pounds to compose and present two operas for the upcoming season. It was a hard choice, but his recent experience in Dublin—and his disastrous opera season of 1741—had convinced him that the future lay with oratorios.

The decision to turn his back on the offer, once made, was confirmed when friends told him one of the backers behind the offer was a strong supporter of the prince. This confirmed his fears that the offer had been intended in some way to undermine him. His mind swirled with possible repercussions to the point that he forced himself to erase the offer from his mind and accept that he'd done the right thing.

When he was not working on *Samson*, Handel completed some concertos and smaller novelty pieces commissioned by various friends and followers. Infused with new enthusiasm, he worked through the autumn and finally set aside the date of February 18 the following year at Covent Garden theatre for *Samson*'s debut.

All along, though, he yearned to bring *Messiah* to London. Instinct, and the Irish reception, had convinced him it would succeed, but lingering fears of disapproval from the Church hierarchy, as well as the prince's known opposition, held him back. Admirers asked about it often, only to receive profuse thanks for their interest and enthusiasm and a vague answer, pleading an excess of work to complete first.

Liar and fraud, he reprimanded himself after one such discussion. *You haven't the courage to risk it because you are now too comfortable, basking in praise and not upsetting the cart with a controversial production.*

His discomfort was enhanced by the continued criticism from Jennens. Mutual friends increasingly commented on Jennens' angry statements, written as well as verbal, lambasting Handel and particularly *Messiah*. Debuting it in Dublin seemed to have been the trigger, but Handel realized that his decision not to visit Gopsall Hall was another flame of annoyance.

He dug out a letter Jennens had sent criticizing the work and demanding that the opening Sinfonia be dropped. Other pieces, Jennens declared, needed to be reworked and the book of music sent to him was unprofessional and unworthy, replete with typographical errors caused by the Dublin printer.

While the breakdown of this relationship bothered Handel, he knew *Messiah* was worthy of performance as it stood. Dublin had proved that. As he did with most of his music, he tinkered with some of the pieces and modified several to soothe Jennens' complaints, though he outright refused to drop the Sinfonia.

The constant niggling criticism, however, had a reverse affect. Handel became convinced that if Jennens actually heard the music, he would understand its power and fully appreciate it. That thought added fuel to the fire driving Handel to a decision.

On an unseasonably warm and clear February day, Handel left the house and walked to St. George's once again. The sun warmed his skin and he glanced up, noting there was not a cloud dotting the sky. He passed throngs of sellers and passersby, a number of whom recognized him, and nodded and remarked on the fine weather. Some stepped aside and bowed while an older bread-seller curtsied and almost tipped her whole basked of breads and buns.

Inside the church, he ascended the steps to the organ's keyboard and began another impromptu performance to the delight of those in the church and the many who had followed him inside in expectation. Handel was oblivious. His mind was on another plane, part in prayer and part wrestling with his dilemma.

He was excited. *Samson*'s debut at Covent Garden had been another remarkable triumph.

Horace Walpole, the writer son of the recently resigned Prime Minister Robert Walpole, had written, "Handel has set up an oratorio against opera, and succeeds!" A few days later, Walpole told his friends, "The oratorio gave me a sense of heaven, where everybody is to sing whether they have voices or not."

The praise from Walpole and others confirmed Handel's decision to stop writing and performing operas.

As he left St, George's, his mind was finally made up. The end of the 1742–43 season was almost at hand, and in another month or so it would be over.

Back in his Brook Street premises, he quickly arranged three more performances of *Samson* and began quietly promoting *Messiah*, arranging for its London debut at Covent Garden. Within two days he had confirmation from both Christina Avolio and Susannah Cibber that they would sing it if he wished. Susannah's ready response in particular pleased him. She'd responded warmly to his persuasions and had indeed returned to London and renewed her career.

The end of the winter performance season coincided with Lent, which was perfect in his mind. *Messiah*, he felt, was a decidedly Easter work, with the resurrection and ultimate triumph as the central theme. He decided on March 23 and began quietly promoting it.

Opposition came swiftly, as he'd feared.

Bishop Edmund Gibson, a prickly man at the best of times, exploded when he heard of the plans to stage *Messiah* in a theatre. He raged verbally and in a flood of letters to newspapers about what he called the profanity, if not blasphemy, the production represented. He called on all his parishes to condemn Handel's plans and urge parishioners to stay away from any such performance. His Sunday sermon at the abbey the week before had been a particularly fierce denunciation of the perfidy of base secularism seeping in and devouring the sacred.

At Cliveden, the Prince of Wales read a copy of Bishop Gibson's sermon and chuckled. Gibson was notorious and touchy, as the prince had personally discovered, but the man could be used.

Frederick contemplated ways in which he could harness the bishop's opposition. Now that he could no longer rely on Ilchester, he knew a deft touch from his newest recruit, the Marquis of Templecombe was needed. He'd found the marquis smarter and more adroit than others in his orbit, one who, while pliant, often opted for a more subtle approach. Certainly, that had worked the last few months as he'd negotiated an increase in the prince's parliamentary allowance. Walpole himself had resigned as discussions were wrapping up and, to the prince's surprise, Templecombe had even persuaded the King to reluctantly endorse the increase.

A summons brought Templecombe to Cliveden by noon the next day. As the marquis discussed the situation with the prince, he urged his master to follow the suggestions of Lord Ilchester and coat any plans with buckets full of honey.

"Your Royal Highness must be seen as a reasonable and positive force in the nation's future," said Templecombe. "This dispute between the musician and Bishop Gibson offers you a chance to question Handel's suitability as a cultural cornerstone in Britain while also exhibiting your Royal Highness' great cultural sensitivity and appreciation."

Frederick shot a puzzled look at his lackey.

Templecombe sighed under his breath. One thing he'd learned since joining the prince's entourage was that Frederick was not the most astute individual. Subtlety was a weapon unknown to him. All his life he'd bludgeoned people into doing his will.

Templecombe paused, scratching his eyebrow as he sought to explain. "I mean, sir, that you must raise yourself above this matter. Let others fight the fight against Handel."

"That's what Ilchester and Dawlish were supposed to do," the prince snapped. "And where has that got us? Nowhere, Templecombe, nowhere. Maybe we should look at finding some way of deporting the man back to Germany and be done with it."

Templecombe shook his head firmly. "That's what a prince unbound by laws in some barbarian nation might do. You, sir, are a prince of this realm and its future king. You must rise above those feelings, however strongly you may perceive them. As the upholder of the rules of law you must be seen to be above such base reactions and instead show Parliament and the nation that you are a true and good leader with the best interests of the nation at heart."

Templecombe knew he was walking on the sword's edge with a man whose volatile temper could explode at any minute. He felt trickles of sweat running down his back.

"My suggestion, sir," Templecombe added, "is that you use this situation to applaud rather than lead criticism of Handel as un-British and un-Christian, thus aligning yourself with Bishop Gibson's position."

Frederick snorted. "Un-British he most certainly is. But un-Christian? For heaven's sake, the man is planning another performance of a piece called *Messiah* which uses only the words of Scripture." He shot a gloomy look at his man. "I cannot see how we convince people of that."

"By piggybacking on Gibson's accusations of blasphemy and highlighting them, sir," the marquis explained patiently as the prince and began to pace the room. "Holding a performance with such a sacred name and words in the bowels of a playhouse and with bawdy men and women more used to drunken and profane music and plays is surely blasphemy, as the bishop says. Is it not, sir? Why, the very thought would be like a minister preaching the gospel in the taproom of a louse-infested inn filled with the lowest and vilest of people! They would be underserving of such. If you then compound the criticism by stating that position from your perspective as a music lover, you accomplish the same effect on the public in a softer, gentler way. But the genteel people, the ones you want to sway to your viewpoint, will understand and flock to your side, adding to the criticism until it reaches a crescendo and the German is defeated. It matters not what the masses of gin-soaked ruffians and their women think."

Templecombe looked up and smiled.

"You will have won without hammering the man, upsetting his performances or sabotaging his advertising," the marquis added. "You will have won with honey."

The prince still stalked around the room, thinking and occasionally glancing at his man with a perplexed look. Finally, he sat down across from Templecombe.

"I like the thoughts, sir, but the people already know my antagonism towards Handel," the prince pointed out. "If I suddenly change my spots... well, they'll be suspicious."

"That, sir, is why you must rise above the fray. Someone else must take up the cause while you refrain from comment of any kind. Opposition must come from sources other than Cliveden or your person."

"What do you suggest?"

Relieved, Templecombe pushed ahead. "You have a dinner party this evening, sir. Very quietly in your conversations with your guests, let them know that you are disturbed by the rumors that a sacred work might be performed in a playhouse rather than church. Make no mention of Handel or the title of the work. Say that you've been impressed with Bishop Gibson's astute views on this matter and how much you appreciate his wisdom and Christian leadership."

The prince nodded

"Very delicately muse that this matter needs to be considered very deeply by all who love music," Templecombe continued. "One thing is certain, sir. You have a strong reputation as a lover of fine music and your guests know it. Why, was it not you who invited Mr. Arne to perform his music here at Cliveden? And while here, did he not introduce one of the finest and most heroic compositions ever, *Rule Britannia?* And were you not his patron for that?"

Frederick smiled. Yes, he did indeed have a glorious reputation as a patron of fine music and the arts.

"Above all, Sir," Templecombe rapidly went om, "you must not order your guests, or even ask them, to support your position on this matter. This is where you must be very subtle in your words and tone. You are only quietly pondering a most troubling issue. Let them make their own decisions to speak about the issue elsewhere. Let them take up the cause to protect the sanctity of the church!"

A sly smile crept across the prince's face. "I like it, sir. They take up the cudgels and I stay out of the fight. Yes, I like it!"

Frederick jumped up and strode across the room to fill a glass of wine from a decanter.

"One other suggestion, sir," Templecombe added. "Since we are to use others to fight the fight for us, we need to broaden the base of your support. I recommend that we also use the broadsheets to press the arguments against such a production."

"And how, pray, do we do that?"

"Someone writes a letter to the broadsheet newspapers under an assumed name, decrying the scandal of such use of Scripture and supporting the Bishop's well-thought-out opposition to it. Several of those kinds of letters from a variety of sources will soon sway opinion against the production and in favor of your own views."

Frederick took a long drink and refilled his glass. Templecombe remained silent while the prince chewed the advice over in his mind. A clock ticked solemnly in the background as Frederick paced, drank, and paced some more.

Finally, he stopped and placed the glass on a table as he turned and pointed to Templecombe.

"You, sir, shall write the letter. You know what to say and, more importantly, how to say it." He resumed pacing while Templecombe stared at him, surprised by the sudden turn of events. "You cannot use your own name, of course, as you said. But you do have a way with words. It will be a real shot across the bows." The prince chuckled, beaming at the marquis. "You can do it, sir. Look how you have persuaded me!"

Seeing no way out, Templecombe rose from his chair and bowed. "As you wish, Your Royal Highness."

"A name. We must give you a name that resounds with thought and intelligence." Cupping his chin between his thumb and forefinger, he suddenly clapped his hands in delight. "Philalethes! Lover of truth." Frederick roared with laughter, pleased with what he considered to be a brilliant idea. "The Greeks have given you your assumed name, sir. Now go and write a letter to end all letters and let us stop this abomination."

Templecombe showed a leg and backed out of the room, his head spinning. He'd planned to weave the spider's web of course, but at no point had he thought he would become the chief spider.

Handel wrestled with the ramifications of his decision. He reminded himself again that this time he had no strong ecclesiastic support from church leaders as he'd had in Dublin. Further, Gibson was no weak and doddering Dean Swift. He was a strong, vocal, and fierce opponent.

As he spoke to friends and listened to conversations at luncheons and dinners, he began to understand that much of the concerns about the work revolved around its title. For a sophisticated but entrenched London society, calling it *Messiah* and presenting it in a theatre was like waving a red flag in front of a bull, baiting them into a fight, no matter his own sincere and lofty motives.

Perhaps if he removed the sting a bit, it might soften the opposition.

Handel immediately arranged for advertisements in the most critical newspapers announcing "A New Sacred Oratorio" and added that there would be an organ concerto as well as a violin solo by Matthew Dubourg.

The next day, a long letter appeared in the *Universal Spectator*. The anonymous writer, one called Philalethes, gently railed against the performance. Handel was shaken by the length and strenuousness of the arguments employed as he read the diatribe.

> An oratorio is either an "Act of Religion" or it is not. If it is, I ask if the playhouse is a fit temple to perform it, or is a company of players fit ministers for God's word? If it is not an act of religion, what an act of profanation of God's name and word is this?

Philalethes called himself a professed lover of music and in particular of Mr. Handel's performances. He also claimed to be a great admirer of church music and challenged the performance, reminding readers of the advice of the psalmist to serve the Lord with fear and rejoice unto him with reverence, an act, he suggested, that would not be possible in such a location. He asked,

Can the sacred word of God be performed by a set of people unfit to perform so solemn a service?

He even invoked the commandments, charging that performing the oratorio on the proposed performance day of Saturday violated the third commandment to keep the Sabbath Day holy, that anything of such a sacred nature should be retained for Sundays.

Handel read the letter to Matthew Dubourg, mostly as a sounding board for his own fears and misgivings.

"This is altogether too intellectual an objection and will require me to respond in equal fashion," Handel complained. "And I cannot do that. A musician I am, not an academic, Matthew. But this must be answered."

Dubourg smiled. He'd just arrived at Handel's home clutching a newspaper and had not had a chance to share it with Handel before the computer had begun ranting against Philalethes and reading the letter aloud.

"Mr. Handel, sir, allow me to share this with you." Dubourg laid the paper open. "You do not need to fear. You don't need to respond yourself. Others, equally intellectual and academic, will do it for you. Look here!"

He jabbed at a response to Philalethes printed that morning. The response took the form of a poem.

"There's your answer," Dubourg said. "Many of your friends are already responding, to do battle with this person, whoever he is. They will lay out the argument for you. Look, this respondent makes it clear that the argument about sacred music in a theatre is a trivial one, made all the more ridiculous by showing that your music will open up new ways to worship. Read the last few lines. He says your music will give new grace to virtue and will sanctify the place and will turn the place from a hell to a heaven. That's the response, Mr. Handel. You are opening up new audiences to God's word. A great number of people realize it and are willing to support you and argue for you. You're giving grace to the people and allowing them to hear it. Perhaps for the first time. No, you cannot let these pitiful and petty sycophants of the church stand in the way. Your *Messiah* is wonderful and will have as great an impact here as it did in Dublin. Don't stray from your plans. I believe, as you do, that God gave you this music. You cannot bury it. It must be heard."

Surprised at his own vehemence, Dubourg suddenly fell quiet, worried about Handel's response. All he got was a nod, a smile, and a firm "Well then, we should get down to the theatre for rehearsals then, shouldn't we?"

Messiah was on.

CHAPTER TWENTY-THREE

IN WHICH LONDON HEARS MESSIAH

Handel walked around the luxurious interior of the Covent Garden Theatre, inspecting the vibrant and beautiful setting. It was more a case of nerves driving him to do something other than sit, because there was no real need to inspect. He glanced on stage. There, he could see the stark arrangements, chairs for the performers, plus his own harpsichord he would conduct from.

Covent Garden Theatre was grander in scale and design outside and in than the Musick Hall in Dublin, he mused, even though it was ten years older. The rich gold leaf decorations on plaster complemented the deep red brocade curtains. Although it was afternoon, the decorated oil lamps had been lit, casting shadows and light across the three levels of balconies that towered over the main level where a good number of attendees would stand.

As was the case in Dublin, the pit area in front of the orchestra would be jammed if ticket sales were any indication. Certainly, the seats on all three balcony levels were already sold. It would be a full house, despite the best efforts of Gibson and others to persuade London's nobility and theater-loving crowds to stay home.

Handel told himself that three types of people would attend: those who were enamored of his music and faithfully attended all his productions, those who came out of curiosity as to the nature of a sacred oratorio in a secular setting, and those who knew neither his music nor the criticisms he endured, but merely wanted to see and hear this new type of production. The last group, he knew, were more attracted by the controversy than they were by any musical interest.

From overheard conversations the past few days, he realized too that even those who were attracted by the blossoming trend of enlightenment, emphasizing scientific and rational thinking as opposed to religious or mystical teachings, were intrigued by the novelty the production promised.

One thing he was grateful for. Neither he nor his myriad of friends and supporters heard any rumors of gangs of thugs seeking to disrupt the evening, nor over the past week had any posters been ripped up. So far the only meaningful opposition had come from Bishop Gibson's missives to various newspapers and the distribution of printed copies of his sermons lashing out at the "pernicious abomination that was the marriage of theatre and church embodied by Mr. Handel's sacred oratorio." It seemed few, however, were persuaded. And there had been an equal number of letters fully supporting the proposed performance.

He climbed the stairs to the third level and stood at the back, facing the assembling musicians. As they tuned their instruments, he was more than satisfied with the sweet sounds the theater projected, even over the normal bustle and conversations that accompanied any pre-concert period.

Everything seemed well. The only thing that concerned him was the silence that had greeted his invitation for King George to attend the performance. It had been sent three days ago in a deeply personal letter. Doubts had begun to creep in at His Majesty's lack of response. He wondered if the King was angry that he had left London for more a year. Or perhaps he was tired of the controversy that surrounded his patronage of Handel. Perhaps he even agreed with the bishop and his supporters that sacred music had no place in theatres.

All day, the doubts had crept in and chipped away at his confidence. Now, when he needed to project that confidence and conduct with authority, he was having second, third, and even fourth thoughts about his temerity in writing such a composition.

If only Jennens had given me another libretto, he told himself.

As he waited in the highest reaches, he scolded himself for having the audacity to tackle such an auspicious and holy topic. Who was he, a simple musician from the village of Halle in Saxony, to dare trifle with such lofty subjects? Better surely that Kapellmeister Johan Bach should have done it, not a man who writes mere entertainments.

The words "you of all men are not worthy" unexpectedly flashed through his mind, followed swiftly by a quiet understanding that he was not the one to judge worthiness. All he needed to do was obey.

Which I did, he told himself.

He sighed, knowing the die had been cast, and headed down the stairs.

Winding his way backstage, he shook his head at the thoughts crowding his mind. George Frederik Handel, the man most people, be they friend or enemy, believed to be the very epitome of ego and confidence, was now a churning mass of nerves. His stomach lurched and a slight waft of nausea caused him to grasp a pillar and pause while he regained his equilibrium. He tried to quell the upsetting worries and calm his mind for the performance.

In short order, Handel was in the wings. Members of the orchestra and chorus passed by, bowing and curtseying, acknowledging him as they took up their places. He glanced out of the wings and surveyed the audience that was already pouring into the theatre. The noise of their conversation increased as more and more people came in. He looked up and across the towering balconies and jerked with surprise when he saw a stern-looking Charles Jennens take his seat.

Bless me, he thought. *I sent him an invitation and ticket but certainly did not expect to see him take up the offer.*

He smiled to himself and hurried backstage, calling out for a quill, ink, and paper. He quickly penned a short note expressing his gratitude and best wishes to Jennens, expressing his hope that the librettist would enjoy the fruits of his most excellent labors. He then stopped one of the theater's backstage hands and asked him to deliver the note, pointing out Jennens in the crowd. The boy set off.

By now the theater was near capacity. He shot a quick glance towards the royal box, which sat disappointingly empty.

Handel peeked in a mirror and straightened his wig. Before he could move, his manservant John, who normally stayed home for debut performances, stepped up and with a small hand brush swept it quickly and efficiently over Handel's rich velvety brown and gold coat, waistcoat, and breeches. John knelt and, using a rag he produced from his deep pockets, gave the black-buckled shoes a final quick shine.

"Thank you, John. I am pleased that you came."

As he spoke, Matthew Dubourg appeared at his side. "Almost time, Mr. Handel." He pointed towards the stage. "The lads are already turning up the flames on the stage lamps." He extended his hand to Handel's and gave it a firm, confident shake. "This will be a performance for the ages, Mr. Handel. It will change London and people everywhere. I feel it in my bones, and I thank you for the privilege of inviting me to participate."

The man's grin was infectious. Handel, a basket of insecurity, answered with a beaming appreciation of the man's kind words.

"Yes, Matthew, I believe you may be right. It transcends any other I have yet written, or will write, in the future." His grin grew larger until it transformed the frowning, worried visage into one of peace and contentment. A growing revelation surged through his mind. "Whatever men say, and whatever concerns I may have, I can say that I am satisfied. I have done my best." He gripped Dubourg's hand tightly. "Thank you for your kind words, your patience, and your musical talent. Now, go and give the performance of your life."

As Dubourg strode out to take his place amidst applause, Handel heard a noise behind him. Turning, he saw Susannah Cibber and Christina Avolio quietly clapping their gloved hands.

"We too thank you for the privilege, Mr. Handel," Susanna spoke as Christina nodded approval. "And we too will give the performance of our lives."

They stepped around him and swept onto the stage, also to loud applause.

Handel waited while Dubourg did a final tuning of the orchestra and then sat.

A hush swept over the crowd. The shuffling of feet and chairs disappeared. Handel stepped out from the wings and slowly made his way towards his harpsichord, accompanied by thunderous ovation. He stopped beside his bench and turned to face the audience, bowing deeply as he did so. He looked up into the balconies and across the crowd standing jammed together in front of him and bowed deeply once again.

As the applause died away, he took his place on the bench. He was just about to raise his hands to begin the Sinfonia when suddenly Dubourg, the orchestra, and singers leapt to their feet.

A huge rustling of feet and chairs as well as clapping began. He lurched around and abruptly stood to face the royal box. To Handel's amazement, the King acknowledged the crowd with a bow then he quietly took his seat, along with his retinue.

As soon as the King was seated, the rest of the audience quieted and the performers retook their places. Only Handel remained standing, maintaining eye contact with the King as he again bowed deeply towards the royal box. He smiled to himself, warmth seeping quickly through his entire body.

Seconds later, he raised his hands again and the deep slow notes of the strings began.

As they worked through the various arias, choruses, recitatives, and other pieces it was obvious that a hush enveloped the audience. Apart from the occasional cough or sneeze, there was very little noise. Handel couldn't look around to see the audience reaction, but he could sense it. They were moved and did not want to miss a single note.

If it was quiet before, the theatre descended into total silence as Susannah Cibber rose and the orchestra began the mournful notes of "He was despised and rejected." Word of her performance in Dublin and Delaney's reaction had them waiting in anticipation.

Whether the London crowd were respectful of the piece or just plain curious to see if she was as good as advertised, Handel could not tell, but the stillness told him that she may indeed be reaching the hearts of even the most cynical critics.

As the last notes died away, he saw tears trickling down her face. Before there could be any interruption, the chorus stood immediately and with the orchestra began the mournful *"Surely he has borne our griefs."*

The silence in the theatre was deafening. Subconsciously Handel reminded himself they were now near the end of part two. He was looking forward to his beloved Hallelujah Chorus, as he did every time he played it. It transported him and helped him soar, even when he played it just to himself.

They'd reached the middle of the piece when he suddenly heard a shuffle of feet and was astounded when he saw Dubourg and those members of the orchestra who could struggle to their feet. He whipped his head around, saw people all over the theater standing, and glanced up at the royal box, astonished to see the King himself standing. Neither he nor the performers missed a beat; they remained standing until they finished the grand final "Hallelujah!"

Spontaneous applause broke out as the King and his subjects resumed their seats. Only those on the main floor, who'd been standing all the while, remained on their feet, and they too were applauding wildly.

There was a short break written into the score between the second and third parts. As they waited for the crowd to settle, Handel glanced quizzically at Dubourg.

"We were playing 'King of Kings' when His Majesty suddenly stood up, so we had to as well," Dubourg whispered.

Before he could grasp what had just happened, Handel steeled himself to concentrate, nodded to Christina Avolio as she stepped forward, and commenced conducting as she began singing *"I know that my redeemer liveth."*

The final triumphant Amens at the conclusion of the performance had hardly died away before deafening applause began raining down. Handel stood and bowed, bowed again, and gestured for the orchestra and singers to do the same.

He looked first at the royal box and was gratified to see a smiling King George applauding and smiling. He turned to face the King and bowed deeply yet again. The seated portion of the audience stood once again as the King got to his feet and left the box.

When he was gone, Handel looked for Jennens and saw him smile as he clapped. Handel felt relieved and vindicated. Their differences over style might linger, as would the sting of his Dublin debut and lack of courtesy in visiting Jennens at home, but he would apologize profoundly for his mistakes and beg forgiveness that would, he trusted, be given. For now, it was enough that Jennens had been able to get beyond reading the musical score and actually hear its power through the instruments and voices.

Backstage, he received another ovation from the performers and theater workers from the manager, John Rich, to the humblest stage boys and porters. Dubourg bowed before him and then enthusiastically shook his hand. Susannah and Christina both curtseyed, enormous smiles on their faces. All around, the excited singers and musicians buzzed with excitement and joy at their performance and the reaction to it.

Handel quieted them and thanked them profusely. He then did something he'd never done before: he shared some of his concerns and besetting worries about the acceptance of the oratorio.

Before he could get much further, one of the wind players shouted, "Well, you got your answer, Mr. Handel. They loved it!"

There was much laughter and renewed applause from the company.

Handel hushed them. "I am grateful for all your support and hard work. Mr. Dubourg promised the performance of a lifetime tonight, and all of you accomplished that. But my concerns were not about you, or the music. It was not even about whether a lot of tickets were sold or that people enjoyed it." He paused a moment. "It was about whether I—and yes, you—were worthy. The subject is so powerful and inspiring, I wondered were simple humans like us truly worthy of writing or singing or playing it."

He looked around at the suddenly quiet and serious group.

"I have my answer. None of us is worthy at all. But we have been privileged to be used to tell the grand story of redemption in a new way. I for one am grateful and humbled by that knowledge." Looking around, pausing ever so slightly on Susannah, he softly added, And I know others are as well."

As he finished, he noted their smiling faces, nodding heads, and not a few tears. He could think of nothing more to say, so he merely bowed deeply at them and walked off.

The next morning, Handel finished his breakfast with a good hot cup of coffee. He was eminently satisfied with the reaction to *Messiah* but knew it was a muted success compared to the triumph that taken place in Dublin. The entire city had been overwhelmingly supportive of the work then, but last night, and the battles leading up to it, had shown that London was still a challenge as far as his sacred oratorio went. His friends and supporters had been appreciative and enthusiastic last night, however, and even Jennens had sent a note around this morning congratulating him, though he still quibbled about some of the pieces.

Despite the wondrous reception, he knew London was a difficult city to win over to a new style of music or performance. It was a city that prided itself on its sophistication and relished intellectual battles as much as anything. The added encumbrances of high church opposition and the ongoing cultural battles waged by King and prince had imposed a dampening effect on the people's enthusiasm for any work—art, writing, or music—that trod into that debate.

No, he realized, it would take London longer to embrace *Messiah*. But that was all right with him.

Much as he enjoyed public appreciation and enthusiasm, it was no longer the major driving energy behind him. *Messiah*, he realized, had a higher purpose than creating fame and accolades. That might come with his earlier works, and hopefully, his later ones, but this one was different. It stood alone on a mountaintop in his mind. And there it would remain.

Perhaps one day, he mused, it would develop its own niche and audiences would appreciate it for what it was.

If it is performed at least once after my death and thus transcends me, I will be happy, he thought.

He was still in this melancholic mood, sipping another cup of coffee, when there was a loud hammering at the door. He heard John scurry to the door, detected some muted voices, and then the door closed. He looked up as John hurried in, waving a piece of paper.

"Mr. Handel, a command from His Majesty."

John laid the note in front of him. It was indeed from the King himself and, though phrased as a request, Handel knew it was indeed a command.

"Well, John. You'd best assemble my finest wig and clothes and help me dress. It seems His Majesty has invited me to visit this afternoon."

Although his response was calm, inside Handel churned. A myriad of thoughts went through his mind. Above all, he wondered, why had the King stood in the middle of the performance? Handel understood that once he had, the audience and performers had no choice but to follow suit.

"But why did he rise?"

Unknowingly, he had asked the question aloud, only to be shocked at John's flippant response.

"Maybe he suddenly needed the privy."

A stern glare from Handel cut the thought off.

John outdid himself. Somehow between finding, brushing, and straightening Handel's dark blue coat and breeches with white trim, along with an elegant cream tapestry-like waistcoat, white stockings, and perfectly coiffured white wig, he also found time to arrange for an elegant coach to take his master to St. James' Palace.

"You've been called before the King, sir," John said when Handel groused about the additional expenditure. "So you must travel in a style appropriate."

The trip to St. James' Palace was reasonably quick, given the crowded streets. When they arrived, he was quickly ushered up the stairs into the King's private quarters, a section of the palace he'd never visited before.

After he was announced, Handel said, "Your Majesty," showing a leg and bowing low. He held the position while still at the door until he heard the King command him to enter. He stepped into the room, showed a leg again, and bowed just as low. He saw King George gesturing him to a light blue sofa with a warm, welcoming smile.

Two elegant footmen stood at the back of the room, staring straight ahead, not moving a muscle. Other footmen bustled about on various duties.

"Welcome to the palace again, Mr. Handel." The King took a seat in the elegant armchair opposite him, timing it so that he was seated first and thus allowing Handel to follow. "May I thank you personally for that delightful and most profound entertainment last night. It truly was wonderful."

Handel flushed with pleasure. "Thank you, Your Majesty. And may I say how grateful and pleased we were that Your Majesty graced our oratorio with your presence."

The King waved the comment off. "It was a very moving thing, sir. Very moving."

As the afternoon proceeded with a slow grace, the conversation ranged from Handel's visit to Ireland and the resulting accolades to the previous night's presentation. Handel began to relax.

At the King's request, a footman brought in a carafe of red wine and two glasses, pouring one for the King and one for the visitor.

"The Duke of Devonshire urged me to attend as soon as you presented it in London," said the King. "He informed me of some of the difficulties you faced, but he also told me of the enormous positive response you received. I'm glad you performed it here at last. I know, of course, that Bishop Gibbons had misgivings, but then he has misgivings about everything, as I have personal reasons to know."

He sipped his wine. "Why I was persuaded to appoint that man to the bishopric of London, I do not know. He's been nothing but a hindrance and complainer since he took up the post."

The King proceeded to take apart the bishop's arguments against *Messiah* piece by piece, along with pointed and sometimes bitter side comments about the prince and his supporters.

Handel nodded to indicate he was listening, but inside he squirmed. He'd never before been privy to such deep conversations in the King's presence. The few other times he'd met the King, the conversations had been fairly innocuous, touching on music, social galas, and the like, but never matters of state. He had no idea how to respond.

The King smiled at Handel, realizing that the depth of discussion was making him uncomfortable. It was time to slightly change the topic.

"I must apologize for standing in the middle of the performance," he said quietly, "but I do not regret doing so."

Handel cocked his head, wondering where this was going.

"I had no choice. I suddenly realized that above all else, I felt like I was in the presence of the King of Kings." He smiled. "I had no option but to stand. It was my duty. I do regret, however, that protocol meant that everyone else had to stand the moment I did and thus disrupt the performance." He chuckled. "I must confess that as moving as the moment was, it was amusing to see some of the orchestra struggling to stand without knocking over their music stands or losing their place." His smile grew into a huge grin. "Please let them all know that I was impressed with their ability to do so!"

Handel's mouth dropped open and he hastily shut it, realizing he had to stop gawping.

"Thank you, Your Majesty. I will indeed inform them." He put his glass down. "When I wrote that particular chorus, I too was moved beyond speech. I myself felt that I was in the presence of the King of Kings."

"Then we are agreed, Mr. Handel. This oratorio is a piece of music that surpasses the level of entertainment you usually produce. I give you my heartiest thanks for a profoundly inspiring evening. I am glad that you ignored the bishop's paltry arguments as well as His Royal Highness' blasted moanings." He placed his empty glass to the side. "I pray that God will bless this music and that it will live on in repeated presentations for many years yet to come. You, sir, have produced a very fine entertainment."

Handel looked up, wondering how he should respond. It was important that the King understand how differently he felt about this music compared to everything else he'd composed. But he did not want to insult the King's praises either.

"Thank you, Your Majesty," Handel said, thinking quickly. "Your words are truly humbling. But in all honesty, Your Majesty, your praise should not be for me. I was merely a tool. Nor did I seek to simply entertain my audience. I sought to make them better!"

The King stood and Handel hastily rose as well.

"You did indeed, sir. You did indeed better mankind. And I, not the King, but I, George, am humble enough to say that it moved me and made me better."

Handel was speechless. He could barely keep his emotions in check, feeling tears begin to well up.

He was grateful when the King gestured to the door. Handel bowed deeply once again, and backed slowly out of the room, stopping several times to bow again.

A whirlwind of emotions and thoughts grabbed him as he walked out of the palace precincts and stepped out into the crowded, noisy bustle of the city streets.

In the carriage, he bowed his head and silently prayed his thanks, grateful for all that had transpired.

He was content.

AUTHOR'S REFLECTIONS

IN WHICH THE AUTHOR PROVIDES SOME INSIGHTS INTO MR. HANDEL'S STORY AND KEY ASPECTS OF THE HISTORY OF WRITING MESSIAH

It is said that truth is often stranger than fiction. If I can bend that cliché a bit, it might be said that truth often lends its way to fiction and makes the fiction stronger. That is certainly true in the story of George Frederik Handel's creation of his masterpiece *Messiah*, as well as the story of those people who surrounded him at the time.

Handel first presented *Messiah* to London audiences in 1743. Throughout the remainder of the 1740s, he presented it only occasionally. Although London audiences were initially reluctant to fully embrace it, the work slowly grew in popularity and steadily gained audiences. By the 1750s it was a frequent Easter event. Through the remainder of the eighteenth, nineteenth, and twentieth centuries its popularity grew. Today *Messiah* is considered one of the finest ever classical music compositions. It has become a Christmas centerpiece for orchestras and choirs around the world.

This is a work of historical fiction, so naturally some of the peripheral characters are fictional. However, by and large most of the people in this novel are real. I have tried to characterize them as history has recorded them.

The dispute between King George II and his son and heir Frederick, Prince of Wales, was real; the hatred they felt towards each other was palpable. It really was a dysfunctional family. Tradition dictated that the birth of a royal child be observed by authorities as well as the king and queen so there could be no question of "exchanged" children at the time of birth. Frederick was so angry with his father that when his own wife, Augusta, was about to deliver their child, he whisked his pregnant wife away from Hampton Court Palace in the middle of the night so his father would not be present at the birth.

As a result, Frederick was banished from court. When George II's wife Charlotte was dying, he retaliated by refusing permission for Frederick to pay last respects to his mother, for whom Frederick still had warm feelings.

Frederick worked hard to undermine his father at every turn. George II was German, but Frederick had been born in England. He was sent by his father to serve for a number of years as the ruler in his father's province of Hanover, Germany. Frederick hated it and wanted to return to England. He resented what he considered his exile. Once he finally did return, he wanted to undermine any German or European influence in Britain. Handel drew his ire because he was German and specialized in Italian opera. He was also generously supported by the King. Frederick automatically strove to undermine Handel and see that he left Britain, thus removing "foreign" influences.

Twice Frederick circulated false rumors of his father's death, so desperate was he to become king. He did it once after George's ship ran into storm troubles in the English Channel; Frederick claimed the King had drowned. Another time, George was ill with what would now be called a bad cold and cancelled several engagements. Frederick put it about that the King had died. His lust for the throne was unmistakable.

Frederick was dissolute. He drank excessively and was a renowned womanizer, sharing mistresses with friends and allies. The concept of kingship and statesmanship was beyond him. Fortunately, despite the Duke of Devonshire's gloomy pessimism in this book, Frederick never became king. He died at Cliveden House in 1751 at the age of forty-four, apparently from a burst abscess in the lung. It was caused by a hit from a cricket ball during a spirited game.

There was an anonymous letter-writer who called himself Philalethes (Lover of truth) who wrote a stinging indictment of Handel's decision to perform his oratorio in a public theatre and sent it to London newspapers. That person was never identified and remains anonymous to this day. I decided to speculate on his identity and write it into the story.

When George II finally died in October 1760 at the age of seventy-seven, it was Frederick's oldest son who succeeded and became George III.

A combination of events and situations drained Handel in 1740 and 1741. At that time, he seriously considered quitting his beloved England and returning to Europe.

As impresario as well as composer, Handel bore all the expenses of his productions. He hired and paid the soloists and musicians. He hired the theatre. He paid for the staging, the advertising, and all incidental expenses. Italian operas, however, were going out of style and being supplanted by other forms, especially English language operas such as *The Beggar's Opera*. The Prince of Wales championed such music. He also supported English composers like Thomas Arne. The prince's dislike of Handel and his approval of the hiring of gangs of thugs to tear down Handel's advertising and disrupt performances led Handel inevitably to the brink of bankruptcy.

At the time when this novel begins, Handel was weeks away from debtors' prison. Only the friendship of people like the Duke of Devonshire kept the wolf from the door. Additionally, he'd suffered what would nowadays be considered a stroke that partly paralyzed his right hand and arm for a time. It was combination of these and other events that threw him into a deep depression that he only began to climb out of when he received Devonshire's invitation to present a season of concerts in Dublin.

William Cavendish was the second Duke of Devonshire and the real founder of the family home called Chatsworth, which is still the home of the Duke of Devonshire and a major tourist attraction in Derbyshire in the heart of the Peak District. He was Lord Lieutenant of Ireland, the King's governor, or Viceroy, on that island. Dublin was indeed the second largest and greatest city in the kingdom and a vibrant center of culture.

Susannah Cibber, like Handel, was at the bottom of the pit. An accomplished actress and singer, she was married to a man who abused her verbally, physically, mentally, and sexually. Theo Cibber owned a theatre and styled himself as her manager, thus keeping all her salaries to himself and giving her little. He gambled and drank most of it away, often selling her clothing and possessions to generate cash when it was needed.

There are differences of opinion about how willing a participant she was in sexual activities with her husband and others. What is known is that she became William Sloper's mistress, which in turn led to Theo Cibber's lawsuit charging adultery and demanding hundreds of pounds in damages. The grisly details that formed much of the court case were the fodder for public consumption in the newspapers of the time. It was the equivalent of watching today's celebrities be destroyed on social media.

Even though women had very few rights and almost no legal protection, Theo Cibber was the big loser in this public scandal. Although the court found her guilty, Theo was only awarded five pounds in damages, a paltry amount even in those days. She fled the London theatre scene and eventually wound up in Dublin without Sloper, a situation I speculated upon in this book.

Handel did indeed persuade her to sing at the Dublin debut of *Messiah*. Because of her public experiences, he felt she would excel in the role. He knew well her capabilities, having hired her many times for a wide variety of previous productions. His expectation was that she would, as one contemporary put it, sing to the heart and not just the ear.

Charles Jennens, the man who "wrote" the libretto (perhaps "arranged the order of Bible verses" would be better) was an odd duck, to say the least. He was wealthy beyond measure, not needing to work a day in his life. Which was just as well. As a non-juror, he could not support or pledge allegiance to the Hanover dynasty, believing that the Stuarts were the true kings, even though as a devout Protestant he despised the Stuarts' attempts to reverse the tide and bring Britain back into the Roman Catholic fold. To him, the Stuarts and no others were God's ordained rulers, end of story. It meant all normal occupations of men in his class—politics, military service, diplomacy, or other government service—were denied him. Instead he collected art and books, considering himself an intellectual and quasi-theologian. He also considered himself an astute lover of music, thinking he was both a musical critic of the highest level as well as a librettist. He was a big fan of Handel's work and wrote several librettos for Handel. His most successful, apart from *Messiah*, was probably *Saul*.

Unfortunately, he was also a very prickly character. He constantly fell out with friends over disagreements on politics, theology, art, and obviously, as noted in this book, music. When people countered his opinion on any topic, it led to snide and bitter responses, usually delivered through third parties rather than directly.

Jonathon Swift is best known as the author of *Gulliver's Travels*. He was Anglo-Irish and had an icy wit that poked away at the hypocrisy of church and state in pamphlets, essays, articles, and books. He was indeed one of Ireland's leading thinkers, satirists, and writers. He was also the dean of St. Patrick's Cathedral. At the time Handel arrived in Dublin, Swift was suffering from dementia and other illnesses on and off, markedly getting worse each month. He died within a year and a half of these events. He did indeed try to block Handel from using the choirs of both cathedrals, as described.

The Vicars Choral that Swift referred to were the core singers of the choirs in both cathedrals. They were professional singers and musicians granted the status of ministers on the cathedral staff and paid accordingly. They were used to bolster the other volunteer choir members on special occasions and shared duties in both cathedrals. Wynne was right when he said that if they were forbidden to participate, the remainder of the volunteer choir members had neither the numbers nor quality required for such a monumental presentation. Interestingly, even in a city as large as Dublin, the two cathedrals are fairly close to each other, around five city blocks. While an unusual situation, they have different roles. St. Patrick's is the cathedral of the national Church of Ireland (Anglican). Christ Church, while also Anglican, is the cathedral for the city of Dublin.

Swift almost singlehandedly scuppered the whole thing. Nobody knows why, nor do they know why he changed his mind, so I let loose my creative side.

Where they fit, I have included portions of the actual letters, advertising, notes, and other materials and communications between the principals of this story. I left such materials in their original format, with that era's spellings, capitalizations, grammar, and style. Included in this is the actual wording of the note Swift wrote to his dean.

Handel was a larger than life character and lived accordingly. Stories abound of his prodigious appetite, raging temper, demand for perfection, and refusal to be cowed by fellow composers, theatre owners, nobles, and the like. Where they fit with the story, I worked in such anecdotes. He did indeed hang a diva out a window. He did verbally grapple with a singer in Chester. He did frequent St. George's in Hanover Square and play the organ, almost using it as his personal toy. There are many other anecdotes blended into this story—and many, many more that did not fit within the timeframe of this book.

I have tried to emulate the style of writing and book production from those times, thus including chapter introductions that give readers a foreshadowing of the contents of that chapter. This novel also follows the style and wordings Handel used on separating the parts of Messiah. I too present this book in three parts.

Handel, always a generous man, was ever willing to give to and support a wide variety of charities. He began doing annual fundraising performances of *Messiah* for the Foundling Children's' Home of London, created by a retired sea captain, Thomas Coram, who was an interesting character in and of himself.

On Handel's death in 1759, fittingly at Easter, at the age of seventy-four, he was a wealthy man. He'd never married, so there were no heirs. He left a bequest to his servant John, and also funds for his burial. He generously left the rights to *Messiah* to the Foundling Hospital, which holds those rights to this day.

Despite Frederick's intense dislike of Handel, his son, who became King George III, was an unabashed fan of the composer, and especially *Messiah*. Presentations of the work increased during George III's reign. He was instrumental in the decision to bury Handel in Westminster Abbey, helping persuade the archbishop and his grandfather King George II. A monument to Handel can now be seen in the Abbey's Poets Corner. The memorial has a marble image of him holding a scroll with part of the Hallelujah Chorus inscribed on it. He is looking toward heaven with one hand raised, pointing.

Although Handel was a very public figure, he was also a very private man. He wrote very few letters, had a small number of close friends, both male and female, and never married. He was raised in Germany as a Lutheran but switched to the Anglican Church when he arrived in England and became nationalized. Because of his reluctance to expose and record his deepest personal feelings, very little is truly known about the depth of his faith. It is known, however, that writing *Messiah* changed him. He did declare to his servant John, and later to others, that he believed he saw heaven and God himself while writing the Hallelujah Chorus. The entire work is profoundly spiritual, and Handel was deeply impacted by it.

Historians debate whether King George II really attended the first London performance or that he stood during the Hallelujah Chorus, thus creating today's tradition.

However, I looked at the matter logically.

Royal outings in those days were not the extravagant events they are today. They were not planned months or years in advance. There were no major security issues requiring massive protection squads and advance screening and planning. George often went riding alone in parks and public areas. He often decided to attend theatres and other events on a whim. And he did so with little fuss or fanfare, though most theatres had royal boxes adorned with the flag just in case. Such visits and activities were not meticulously recorded and discussed as they are today.

I have no trouble believing that George was aware of the production and decided, on the spur of the moment, to attend.

It was and is protocol that people are never seated if the king or queen stands. Since the tradition of standing for the Hallelujah Chorus is so ingrained today, it makes sense that someone, most likely King George II, stood on hearing the chorus as I have described. Everything else flows from that. Remember, although the Age of Enlightenment was beginning, this was still a deeply religious era and monarchs believed that their rule was ordained, or at the very least blessed, by God. It therefore made eminent sense to me that a deeply religious king would stand in the presence of *his* King, Jesus, in turn causing the audience to stand.

That Handel did indeed write the entire score for Messiah in twenty-four days is remarkable, yes, but not unheard of for him. Once he got stuck into a work, he apparently did so feverishly until he finished. He usually took even less time to complete a concerto or opera.

I'd like to think that he spent *more* time composing *Messiah* simply because of its profound subject matter.

One of the reasons he was able to work so quickly is that he was one of the original recyclers! He would rework melodies and pieces he'd written for previous compositions and make brand-new material out of it. He also, like many other composers, leaned heavily on the huge variety of folk music and songs that laced society of the day.

Handel was never fully satisfied with *Messiah*. Up to the time of his death, he was always reworking certain parts, changing the ranges on solo pieces to better suit the voices he was hiring, tweaking tunes, and massaging melodies.

Handel perceived *Messiah* as an Easter oratorio. He always performed it around Easter and the Lenten season. How and when it became a Christmas standard would have puzzled and amused him. He would appreciate the worldwide acclamation, certainly, but I'm sure he would be wondering, "Why Christmas?" The birth of Christ is actually a minor portion of the piece, while the resurrection and its triumphant aftermath is the focal point.

It must be understood that this novel was written for ordinary people like me. It is not purporting in any way to be a biography. The historian or biographer who insists on absolute factual, chronological dissertation, complete with footnotes, will be disappointed with my book. I get that.

Nor is the book intended for the musical expert or true aficionado. I'm sure I've made musical errors and that such people will be annoyed at the way I've described it. Or they will be unhappy with the unprofessional, non-musical terminology I've used. I have the greatest admiration for anyone who can play a musical instrument or have a good enough voice to sing. I don't. Musicians and professional singers will likely criticize this book for being too simplistic. I get that too.

But this was never intended to be a biography or musical critique. I know there are many like me who merely enjoy and appreciate great music. This book is for them. It is simply the story of a man who slid from adulation and wealth to the bottom of the pit and then persevered and made his way back up to the top, guided and aided by divine grace. I trust readers will view it in that light.

Messiah is a moving, uplifting, and triumphant work. The words of Scripture, melded with the amazing music, lifts it above most other classical works.

I am amazed when I see videos of concerts performed around the world, whether from Brazil, Holland, Japan, China, or other places. I often notice people standing for the Hallelujah Chorus, with many in the audience singing along in English. They represent all ages, nationalities, and different first languages. I remember sitting in London's Church of St. Martin in the Fields one Easter, enjoying *Messiah*. A man in the row behind us sang the entire Hallelujah Chorus in a cultured English accent. After the performance, I turned to congratulate him on his voice. I found out that he was Italian and knew no other English than the words he'd just sung!

Such is the impact of *Messiah*. Very few classical works have that kind of power and acceptance.

The composer Ludwig von Beethoven declared that Handel was his favorite composer. The only English *he* knew were the words to the Hallelujah Chorus! He said, "Handel is the greatest composer who ever lived. Mozart, Bach and Haydn would never stand a chance. I would uncover my head and kneel down before his tomb."

High praise indeed from one of the greatest classical composers himself.

—Barrie Doyle
September 2019

Printed in the USA
CPSIA information can be obtained
at www.ICGtesting.com
LVHW051408141223
766325LV00002B/278